FRENCH
KISS

Get your drama on with the girls of

FRENCH KISS
in their first escapade

French Kiss

Aimee Friedman

SCHOLASTIC INC.

New York Toronto London Auckland Sydney
Mexico City New Delhi Hong Kong Buenos Aires

For Gérard

No part of this publication may be reproduced, stored in a retrieval system, or transmitted in any form or by any means, electronic, mechanical, photocopying, recording, or otherwise, without written permission of the publisher. For information regarding permission, write to Scholastic Inc., Attention: Permissions Department, 557 Broadway, New York, NY 10012.

ISBN 0-439-79281-9

Copyright © 2006 by Aimee Friedman

All rights reserved. Published by Scholastic Inc.
SCHOLASTIC and associated logos are trademarks and/or registered trademarks of Scholastic Inc.

Book design by Steve Scott

12 11 10 9 8 7 6 5 4 3 2 1   6 7 8 9 10 11/0

Printed in the U.S.A.
First printing, January 2006

Acknowledgments

Boundless thanks to Jean Feiwel and Craig Walker, for their unflagging support, and to Maria Barbo, for her brilliant editorial guidance and *joie de vivre*. I am greatly indebted to Beth Dunfey, Shannon Penney, Steve Scott, Susan Jeffers Casel, Kristin Earhart, Lisa Sandell, and all my wonderful colleagues and friends at Scholastic. *Un grand merci à mes amis français,* most especially the Bouskela family, for their Parisian hospitality. I am equally grateful to my charming friends Stateside, particularly Nicole Weitzner, Jennifer Clark, Jon Gemma, Elizabeth Harty, Martha Kelehan, Emily Smith, and Jaynie Saunders Tiller, for putting up with me so gracefully. I also offer a bouquet of thanks to Nicolas Medina and Richard Parker for, respectively, the helpful information on the Eiffel Tower and Wimbledon. And, finally, all my thanks to my fabulous family: my lifesaving sister and brother-in-law, and my divinely patient parents.

You will do foolish things,
but do them with enthusiasm.
— Colette

I'm in Paris. *Don't you worry about me.*
— Carrie Bradshaw

CHAPTER ONE
Ooh La La

"Tomorrow," Alexandria St. Laurent announced to her best friends, Portia and Maeve, over sushi in the school cafeteria. "I am taking a 'me' day." She flashed a sparkly grin, tossed her silky white-blonde hair over one shoulder, and reached for the wasabi. Not that Alexa needed any more spice in her life; her pulse was already racing with excitement.

"Why?" Portia snapped, raising one thin, dark eyebrow. "Tomorrow's the Friday before spring break. Ms. St. Laurent can't be bothered to show up?" Scowling, Portia shook out her chestnut ringlets and boldly plucked a cigarette from her patent leather clutch, just daring Mrs. Jacobson, the assistant principal, to bust her ass for smoking.

Alexa rolled her sapphire-blue eyes and tugged on

1

one dangly crystal-encrusted earring. "Portia, you know I'm swamped." Cramming her fuzzy shrugs, silk camisoles, and spike-heeled shoe collection into her Coach bags was the *least* of Alexa's worries. She needed a manicure, a seaweed facial, and — since she was about to spend one full, delicious week with her olive-skinned, drop-dead sexy boyfriend — a Brazilian bikini wax.

Alexa St. Laurent took her vacations very, very seriously.

Especially this one. Because she and said boyfriend, Diego Mendieta, would be celebrating their one-year anniversary — a first for Alexa — in Paris.

Oui. Paris. Also known as Alexa's favorite city in the world. With a shiver of anticipation, she closed her eyes and summoned up the light-spangled romantic bridges, perfect for late-night kissing; the cozy corner cafés, where couples held hands over flutes of sweet kir; the hidden, narrow streets, made for getting wonderfully lost. . . .

"Oh, God," Maeve wailed, jerking Alexa out of her Parisian reverie. "You're going to have the *best* time, Alexa, while *I'll* be here all alone —" Breaking into sobs, Maeve pushed her sushi aside and dropped her head onto the sleeve of her striped Stella McCartney boatneck, her wavy red hair falling over her tear-stained face.

A group of gossip-hungry junior girls in short

Princy skirts and Tylie Malibu boots scuttled past, gazing in curiosity at the holy Alexa-Maeve-Portia trinity. In the halls of Oakridge High School, the three girls were practically celebrities. Alexa had once lapped up the attention, but now, by March of her senior year, she was growing weary of the spotlight. Sometimes she wanted to don her oversized shades and Gucci head scarf and go into hiding.

As Maeve continued to sniffle and sob, Alexa bit her glossy bottom lip, trying not to snort. Maeve had split with her longtime boyfriend, Misha, in January, but still acted as if the pain were fresh. The two of them had been planning a deluxe spring-break jaunt to Bora Bora, but when Misha had ditched Maeve for her (now former) BFF, Sabina, the vacation plans, needless to say, crumbled. Now, any time the subject of spring break came up, Maeve would dissolve into a quivering mess. Alexa was done with her friend's whole melodrama.

And, really, too wrapped up in her Paris trip to care.

After all, for Alexa, Paris was more than just a destination — it was her hometown. She had been born, and grew up, steps from the Champs-Elysées, but her fabulous French lifestyle — flaky croissants every morning, a view of the Seine from her bedroom window, designer boutiques around the corner — had come to a tragic end at the tender age of seven. It was then that her father's architecture job had whisked the family across the ocean to, of all places, suburban New Jersey.

For the next eleven years, Alexa's persistent homesickness had only been alleviated by a few, all-too-short trips back to see her French side of the family: her rolling-in-euros aunt and uncle, Aziza and Julien St. Laurent, and their two kids — her cousins, Pierre and Raphaëlle. In fact, on *this* trip, Alexa had planned for her and Diego to stay with said cousins in their funky Le Marais flat. But because the St. Laurents would be at their country house in Avignon for a long weekend, Alexa and Diego would have to spend their first three days in a hotel — which Alexa actually *wasn't* thrilled about. In Paris, she resented anything that made her feel even remotely like a tourist.

"Sweetie, you'll survive in Oakridge for a week," Portia was murmuring as she patted Maeve's plump, ring-bedecked hand. "It's not like *my* break's going to be all that fabulous." At this, Portia cast a quick, withering glance in Alexa's direction.

Alexa felt a cold tightening in her stomach. She detested arguing with her friends, but she was also never one to shy away from a confrontation. "Is there a problem, Portia?" Alexa asked coolly, toying with the bejeweled buttons on her fitted periwinkle Nanette

Lepore blazer. Portia would be spending the week on her parents' yacht off the coast of Bermuda — hardly slumming. Besides, Alexa thought, it was Portia's own fault for waiting until the eleventh hour to make her plans.

"Hmm. Now you notice?" Portia retorted, narrowing her yellow-brown eyes at Alexa while twirling the unlit cigarette between her fingers. Then she turned back to Maeve and draped a skinny arm around the weeping girl's shoulders, playing up the oh-so-sympathetic-friend role.

What*ever.* With a dismissive sigh, Alexa crossed her long, denim-clad legs and poked at her avocado roll with a slender finger. She was so not going to feed into Portia's mysterious bout of bitchiness, which, now that Alexa thought about it, had been building all week. Yesterday, Portia had blown off Alexa's suggestion that the two of them drive to New York City for a Marc Jacobs sample sale with an icy "Why don't you ask Mr. Princeton instead?" That was Portia's nickname for Diego; he was a freshman at the university and, in Portia's opinion, way too arrogant about it.

And, in Alexa's opinion, Portia was just jealous because *she'd* never had a college boyfriend.

"Ooh la la, Alexa St. Laurent! Why ze sour face?"

Alexa turned in her orange plastic seat, her spirits immediately lifting. The laughing, melodic voice could only belong to one person: Holly Jacobson. Bestest childhood friends, Alexa and Holly had drifted apart in middle school, only to become kind of close again after spending a whirlwind week together in South Beach last year.

Sure enough, there stood Holly, her light-brown ponytail bobbing as she tried to balance her lunch tray against her hip, adjust her backpack on her shoulder, and smile at Alexa all at once. Holly's tray bore a whole-wheat turkey sandwich, a bag of soy chips, an apple, and a bottle of Gatorade — the typical sporty-girl lunch, cobbled together from the cafeteria's blah options. Students weren't allowed off campus for lunch, but Alexa and her crew had deftly worked around that rule: Every morning, they'd stop by the Oakridge gourmet food shop for sushi, fennel salad, or brie, and store their treats in Maeve's portable cooler until lunchtime.

For a split second, Alexa wondered if Holly planned to join her table, and she felt a pinprick of concern. Alexa and Holly rarely, if ever, associated in school. They occasionally chatted on the phone and sometimes met for lattes over the weekend — but always just the two of them. Alone. It was kind of ridiculous, really; Alexa often felt as if she and Holly were carrying on an illicit affair. Now, she sneaked a precautionary glance at her friends; Maeve, oblivious as ever, was blowing her nose, but Portia was regarding Holly with a cruel smirk.

If Holly noticed Portia's less-than-welcoming expression, she didn't show it. "I was on my way to sit down," she told Alexa, and gestured across the cafeteria to where most of the senior athletes were gathered at a long table. "But then I noticed you pouting over here," she went on with a grin. "Shouldn't you be all giddy about *Paree*?"

Alexa laughed, her earlier irritation dissolving. Leave it to sensitive Holly to pick up on her pissiness from a mile away. Plus, Holly had a point: Why was Alexa even *allowing* any weirdness with Portia to bother her, considering the yummy adventures that lay ahead? Brushing off her brooding, Alexa reached up to squeeze Holly's elbow affectionately. "I'm over the moon, *chérie*," she replied breezily. "I was just trying to figure out which nightclub Diego and I should visit first. Decisions, decisions . . ."

Holly nodded, her freckled cheeks coloring, and Alexa felt the tiniest stab of guilt. Once upon a time, Holly had harbored a huge crush on Diego, and she'd even been the one to innocently introduce him to Alexa. Though Alexa knew for a fact that Holly was good and over Diego — randomly enough, Holly was now dating *Alexa's* ex, Tyler Davis — the past love triangle remained a source of slight friction between the two girls. "You must be psyched for London," Alexa added, smoothly changing the subject. "You're leaving tomorrow night, right?"

"*London?*" Portia cut in, and even Maeve abandoned her Kleenex to glance up at Holly in surprise. "As in, London, England? Why are *you* going there?" Portia asked, leaning back in her seat and blatantly looking Holly up and down.

Alexa couldn't help it — she, too, sized up her old friend. Last year, a standard Holly ensemble would have been Puma racing pants, Sauconys, and a gray Oakridge High Track & Field T-shirt. Today, Holly was wearing a burgundy cardigan over a fitted white V-neck, tan bell-bottom cords, a big-buckled belt, and wine-colored crushed velvet flats that Alexa had seen — but scorned — at the Nine West in the Galleria last week. *Not half bad,* Alexa decided. Also, Holly had recently grown out her chin-length hair, so that it fell to her shoulders, and her once short, straight bangs now framed her face in soft, flattering layers.

Still, it wasn't only the outfit and the new 'do that made her old friend look different, Alexa realized. The once super-shy Holly now gave off a confident vibe that turned her gray-green eyes bright and, apparently, lent her enough boldness to stop by Alexa's lunch table in the first place — something the old Holly would *never* have dared.

But now that shyness seemed to be returning under Portia and Maeve's scrutinizing gazes. Alexa looked on sympathetically as Holly shifted her weight from one foot to the other and studied the tiled floor. "Um, it's not really London," Holly amended, her face turning progressively pinker. "The girls' track team — we're, I guess, attending this international meet in Wimbledon? And since I'm, uh, the captain . . . I need to, you know, go . . ." She shrugged and Alexa sighed, wishing Holly could finish the sentence without fumbling so much.

"I love Wimbledon!" Maeve cried, her round hazel eyes lighting up. "I've been there zillions of times to see Andy play." She rested her chin in her hands dreamily while Alexa fought back a giggle; Maeve's hopeless obsession with Andy Roddick was legendary.

Portia flicked her hand as if there were an invisible mosquito buzzing around their table. "I have, too, but come *on*, Maevie. It's such a drab little village." The corners of her Urban Decay–stained lips curved up in a smile. "Though that makes perfect sense for you, doesn't it, Holly?"

"Portia . . ." Alexa warned, rolling her eyes. She was sick of having to navigate the treacherous waters between her friends and Holly.

Holly swallowed hard and tightened her hold on her lunch tray. Alexa could tell from the set of her mouth that Holly was pissed, but Alexa also knew

9

her timid friend would never fight back. "I should go," Holly muttered, backing away. Then she glanced at Alexa, and her face brightened slightly. "Hey, Alexa, call me if you want while you're in Paris, okay?" she offered. "I'm getting one of those world phones so I'll be able to use my cell."

Only because your overprotective parents are making you, Alexa thought, smiling and fluttering her fingers up at Holly. Alexa knew that the chances she'd actually contact Holly were slim to none — why would *any* sane girl take a break from Paris and her boyfriend to place a phone call?

Twirling a strand of flaxen hair around one finger, Alexa watched as Holly hurried over to the jock lunch table. She took a seat across from her track team cocaptains, Meghan and Jess, and next to Tyler Davis. Holly turned and said something to Tyler that made him laugh, and then he leaned in and kissed her. So *that* was where Holly's confidence came from, Alexa mused, as Holly casually reached over and stroked the back of Tyler's neck. *Have they done it yet?* Alexa wondered, suddenly intrigued.

"Ugh," Portia groaned, breaking into Alexa's thoughts. "Dork central. *Please* tell me you girls noticed those lame Nine West flats?"

Maeve nodded sagely, her crying jag forgotten. "Bad news. I mean, yeah, everyone knows that Tyler

Davis has lifted Holly Jacobson a few rungs up the social ladder," she added. "But, Lex, it's probably not too smart to be seen with her, don't you think?"

"*Excuse* me?" Alexa snapped, anger flushing her peaches-and-cream skin hot as she studied Portia and Maeve across the table. "Last time I checked, Maevie, it was *not* your job to dictate who I do or do not talk to." Alexa was absolutely over that petty high school mentality. Ever since getting accepted early decision to Columbia in December, she'd been living with one pencil-heeled Christian Louboutin boot in college. And, of course, she'd grown accustomed to lounging in Diego's dorm room every afternoon and attending Princeton parties every Saturday night. Not for the first time, the large, brightly lit Oakridge High cafeteria seemed tiny — suffocating — to Alexa.

And suddenly, so did her friends.

"I'm sorry, Lex, but —" Maeve began, looking huffy.

"I so don't need this bullshit right now," Alexa declared, reaching down to scoop up her purple suede Michael Kors satchel. She pushed her chair back.

"Fine," Portia said silkily, snatching up her silver-plated lighter from the table. "Go run off to Mr. Princeton. He's all that matters to you anyway — right, Alexandria? You're so high on the fact that you have an older boyfriend that you don't give a damn about leaving your best friends in the lurch for our *last* spring break together." Portia slid the cigarette between her lips and lit it, her 'trembling fingers betraying her fury.

Aha! Alexa thought, pausing mid-escape. So that explained both Portia's hostility *and* why she'd held off on making vacation plans for so long. She'd been expecting that Alexa would — what? Invite the girls along to Paris? Scrap the incredible plans she and Diego had made forever ago so the three of them could fly to Panama City and spend a week dozing on the beach? Last year, South Beach had been a much-needed sun-splashed change of scene from wintry, ordinary Oakridge. But this year Alexa craved a different kind of experience. And she'd already made that crystal-clear to her friends.

"Nobody told you to wait for me," Alexa shot back, meeting Portia's glare. "You knew I was doing Paris with Diego. Besides, don't be so dramatic, Portia — we can still go away on spring breaks together when we're in college." *But can we?* Alexa wondered. *Will we still be as close by then?*

"That's not the point," Maeve jumped in, glancing questioningly at Portia, who gave a quick nod of approval and blew out a curl of smoke. "We're worried about you, Alexa. You get way too into the guys you date. It's like ... you don't know how to be independent."

"Not independent?" Alexa repeated in horror. She slapped her hand down on the table, her thick ivory bangle knocking against the Formica. "God. How could you say that? Have you even *been* friends with me for these past four years?"

"I don't know," Portia replied softly, removing the cigarette from her mouth and examining the bright orange tip. She flicked her eyes back to Alexa. "Have we? Are we *still* your friends?"

"Yeah," Maeve echoed. "Are we?"

Alexa shook her head, unsure how to respond. She hated feeling misunderstood like this. True friends were supposed to *know* her — to get her. Right? Alexa St. Laurent considered herself the crown *princess* of independence, and she was appalled that anyone — let alone Portia and Maeve — would think otherwise.

But she remembered this tricky issue cropping up with the girls before — their constant complaining that Alexa put her boyfriends over her friend-friends. Since hooking up with Diego, Alexa *had* made an effort to blend her two worlds better — organizing movie nights, throwing an everyone's-invited New Year's bash at her house — but neither Diego nor her girlfriends seemed to take to one another very eagerly. *Maybe,* Alexa realized, as she gazed at Portia and Maeve's scornful faces, *I end up spending more time with my boyfriend because I don't want to spend time with . . . them.*

Alexa was debating whether or not to say these words when the assistant principal, as expected, came barreling toward their table. Uptight Mrs. Jacobson often patrolled the cafeteria at lunchtime, hoping to catch someone doing something illegal.

"Portia Florentino-Cohen," she snapped, gray-green eyes flashing behind her square, red-framed glasses, "extinguish that cigarette right now." Alexa could already hear the kids at the next table — J.D., Tracey, Tabitha, and other popular seniors whom she considered casual friends — laughing over this predictable showdown.

"In a minute, Mrs. J," Portia replied, tapping ash into her empty Diet Pepsi can. "I'm finishing up a discussion with your daughter's very *dearest* friend."

Alexa shot what she hoped was a winning smile at the glowering Mrs. Jacobson — whom Alexa still thought of as "Holly's mom." Poor Holly had the massive misfortune of having an assistant principal for a mother, which, Alexa knew, made her life unfun both in and out of school. At that moment, Alexa could see Holly cringing in embarrassment as she watched her mom from across the cafeteria.

Mrs. Jacobson rolled up the sleeves of her crisp

striped blouse as if she was considering decking Portia. "Let me say, Portia, that I know you are on the wait list for Colgate. One *discussion* with their dean could get you rejected so fast your head would spin."

Nice comeback, Alexa thought, secretly impressed by Mrs. Jacobson's ballsiness. She knew that comment would rattle Portia; despite her parents' generous donations, Portia's college future looked iffy. Even Maeve was more confident about getting accepted to Emory come April. Had Alexa not been so furious, she might have reached across the table to take Portia's hand for comfort.

But Portia only rolled her eyes and stubbed out the cigarette on the side of her can. "Good to know," she said. "I'll just take my activities outside." She stood, gathering her fur-trimmed vest in her arms.

When Mrs. Jacobson finally turned and stalked away, Alexa felt the tension drift back over the table like a cloud of smoke. She realized that, what with all the cigarette commotion, she hadn't answered the girls' question about whether or not they were still her friends.

"Do either of you plan on joining me?" Portia was asking, picking up her clutch.

Deliberately, Alexa lifted her eyes to meet Portia's. "No," she replied, after a long moment of silence. "Not at all." *And that,* she thought, *is my real answer.* Knowing that Portia understood what she'd meant, Alexa swallowed, fighting back the sudden, hot sting of tears. She couldn't stand crying in public.

Portia gave a short nod and swung around to face Maeve. "Are *you* coming, Maevie?" she demanded.

Maeve glanced from Portia to Alexa, blinking. Alexa unbuckled her satchel and busily dug around for her tube of Laura Mercier lip gloss to indicate she didn't care whom Maeve chose either way. When she glanced up again, Maeve was standing and wearing her woolen pea coat, and she and Portia were moving away from the table.

"See you, Alexa?" Maeve called tremulously over her shoulder.

"If she ever decides we're worthy," Portia said, tugging on Maeve's arm and shooting daggers back at Alexa. "Let's *go.*"

Alexa watched the two of them trot out the back doors into the school yard and sighed. Portia and Maeve were doing their typical exaggeration thing; Alexa knew she *would* see them again — even hang out with them — once she was back from Paris. But she also knew that their relationship wouldn't be the same; something irreversible had shifted at that lunch table. Alexa would never feel as tight with the girls as she once had.

Relief sliced through her sadness. In some ways, their fight had been coming for so long that it felt almost liberating to have it out of the way. The only thing Alexa was upset about now was that Portia and Maeve beat *her* to making a grand exit.

But, really, who cares? she realized. What was some stupid schoolgirl bitch session compared to beautiful, sweeping, unforgettable Paris? As she rose to her feet, cleared off the table, and sauntered toward the trash can, Alexa could feel her old optimism bubbling up inside her. Tomorrow, she wouldn't even *be* at school. And tomorrow night, she and Diego would be cuddled close in their Air France seats, sharing mini bottles of champagne and whispering secrets as the sleek airplane zoomed them far, far away from Oakridge.

Heading for the front cafeteria doors, Alexa remembered Holly's words from before and suddenly felt just that: *giddy*. She pictured Diego on the plane, his black eyes sparkling, a slow smile spreading across his face as he moved the armrest up to draw Alexa into his lap. She and Diego hadn't flown together before, but Alexa could imagine him doing something sexy but chivalrous like that. And maybe, when the lights were dimmed and everyone else was asleep, the two of them could indulge in a little beneath-the-airline-blanket action.

Ooh la la indeed.

CHAPTER TWO

Practice Makes Perfect

"I'm going to miss my flight!" Holly Jacobson cried, dashing outside with her duffel bag, her honey-brown hair snapping behind her in the brisk nighttime wind. She raced toward the driveway, ignoring the last-minute warnings — "Don't forget to call us from the gate!" "Set your clock five hours ahead!" "Don't speak to strange British men!" — her parents were yelling from the doorstep.

"We've got plenty of time," her boyfriend, Tyler Davis, said, flashing his trademark relaxed grin as he gallantly lifted Holly's bag and set it in the trunk of his green Audi TT. Holly planted a grateful kiss on his warm, smooth cheek and squeezed his arm.

"But the plane leaves at midnight," she explained, pushing up the sleeve of her fleece and pressing the

GLOW function on her digital wristwatch. It was nine fifteen. "You need to get there at least two hours ahead for international departures," she added, quoting her track team coach, Ms. Graham. Holly felt a prickle of anxiety; she'd never flown overseas before. And as pumped as she was to be traveling to England with her friends, part of her was insanely nervous about being so far from home for a full week.

Not to mention saying good-bye to Tyler.

"We're awesome," Tyler said, opening the passenger side door for Holly. "I can totally make it to Newark by ten if there's no traffic and —" His amber-brown eyes sparkling with mischief, he dropped his voice to a whisper and checked the house to make sure Holly's parents couldn't hear. "I speed."

Holly grinned, sliding into the car. "Tyler Davis, you will never in a million years break the New Jersey speed limit."

And that, Holly thought, waving at her parents as she and Tyler backed out of the Jacobsons' driveway, was *why* her super-strict mom and dad adored Tyler so much — and had even allowed him to drive her to the airport. Tyler was polite in a 1950s-ish way — bringing flowers whenever the Jacobsons had him to dinner, making sure Holly was safely inside every time he dropped her off after track practice, even (to Holly's squirming embarrassment) calling her dad "sir" whenever the mood struck him. Holly knew she was beyond lucky to have such a sweet boyfriend, but sometimes Tyler and his "golly gee gosh!" vibe made her want to roll her eyes.

As they turned onto Beech Street and cruised toward the intersection, Holly let out a big breath. That afternoon, as soon as she and her mother had come home from school, Holly had been caught up in a packing-and-advice frenzy; it was a huge relief to leave her parents behind. Tyler pulled to a stop in front of the red light, and Holly turned to look at him, her heart swelling. His chiseled profile and wavy, dark blond hair were illuminated by the moonlight spilling in through the window. Really, was it any wonder the boy had almost appeared in an American Eagle ad?

Sometimes, when she and Tyler were curled up in his bedroom watching TV or running side by side in the park near Holly's house or even sitting next to each other in calculus class, Holly would glance his way and catch herself thinking: *Tyler Davis. Captain of the lacrosse team. Oakridge High hottie.* My *boyfriend*.

Even after a full year together, she still found this fact nearly impossible to believe.

Holly had never been in a relationship before — actually, before Tyler, she'd barely known how to *talk* to boys. But, despite these moments of incredulous wonder, Holly had discovered she was pretty good at the whole girlfriend thing. Being with Tyler felt as natural to her as breathing; at school, their once-distinct groups of friends had blended easily, forming a formidable sports posse. And outside of school, when it was just the two of them . . . well, that was even better.

The light hadn't changed yet, so Holly leaned forward and lightly traced the line of Tyler's strong jaw.

"Hey," she whispered.

Tyler turned, his face breaking into a smile. "Hey," he whispered back.

At the exact same instant, they leaned in, and kissed.

Holly often wondered why she didn't simply spend her whole life kissing Tyler. Homework and sports and college applications were meaningless compared to the feel of his soft lips, his warm, cinnamony breath, the gentle touch of his tongue against hers.

"Mmm," Holly murmured, nestling in as close as her seat belt would allow. Tyler wrapped his arm around her shoulder, eagerly continuing the kiss, until the blare of car horns behind them ruined the moment.

They pulled apart; the light was green, but Tyler didn't accelerate. "I'm going to miss you so much," he said softly, his eyes sweeping over Holly's face.

Holly bit her lip as the car glided forward. "No kidding."

Tyler was staying in Oakridge over spring break for his do-gooder job at New Jersey Cares, a help-the-homeless organization. The Oakridge High college counselor had encouraged Tyler to sign up at the beginning of senior year, since volunteering always impressed colleges. But, as Holly liked to joke, "Saint Tyler" would have gladly joined such an activity on his own. Besides, he was practically guaranteed admission at his first choice, the University of Michigan, thanks to his skills on the lacrosse field. Holly herself had applied to U Mich — and, at her parents' urging, nearby Rutgers — among a handful of other schools. Neither she nor Tyler knew where they'd gotten in yet, and wouldn't find out for another month or so.

College. Spring break. The world seemed to be conspiring to keep her and Tyler apart. With a sigh of longing, Holly rested her hand on Tyler's knee, feeling the heat of his skin through the khaki fabric. Keeping one hand on the wheel, Tyler reached down and took Holly's small hand in his much larger one, gently tickling her palm, just the way she liked it. When he spoke, his voice was husky.

"Holly? Do you want to stop somewhere and —"

"Practice?" Holly finished, grinning. Her face flushed.

Tyler nodded, swallowing hard, his eyes on the road. "Practice," he affirmed.

"Practice" was Holly and Tyler's secret code word for fooling around. It made sense, Holly reasoned, since the rest of their lives revolved around other, regular kinds of practice, like track and lacrosse.

This, though, was practice for something truly exciting.

When Holly had first started dating Tyler after spring break last year, she'd assumed — based on information she'd read in *Seventeen* — that he'd start pressuring her to have sex right away. But Tyler had taken things deliciously slow, progressing to new levels on a month-by-month basis: April had been about serious kissing; in May, he'd unbuttoned her shirt for the first time; in June, they'd carefully progressed to the undoing-the-belt-buckle stage. One cool evening in October, Tyler's parents had miraculously been away at a wedding and Holly's parents miraculously hadn't been calling her cell every twenty seconds. They were lying half clothed on Tyler's bed when Holly, feeling brave and hopeful and terrified, turned in his arms and whispered in his ear the truth that had been nagging at her for a while: She was a virgin.

Holly had actually been cool with her virgin status — before Tyler, she'd hardly given it a second thought — until her best friend, Meghan, passed her a *Twist* article in Italian class. The article claimed that, apparently, seventeen-year-old virgins were as rare as, say, spotted owls in North America. An endangered species. *I am a freak*, Holly had decided, feeling horrified and forgetting the fact that Meghan, Jess, and *most* of her friends fell into that very same category.

But when she'd made her big confession to Tyler, he'd simply pulled her in closer and murmured that he didn't mind; they could wait as long as she wanted, and he himself had only ever been with one girl, which, when you thought about it, barely even counted.

When Holly thought about it, though, she realized that the *one girl* Tyler referred to was Alexa St. Laurent. Tyler never spoke about Alexa, but Holly knew that the two of them had dated for most of junior year. Holly had practically grown up with Alexa, and especially since their bonding experience in South Beach last year, thought of her as a semi-sister. Holly was certain that Alexa didn't care about Tyler anymore. But sometimes the whole tangled web of connections still bothered her.

Tyler had been as good as his word: He never pressured Holly. But that Friday night, as he parked the car on a secluded dead-end street, under a thick canopy of trees, Holly felt a tingling — part desire, part regret — in her belly. She wished that Tyler wouldn't always be quite so patient. She wished she *weren't* flying off to London as a seventeen-year-old endangered-species. It was funny, but in recent months, Holly had been feeling more like the aggressor, while Tyler was the one who held back — as if they'd switched standard boy-girl roles.

True to form, it was Holly who undid her seat belt first and reached for Tyler, drinking in another one of his knee-weakening kisses. Tyler's hands slid up her sides, over to the zipper on her fleece. Without breaking the kiss, he tugged off Holly's fleece and her black cotton cardigan until she was wearing only her red tank top. Holly drew back slightly to push Tyler's jacket off his broad shoulders and pull his hooded sweatshirt over his head, the better to admire his toned body. The windows were already fogged up, and they were only getting started.

His breath hot against her skin, Tyler planted kisses all up Holly's freckle-dusted collarbone and her neck until his lips reached her ear, which he nibbled on gently. Tyler knew the sensation was one of Holly's favorites. She sighed appreciatively and twined her arms around his neck, breathing in his crisp, clean scent; no matter how hot and bothered Tyler Davis got, he always smelled like fresh soap. Holly tried to wriggle up against him, but the gearshift made it difficult.

"Let's go in the back," Holly whispered, the words slipping out between kisses. Maybe it was the fact that she'd be boarding a plane in an hour and wouldn't be seeing her boyfriend for a full week, but suddenly Holly felt a growing urgency between herself and Tyler that she'd never known before.

Her body made the decision before her mind could even catch up: Tonight, she didn't want to simply practice.

Holly Jacobson was ready for the real deal.

"Now?" Tyler asked, catching his breath. His eyes moved to the dashboard clock; it was ten fifteen. "You were worried about being late for your —"

"Screw it. I'll run to the gate."

Tyler's face lit up. "If you say so." He was reaching for the door handle when Holly touched his arm. He turned back to her, his eyebrows raised.

As butterflies stormed her stomach, Holly took a big, calming breath and inclined her head toward the glove compartment. "Maybe we should . . . take the box with us?"

The box was a box of condoms that Holly and Tyler had purchased together in November on a completely embarrassing expedition to the CVS in the Galleria. Blushing like crazy, Tyler had grabbed the first container of Trojans he could reach and tossed it to Holly, who sprinted to the counter in record time. As Tyler paid the cashier, Holly stuffed the purchase in a plastic bag and raced it out to Tyler's car. It was like they'd been participating in an Olympic triathlon. That, however, was the most action the poor Trojans had seen; they now sat, collecting dust, in Tyler's glove compartment.

Tyler's brown eyes went round. "Seriously?"

Holly squeezed his hand, her pulse quickening. Unable to speak, she managed a slow nod. *Yes.*

Before either of them could change their minds, they grabbed the box and retreated to the back. Holly stretched out across the leather seat — she still had to tuck her legs in a bit — while Tyler tried to arrange himself on top of her without hitting his head on the car's roof. Holly stifled a giggle as Tyler accidentally kicked the side door and muttered "Ouch." She had to admit this wasn't the sexiest setup.

Plus, there *was* something kind of suburban-tacky about losing your virginity in the backseat of your boyfriend's Audi.

But whatever. She and Tyler often had to resort to backseat lovin'; there simply weren't that many places in which to get busy. Whenever they made out in Tyler's spacious room, with its double bed and framed sports posters on the walls, Tyler's mom would inevitably call them to dinner; Holly had come to suspect that Mrs. Davis psychically knew the *precise* moment that Tyler was reaching for the clasp on Holly's bra. Holly's house was worse; her narrow twin bed was even less conducive to hookups than a backseat, and what with her brother, Josh, blasting Eminem next door, and her parents not even bothering to knock . . . impossible.

She and Tyler started kissing, more intensely than before. Soon, Tyler was in his boxers and slowly unbuttoning Holly's jeans, his warm fingers just shy of hesitant.

This is it, Holly realized. Her heart was racing and her palms were sweaty, even if the rest of her was burning up. *There's no turning back.*

"Oh, Tyler," she whispered, closing her eyes. She was aching in the most wonderful way. But suddenly Tyler's touch *was* hesitant. She felt him pause, one hand floating over her belly. By now, Holly was so attuned to Tyler's body — she was sure she knew it as well as her own — that she could always sense the slightest change in him. Her eyes flew open.

"What's wrong?" Holly spoke into his ear. "What is it?"

"Nothing's wrong," Tyler replied, his face in her neck. But Holly could feel his heartbeat, which had been so wild against hers only a second before, slowing down. Her own anticipation began to deflate. Something was off here.

"It's the car, right?" she whispered. When she and Tyler had talked about sex before, they'd both agreed they'd want it to happen in a king-size bed, and hopefully in a room with flickering candles and a door that locked.

"Not really," Tyler said. But then, as Holly's stomach sank in disbelief, he slowly drew back. He pulled away from her, his head narrowly missing the roof again, until he was sitting all the way up.

"Then *what*?" Holly asked, confused. She struggled to sit up as well. How could they have been attacking each other, like, an instant before? "Tyler, tell me."

Tyler brushed his arm across his forehead, not looking at her. A blush was creeping up his bare chest, into his face. "I don't think we should —" He cleared his throat. "I guess I sort of feel like we're . . . rushing."

"Rushing?" Holly echoed. She checked her watch — almost eleven. "Well, I do need to get to the airport," Holly conceded, feeling a prickle of worry about making her flight. "But — I thought you wanted to —"

Tyler shook his head, pushing his fingers through his thick hair. "Not rushing right *now*. More like, in general. You know?"

"No," Holly replied truthfully. "I don't." She slipped up the straps of her tank top, dread building inside her.

Tyler stared down at his hands in his lap. "I've just . . . made that mistake before." He cleared his throat again.

Before? Holly wondered. *With Alexa?* Holly's skin turned cold. She pictured her old friend — her long, fairy-tale blonde tresses and delicate, heart-shaped face; her slinky-sheer designer dresses; her flirty, tinkling laugh . . . Alexa *defined* sexy. And even though Holly had grown a lot surer of herself in the past year, whenever she was around Alexa, she felt pretty much invisible.

How could I not? Holly thought, glancing down at herself. At seventeen, she still looked like a little girl — all freckles and stick-straight hair. Only her decent-sized boobs made her seem remotely mature. But it didn't matter. Alexa was the kind of girl boys always lusted after. *And I'm not,* Holly realized, as tears began to burn her throat. This explained everything. Holly had gleaned enough from *Gilmore Girls, He's Just Not That Into You,* various movies, and countless teen magazines to know that, regardless of the circumstances or the timing, if a boy was attracted to you, he was *not* going to turn down sex.

Holly needed to face the harsh truth: Tyler had gone all the way with Alexa St. Laurent. But he didn't want to go all the way with *her.*

Tyler must have picked up on Holly's mounting misery, because he turned to her and touched her arm. "Maybe we should, um, talk about this. . . ." He trailed off.

"Forget it," Holly said, her voice coming out in a sob. She jerked away, opened the back door, and stormed back to the passenger seat, the bitter March air biting her exposed skin.

"Holly, wait." Tyler was scrambling to get his clothes on.

Holly slammed the door, jerked on her cardigan and fleece, and snapped her seat belt into place. Hot tears hovered on her lower lashes, and her lips quivered. What had she been thinking? That perfect, golden-boy Tyler Davis would want *her*? Just last year, she'd been eating lonely lunches at the unpopular table with Meghan and Jess, worlds away from having a boyfriend.

Tyler got into the driver's seat and immediately reached for her, but, again, she moved away.

"Holly, I'm sorry. You didn't let me — I need to explain the whole thing better —"

"I get it," Holly replied through gritted teeth. "Just drive." Her face on fire, she stared straight ahead at the pitch-black dead end. Suddenly, she wanted to be as far away from Tyler Davis as humanly possible.

Tyler seemed about to say something else, but then he cleared his throat and gunned the engine. In a very un-Tyler manner, he spun the car around and sped back to the main avenue, screeching through yellow lights, until they reached the highway. There, they hit a block of traffic that made Holly count the seconds on the clock and nervously rotate the chunky silver ring on her finger.

"We'll make it," Tyler said.

"Don't talk to me," Holly replied, her voice still shaky.

They drove the rest of the way in silence and arrived at the airport with twenty minutes to spare. Holly's stomach was in knots. Her coach and team-mates were going to kill her if she didn't show. And what would she tell her parents? Before she could leap out of the car, Tyler grabbed her elbow. When she glanced at him, his handsome face was sorrowful.

"Please don't get on that plane all mad at me," Tyler said, his voice choked with emotion. "There's so much stuff we still need to talk about, and just — know that —" He paused, studying her solemnly. "I love you, Holly."

Holly felt her chest seize up. She and Tyler had crossed the overhyped "I love you" hurdle back on — even Holly had rolled her eyes at the predict-ability — Valentine's Day. Still, hearing Tyler speak that phrase — and speaking it herself — always gave her shivers.

But now the words made no sense to Holly's ears. How could Tyler love her and not be into her *that* way? Holly's head spun in confusion.

Since she was deathly afraid of flying, Holly *didn't* like getting on a plane angry at someone. So she leaned close, whispered a quick "I love you, too," and kissed Tyler on the lips. He cupped her face in his hands, trying to hold her there, but she pulled back, opened the door, and jumped out into the night.

"Don't go hooking up with David Beckham, okay?" Tyler called through the window as she raced around to the trunk to get her bag. His voice was half-teasing, half-worried.

"I'll try my *very* best not to," Holly called back with a wave, letting Tyler know, in her way, that she wasn't all-out furious at him.

But maybe she *was.*

There was no time left to ponder the sticky situation. Her thoughts whirling, Holly sprinted into the airport, waited on pins and needles in a long, snaky ticket line (where she squeezed in a phone call home), flashed her passport, raced through security with her carry-on — but got held up when the house keys in her back pocket set off the metal detector — and finally tore toward her gate, thanking her lucky stars she'd worn her Adidas *and* could run like nobody's business. Panting and sweaty, she stumbled onto the airplane at seven minutes to midnight, avoiding the glares of the flight attendants and collapsing into the empty seat between Meghan and Jess.

"Oh, my God! Where the hell *were* you?" Jess cried

"We were so worried!" Meghan added, poking Holly in the ribs.

"I'll tell you guys later," was all that Holly could get out between gasps.

Instantly, Ms. Graham, the usually cheerful track coach, turned in her seat — which was right in front of Holly's — and shot daggers at her.

"Holly Jacobson," Ms. Graham intoned, her curly, ash-blonde bob shaking with anger. "Showing up so grossly late is *not* a good indication of team spirit — or leadership. This had better not become a habit on the trip."

Holly stared back at Ms. Graham in silence. She knew the coach was married (to Mr. Sweeney, the balding golf coach), but Holly was certain that Ms. Graham didn't know what it was like to be caught in the swirling currents of desire and frustration, to gaze into a boy's golden-flecked eyes and wonder what secrets lay there. After what Holly had just been through with Tyler, how was she supposed to care about freaking *team spirit?*

"Of course not," she replied, folding her shaking hands in her lap. "I'm one-hundred-percent committed, Ms. Graham."

She'd do this. She'd get through the week in Wimbledon, throw herself into running, be there for her friends . . . and try her darndest not to obsess over her love life.

A clipped, British-accented voice came over the loudspeaker. "We welcome you aboard this Virgin Atlantic flight, nonstop to Heathrow."

Virgin Atlantic? A wry smile spread across Holly's face as the plane began to taxi. Here she was, crossing the Atlantic, and still a virgin. She wasn't sure if she should burst into tears or burst out laughing. *That's perfect, isn't it?* Holly thought, settling back in her seat for the long flight. *Just perfect.*

CHAPTER THREE

Paris in the Springtime

Taking a deep breath, Alexa opened the French doors and tiptoed out onto the balcony of the hotel. Though she wore only a lace cami and Juicy boy shorts, Alexa didn't shiver in the misty afternoon chill. Instead, she rested her hands on the damp, wrought-iron railing and gazed down, beaming, at the tree-lined boulevard St-Germain.

Petite, slender women — filmy silk scarves knotted around their necks and fluffy Pomeranians peeking out of their Chanel totes — click-clacked along the rain-slick sidewalk in sky-high stilettos. An old man with a baguette under his arm pedaled past, his red bicycle a splash of color against the gray afternoon. In front of the Sonia Rykiel boutique, a teenage couple was making out, staying pressed together even when a

36

fleet of guys on sleek mopeds zoomed noisily up the boulevard. Fragments of French phrases — *"Mais non!" "Ça va, chérie? . . ."* — floated up to Alexa, along with the rich scent of fresh bread from a nearby café.

Alexa's heart soared. She was home.

"Baby, could you come inside? It's freezing."

Oh, yeah. Reluctantly, Alexa turned away from the marvelous view and peered into the dimly lit hotel room behind her. She'd been so caught up in her rapturous return to Paris, she'd — oops — kind of forgotten about Diego.

He was sitting up in the rumpled bed, wearing his boxers and rubbing his eyes with his fists like a little boy. Alexa melted at the adorable sight. Her boyfriend had been so jet-lagged after their grueling overnight flight that he'd crashed as soon as they'd arrived at the hotel that morning. Alexa had curled up beside him for a bit, but it had been impossible to sleep, knowing all the fabulousness that was waiting right outside their window.

Alexa cast one last glance at the kissing couple below. They'd separated and were now arguing loudly, the boy gesturing with his cigarette and the girl sobbing. *So French,* Alexa thought with a smile, slipping back inside. She shut the doors, drew the heavy drapes, and started toward the bed, passing the minibar, the flat-screen TV, and the luggage she'd dropped in front

of the gleaming armoire. Theirs wasn't so much a double bed, Alexa noticed as she flopped down beside
Diego, as two twin beds pushed together, with the nar-
rowest of gaps between them — a typical, if bizarre,
feature of European hotel rooms.

Which was pretty much the only thing Euro *about*
this place, Alexa mused as she stretched out on the
crisp white sheets. The Hôtel Rive Gauche, where
Diego had booked them for the next three days,
was super-posh, very modern, and, in Alexa's opinion, utterly bland. She couldn't *wait* until Tuesday,
when they'd relocate to her cousins' small, shabby-
chic apartment. Alexa vividly remembered the charming
place from her last visit two years ago: the yellow shutters, the claw-footed bathtub, the slanting floors. That,
to Alexa, was the *true* Paris — old-fashioned, artsy,
bohemian. . . .

But, still, it *was* pretty yummy to be all alone in a
luxe hotel room with her boyfriend.

Alexa propped herself on one elbow to study
Diego, who was lying on his back once more and holding a pillow over his face. His smooth, caramel-colored
chest rose and fell steadily.

"Don't go to sleep again, lazy," Alexa murmured,
yanking on the edge of his pillow.

"Cut it out," Diego muttered, his voice muffled.
"I'm really tired."

"Boo-hoo," Alexa teased. She'd noticed that traveling overseas had somehow turned the usually suave, mega-mature Diego Mendieta into a nine-year-old. Feeling mischievous, Alexa slid over to Diego's side of the bed and tickled her boyfriend along his ribs, down his flat stomach, and over to the waistband of his boxers. Finally, Diego started laughing. He lifted the pillow off his face and hurled it right at Alexa. She shrieked and grabbed her own pillow, mashing it in Diego's face until he took hold of her arms and pinned her back against the bed.

"Do I win?" Diego asked softly, his black eyes dancing. He grinned, flashing his deep dimples. His dark hair fell across his forehead as he leaned in closer.

"You win," Alexa laughed, tilting her head all the way back in a gesture of surrender. Her blonde hair fanned out behind her. "Hands down."

"Good," Diego said. He brushed his full lips lightly up her neck, taunting her. Alexa wriggled to get out of his grip, even though she was more than happy where she was. She could feel her skin heating up. Diego's skin, as always, was warm and smelled like Cool Water.

Diego slid his lips up to her mouth, but let them hover there, barely touching hers. Alexa grinned; this was one of their favorite games — to see who would give in first and start the real kiss. When she didn't think she could bear it another second, Diego dove in and kissed her — fiercely. Alexa kissed him back with equal hunger, delighting in the sensation. When it came to hooking up, she and Diego were so in sync that Alexa sometimes felt as if the two of them were giving off actual sparks. Even after a year together, their chemistry was still as intense as ever.

"Alexa," Diego murmured, slowly ending the kiss. He ran his hands down her bare arms and over to her hips, pulling her in even closer. "*Te quiero.*"

Instinctively, Alexa drew back a little. Normally, she adored it when her Cuban American boyfriend spoke to her in Spanish — as he often did when they were together like this. And she did *quiero* Diego, too. But here, in Paris, Spanish felt . . . wrong. Alexa longed to speak her native language — which Diego didn't know a word of, except maybe for *bonjour* or *merci* (but he pronounced even those with a Spanish accent). Alexa turned her head toward the balcony, now hidden behind the drapes. As luscious as Diego made her feel, he couldn't quench her lust for the city outside.

"You okay?" Diego whispered. He rolled to one side and put his arms around her waist, kissing her shoulder. "Listen, I meant to tell you before — I'm sorry about the flight."

Alexa looked back at him and sighed at the regret in his dark eyes. The flight *had* sucked — mainly because Diego had failed to warn her that he sometimes got airsick. When the plane hit a pocket of turbulence somewhere over the Atlantic, he had to keep popping Dramamine pills and making emergency runs to the bathroom — not quite the sublimely sexy voyage Alexa had been envisioning. And, as if Diego's restroom visits weren't mood-killing enough, sitting behind Alexa was a cackling demon child who seemed to take immense pleasure in bopping her on the head with his monster Tonka truck every twenty seconds — that is, until Alexa had finally whirled around to snap at his frazzled nanny in French.

For the rest of the trip, she and Diego had dozed fitfully, banging elbows over the armrest and bickering over the volume on Alexa's portable DVD player. When they'd finally landed, cranky as hell, in Charles de Gaulle airport, Alexa had felt a quick stab of apprehension: What if the flight had been a bad omen for the whole trip?

But then, just as quickly, she had swept the worry away.

"Who *cares* about the flight?" Alexa whispered as she snuggled closer to her beau. "We're here now — so we'd better start making the most of it."

Though Alexa had intended those words as a gentle prod for Diego to get his gorgeous butt out of bed, her boyfriend clearly had a different interpretation.

Grinning, he leaned in and started kissing her again. Figuring Paris could wait a little while longer, Alexa responded happily, wrapping her arms all the way around Diego's back. The two of them started to roll over to Alexa's side of the bed — and Alexa was thinking about how much this felt like some lush romance movie (a French one, of course) — until Diego suddenly stopped.

"What's wrong?" Alexa asked, her skin still tingly from their kissing. She pulled back to gaze down at her boyfriend, who now only had one arm around her waist.

"I'm *stuck*," Diego replied, sounding both amused and annoyed.

Shaking back her tousled hair, Alexa sat up all the way and saw that, in fact, her boyfriend's elbow was tightly jammed between the two twin beds, rendering any movement impossible.

"Oh, no," Alexa whispered, unable to stop herself from bursting into giggles. "We can't leave you like that forever, can we?"

"No," Diego retorted, now looking one hundred percent annoyed. He tried in vain to wrest his arm from the narrow gap, biting down on his full bottom lip. "This isn't funny, Alexa."

Um, yes it is, Alexa thought, fighting back her laughter. Alexa was a seasoned traveler, and though she couldn't stand roughing it, (any kind of camping was a *big* no-no) she was quite accustomed to sleeping in all sorts of conditions. She hoped Diego would be able to deal with her cousins' less-than-swank setup once they left the hotel.

Through various efforts, the two of them finally managed to free a disgruntled Diego from the beds. By then, it was almost two o'clock, and, as far as Alexa was concerned, high time to head out. They dressed — Alexa in a heather-gray Marni scoop-neck sweater and Chip & Pepper jeans tucked into shearling boots, and Diego in baggy cords and his hooded Princeton sweatshirt, which Alexa, appalled, demanded he trade for one of his zillion striped button-downs. To Alexa's slight distaste, Diego's style tended toward conservative/preppy — she preferred guys who dressed more scruffy/sexy — but *anything* beat loud-and-proud Princeton gear.

"Otherwise, we might as well walk outside with giant 'tourist' signs stuck on our foreheads," Alexa explained as she and Diego walked into the corridor and locked the door. "Trust me, in Paris, you want to downplay the whole 'ugly American' thing."

"Ugly American?" Diego echoed as the elevator zipped them down to the lobby. He furrowed his brow, looking confused, but also a little defensive.

On cue, the elevator doors slid open to reveal three

teenage girls in jeans, white sneakers, and dark blue anoraks, all clustered around the front desk. "Can you believe how much bread people eat here?" one of them, whose puffy dark hair was hidden under an Atlanta Braves cap, complained loudly. "Have they even *heard* of low-carb?" "*Here's* the Eiffel Tower!" her blonde, pig-tailed friend was squealing, jabbing at a spot on her enormous city map. "My aunt Doreen said it's the only thing worth seeing in Paris!" The third, a chubby redhead, was accosting the dapper concierge: "*Please* tell me you speak English," she snapped, narrowing her eyes at him.

"Um, them, for example," Alexa murmured, taking Diego's arm as they passed the embarrassing trio. Despite the girls' sub-stylish wardrobes, they reminded Alexa of her friends. She could easily picture Portia and Maeve behaving exactly the same way in Paris — right down to Portia bemoaning how hard it was to stick to Atkins (the French found the idea of diets hilarious), and Maeve assuming no one spoke English (when most everyone in Paris was bilingual). Alexa hadn't been in touch with — or given much thought to — the girls since their blowout on Thursday. Now, she felt supremely thankful that she'd never traveled to France with them.

"Yeah, but we *are* American," Diego was saying

as they cut through the spotless beige lobby. Though Diego's parents were Cuban, he'd been born in Miami, and Alexa knew he considered himself very much American. "I mean, just because you're in a foreign country," he added thoughtfully, "why should you pretend to be something you're not?"

Alexa rolled her eyes as they stepped out onto the wide, windswept boulevard St-Germain. Leave it to Mr. Princeton to turn everything into a philosophical debate. "Darling," she laughed. "That's one deep thought too many for a springtime Saturday in Paris."

Their first stop was Café de Flore, where they lunched on chewy baguettes slathered in butter, fresh mussels, and crispy fries. Two porcelain cups of ink-black coffee sitting on the white tablecloth rounded out the perfect Parisian picture.

"Heaven," Alexa sighed between bites. She'd been craving a visit to Flore. The fabled corner café, with its brightly lit sign set amid a spray of flowers and its crowded, mirrored interior, was one of Alexa's favorites. Legend had it that Picasso used to hang here, so in years past, Alexa would linger over her espresso, smoke a few Gauloises (Alexa didn't smoke, but in Paris, she liked to indulge occasionally), and imagine she, too, was a famous Left Bank *artiste*. Alexa *did* fancy herself a photographer. She'd photographed Paris before, but she hoped she'd have a chance to take some interesting new shots of the city this week.

"Mmm," Diego agreed, reaching for a fry. He was smiling, Alexa observed, and seemed to have recovered from the whole attack-of-the-twin-beds trauma.

"See? Aren't you glad you're *not* cramming for midterms?" Alexa laughed, lifting her delicate coffee cup to her lips.

Although Diego had been totally into the idea of a Paris trip, his spring break fell a month after Alexa's. So it had been a huge effort on Alexa's part to get her stubborn boyfriend to pause in prepping for his biology exams and agree to join her.

"I guess," Diego chuckled, giving Alexa an affectionate look. "If I were at school now, I'd be, like, suffering in the library, instead of sitting here with you —"

"Eating the best food *ever*," Alexa interjected around a mouthful of baguette.

"Though not the healthiest," Diego pointed out. His brow furrowed in concern as he examined the salt-speckled fry between his fingers. "Do you realize how much sodium is in one of these babies?"

Alexa swallowed the last of her coffee, feeling a spark of impatience. Diego was premed at Princeton and loved showing off his vast medical knowledge.

Usually, his drive and dedication turned Alexa on, but now she was *un peu* peeved.

"Relax, Doctor Mendieta," she retorted, toying with one of her oversize silver hoops and glancing out the window at the ritzy passersby on the boulevard. A light drizzle was falling, shrouding the elegant, cream-colored buildings in a thick fog. Alexa had forgotten that Paris in the springtime sometimes felt more like late winter. But what was it her father always said? *Our city is stunning in any season.* It was true; the rain only added to the romance.

Alexa, who hadn't brought her cell along, figured she should find a phone booth and check in back home; Diego had called his parents in Miami earlier that day to tell them he'd arrived safely. But Alexa knew her very French, very chill father wasn't the type to fret over her. And her ambitious American mother, busy being a Manhattan fashionista, had barely remembered to punch Alexa's trip into her BlackBerry. Alexa was an only child, and her parents' culture-clash marriage had crashed and burned soon after the move from Paris to the States. As Alexa liked to joke to Diego, the upside of her occasional loneliness was that she had the freedom to do pretty much whatever she pleased.

Sort of the opposite of Holly Jacobson's life, Alexa mused, thinking of her old friend and wondering how she was faring across the Channel.

"So where to next?"

Diego's voice startled her. Alexa glanced at her boyfriend, who was impatiently drumming his long fingers on the table as he glanced around for their waiter. *Next?* she wondered. They'd only been at the café for an hour.

"There he is!" Diego said, furiously signaling to their waiter. "Can we get the check?" he shouted across the café. A rail-thin woman in a Dior trench coat glanced up from her espresso and *Paris-Match* with a scowl.

Alexa cringed. Couldn't Diego at least *attempt* to speak French?

"What's the rush, baby?" she asked as the waiter disdainfully dropped the tissue-paper-thin bill on their table. She was perfectly content to sit here all afternoon, people-watching and listening to the vintage Serge Gainsbourg playing softly in the background. In Paris, café culture was practically a religion.

"Well, we're only here for seven days," Diego replied, reaching into his messenger bag and — to Alexa's horror — taking out a large, glossy Frommer's guidebook. "We should get in some sightseeing, don't you think?"

Pardonnez-moi?

Alexa stared at her boyfriend, not comprehending.

Sightseeing? Diego knew she was from Paris. By the age of seven, she'd already had the whole Notre Dame–Arc de Triomphe–Eiffel Tower gig down cold. Alexa St. Laurent had seen all there was to see in this city.

"Like — like which sights?" Alexa managed to ask, pulling her pale pink wallet out of her Chloé lizard bag; Diego had forgotten to exchange his dollars for euros at the airport, so she'd been the unofficial bank thus far.

Diego shot her a sheepish grin and ducked his head. When he spoke, he addressed the guidebook in his lap. "Well . . . at the risk of sounding like those girls from the lobby, I've always wanted to, um, go to the top of the Eiffel Tower."

Alexa gasped in shock, her manicured hands flying to her mouth. "Oh . . . my God," she whispered, consumed by shame. Her boyfriend may as well have gotten down on all fours and started chewing on the tablecloth — even *that* would have been preferable to this declaration. "Diego, no. You *can't* be serious."

Alexa had always thought that the Eiffel Tower — all graceful steel lacework — was lovely. But the super-famous structure was also *so*, well, Kodak Moment Number One — not to mention tainted by the gross Tom Cruise–Katie Holmes proposal — that Alexa now considered it no more than a cheesy tourist trap. She'd even torn up the photo of the tower that she'd once displayed on the bulletin board in her bedroom.

"Would you hear me out?" Diego's dark eyes flashed. Both he and Alexa had a certain fire in their temperaments, which worked out nicely for some activities — but could lead to angry flare-ups when they *weren't* getting it on. "You know I was only in Paris once before — for that weekend with my parents and sister. We did, like, the two-second tour of the city, but we didn't even *go* to the Eiffel Tower."

Alexa felt a slow, sinking dread in her stomach that told her this issue wasn't going to resolve itself any time soon. "It's just that there are *so* many better ways to spend our time here," she explained, trying to keep the sharpness out of her tone. "Like walking across the Pont-Neuf or shopping at Collete or —"

Diego silenced her by leaning across the small table and taking her hands in his. "Alexa, think about it," he urged, his expression intense. "We could go at night. You and me, at the very top, the entire city spread out beneath us . . ." He tilted his head, leaned in closer, and softly kissed her pouty bottom lip. "Remember?" he whispered, his dimples showing.

Alexa nodded, weakening. How could she have forgotten? A year ago, she and Diego had shared a breathtaking rooftop experience in South Beach —

and had been together ever since. This trip was supposed to be their anniversary, after all; it *would* be meaningful for the two of them to re-create that magical night.

But Alexa wasn't ready to give in yet.

As a compromise, she agreed to Diego's Frommer's-inspired suggestion that they hit up Montmartre, the funky Right Bank neighborhood where the domed, all-white basilica, Sacré-Coeur, stood. They left Café de Flore, rode the Métro to Abbesses ("The trains are so clean here!" Diego exclaimed loudly while Alexa looked for places to hide), and silently hiked up the steep hill to Sacré-Coeur, the tension still crackling between them.

But being in Montmartre cheered Alexa up; she loved its crooked alleyways and slightly seedy atmosphere. Street vendors hawked piping-hot crêpes alongside miniature replicas of Sacré-Coeur, white-faced mimes performed for wide-eyed children, and wannabe artists perched on stools, sketching at their easels. While Diego made straight for the grand steps of the basilica, Alexa hung back, wanting to scope out the scene some more.

When one of the sketchers glanced up from his easel, Alexa's heart fluttered. Clad in a tight black T-shirt, torn jeans, and scuffed-up boots — the French dirty-boy uniform — he was on the short side, but lean. His ropy body and narrow gray eyes made Alexa think of a hungry cat. A black knit hat was pulled down low over his eyes, almost as if he were going incognito — and there was a smudge of charcoal on his left cheekbone. She bet his lips tasted of Gauloises and cheap beer.

Holding Alexa's gaze — was *he* trying to guess what *her* lips tasted like? — the artist picked up a fresh piece of charcoal and resumed sketching, almost as if he planned to draw her. Alexa, who never blushed, felt a hot redness stealing up her face. She was used to guys checking her out — even today, she'd gotten several sideways smiles from boys on the Métro — but *this* eye contact felt more intense, more personal.

Alexa drew a deep breath, steadying herself. Yes, she'd always had a weakness for seductive French boys, but she was here with *Diego*. And she loved Diego. Didn't she?

Dizzy, Alexa whirled away from the artist's penetrating stare and flew toward the cathedral in search of her boyfriend. When she spotted his dark hair and tall figure, she immediately hurried over, flung her arms around his neck, and buried her face in the collar of his striped shirt, feeling a mixture of guilt and longing.

"Baby," Diego said, clearly startled but pleased. His arms went around her waist and he drew her close, nuzzling her neck. Naturally, since they were in Paris, their cuddling didn't prompt even a second glance from the people milling about on the steps.

"I don't want us to argue anymore," Alexa spoke into Diego's ear, clinging tightly to him.

"Then let's not," Diego murmured. "Let's just have fun."

And, as they started kissing on the steps of Sacré-Coeur, with the setting sun bathing Montmartre in a golden glow, Alexa decided that they would do exactly that. This week would be the best, most wildly romantic one of their lives.

If only Diego would get over the stupid Eiffel Tower.

CHAPTER FOUR

A Royal Mess

"Is that Prince William?" Holly's best friend, Meghan, asked, pointing to a blond boy in a navy blue sweater who was leaning against the bar, drinking a bottle of Theakston's beer.

Holly groaned. "I hate to break it to you, Meggie," she replied, reaching for the pitcher of ale, "but what would the extremely hot heir to the British throne be doing in a dinky pub in Wimbledon?"

From the moment the girls had arrived in England two days before, on Saturday, Meghan had been spotting members of the royal family everywhere: at the run-down faux-Victorian hostel where the team was staying, at the local fish-and-chips place, even on the running track at Wimbledon Park. Her obsessing was starting to wear on Holly's nerves.

"The same thing *we're* doing," Jess chimed in, plopping down on the wooden bench across from them with a fresh pitcher. "Getting sloshed." Grinning, she filled her mug to the brim, then clinked it against Holly's. "Cheerio."

Holly toasted Jess back and tentatively sipped at the cool, foamy ale. She wasn't a big drinker, but in England, where the drinking age was eighteen, and no one seemed to card, it was hard to resist. In fact, *all* the members of the Oakridge High girls' track team — on their blissful free hour before curfew — were scattered throughout the Fox Run Pub. Disregarding the fact that they weren't supposed to drink while competing, the girls were drowning their sorrows in pints. That morning, they'd lost miserably to the annoyingly svelte, über-blonde German team.

Of course, Holly — team captain and perpetual guilt magnet — blamed herself.

While Jess and Meghan continued to swoon over the Prince William clone, Holly tuned them out, set down her pint, and rested one freckled cheek in her hand. For the millionth time that night, she rotated her sore ankle beneath the table and mentally replayed the awful events of that morning.

Ponytail swinging, heart thumping, she'd been pounding up the track as her teammates screamed her on. But then she'd felt it — sharp and sure as the

55

stitch in her side: She was off her game. Holly had been feeling fuzzy and distracted ever since she'd gotten to England. But she hadn't expected her condition to worsen on the track. As Holly's legs slowed, the pompous captain of the German team — Brünhilde or whatever her name was — shot by her. Holly's stomach dropped, and her knees followed; as her left ankle turned, she stumbled and fell, slapping her hands against the crimson-colored track. A hush fell over the stadium.

It was the most mortifying moment of Holly Jacobson's entire life, not counting the time a random boy had seen her naked in South Beach last year.

Shaking, she'd picked herself up and limped across the finish line — dead last.

"Jacobson," Coach Graham had barked, storming over. "You were a mess out there!" In a matter of days, Ms. Graham had morphed from friendly, Go-Team-Go! coach into Psycho Drill Sergeant.

Holly had tried to catch her breath as the rest of the team gathered around her, asking if she was okay. She'd sought out Meghan's and Jess's concerned faces in the crowd and lifted her shoulders at them in a helpless *I suck, don't I?* gesture. More than anything, Holly hated knowing that she'd let her team down.

Frowning, Coach Graham had led Holly through the crush of Oakridge girls, over to the nearest wooden bench. She'd promptly sat Holly down and expertly prodded her achy ankle.

"Ouch," Holly had whispered, wincing and turning her head away. Pieces of hair that had escaped from her ponytail stuck damply to the back of her neck, her green uniform felt itchy, and her palms burned. Holly had been running track for the past four years; she was used to enduring discomfort, even pain. Tiger Balm and Icy-Hot could be a girl's best friends. But now, Holly didn't want to deal with the recovery process. She was sick of always worrying about injuries. And she bet that Coach Graham would make a huge deal out of this latest one.

"It's not sprained, but you need to stay off it," Coach Graham had pronounced, confirming Holly's fears. After applying an ice pack to Holly's ankle, she straightened up and crossed her arms over her chest, glowering. "Though you shouldn't have any problems walking, doing any running would be a terrible idea now." She cleared her throat and gave a decisive shake of her curly ash-blonde bob. "I don't think you'll be able to compete for the rest of the week."

Thud. That had been the sound of Holly's heart completing its slow descent. She'd stared up at her coach in disbelief. Not being able to run was the worst punishment someone could inflict on Holly Jacobson; it was only while in motion that she felt in control of her life. And running always provided a blissful distraction from whatever problems Holly might be grappling with at the time. Holly couldn't bear the thought of a week spent sitting lamely on the sidelines, watching as her teammates sped up and down the track, trying to cheer them on despite the lump in her throat.

Because then she'd have *lots* of free time to dwell on that one big problem she was dealing with.

"I'm — I'm fine," Holly had protested feebly. She'd reached down, feeling with her own fingers how swollen her ankle was. "Just give me, like, another day —"

But Ms. Graham had already interrupted with a litany of reasons as to why Holly had to remain benched — though she *was* expected to attend every single practice session and competition, of course. As her coach rambled on, Holly had stared dreamily at the dark green treetops that ringed the track, suddenly filled with the desire to run. Not in a race this time, but as a means of escape. Holly imagined herself running and running, leaving Wimbledon and the rest of England far behind. Only she didn't want to run home, to her parents and Oakridge. She wanted to go someplace where nobody knew her and didn't care in the slightest about track and field.

"The thing is, Jacobson," Coach Graham had said, her voice stern. "Your head has been in the clouds from the minute this trip began. Honestly, I'm not surprised you fell today." She'd taken a step closer, blocking Holly's pleasant view of the treetops. "What's been throwing you off? I want an explanation."

Holly had blown her bangs up off her forehead, at a loss. What reason could she possibly offer her coach? *Jet-lag? PMS? Torn tendon?* Or . . . the truth?

Tyler.

Now, sitting with her friends in the crowded pub, listening to the rhythmic beats of Dizzee Rascal, and watching guys and girls snog at the bar, Holly felt a deep pang of longing. Tyler Davis may have caused her fall that morning, but she still missed him like crazy.

Tyler had called her only once since she'd been in England, on Saturday night, and they'd suffered through The Most Awkward Conversation in the History of Dating. (The highlights, as Holly remembered, had been "Um" and "Yeah.") Then, when Tyler had blurted "Do you want to talk about, you know, the car?" Holly panicked. She'd been agonizing nonstop over what she'd termed "the car-tastrophe" — but *discussing* it was a whole different beast. What if Tyler confirmed her worst fears ("You're no Alexa St. Laurent!"), and Holly started crying? So, swallowing her hurt and confusion, she'd made up some feeble excuse about needing to go stretch, and abruptly clicked off.

If running was Holly Jacobson's greatest talent —

and that definitely felt questionable now — then her second greatest was avoiding confrontations.

The proof? For an entire year, she'd avoided getting into a single real argument with her boyfriend. There had been tensions over minor matters, like which movie to rent (Tyler nixed anything with subtitles; Holly hated horror) or what kind of food to take out with the movie (Tyler was only happy with Applebee's or Arby's; Holly preferred Middle Eastern or Indian). But Holly was so adept at smoothing out these wrinkles in their relationship, and Tyler was so laid back, that no misunderstanding ever turned too serious.

Now, their transatlantic tension felt suspiciously like an actual fight.

Holly reached under the beer-sticky table for her blue Vans tote and, almost out of habit, withdrew her red T-Mobile.

Still no messages.

She knew she could call Tyler herself, or e-mail him from the local Internet café, but — not to get all Wimbledon or anything — Holly felt like it was totally Tyler's serve. After all, *he* was the one who'd rejected *her* in Oakridge. She sighed heavily.

"Oh no — does your ankle hurt?" Meghan asked worriedly, glancing at Holly.

Holly shook her head, looking back at her cell. *Just my heart.*

"Girl, what is *up* with that phone?" Jess asked, leaning across the table and grabbing the cell. "It's been, like, glued to your hand since Saturday."

"Stop, Jess — give it back," Holly pleaded, reaching across the table. Chuckling, Jess hurriedly passed the phone to Meghan, who stuffed it into the pocket of her Champion hoodie. A group of shaggy-haired guys drinking Guinness at a nearby table laughed at their antics, and Holly's face burned; she and her friends must have looked like kindergarteners fighting over a toy. Why did hanging out with Meghan and Jess make her feel so *young* sometimes?

"Tell us what's going on and we'll give it back," Meghan challenged, her brown eyes sparkling.

Holly bit her lower lip, hesitating. She'd fully intended to spill the Tyler story to her best friends, but for some reason, she'd held off. Back in the day, Holly used to tell the girls every detail of her humdrum life — unrequited crushes, failed exams, gym class triumphs — and they'd always reciprocated with their own similarly benign tales. Since she'd met Tyler, though, Holly had found herself leaving out certain juicy details. And on this trip, she'd kept completely mum. It wasn't like Meghan and Jess weren't sympathetic listeners. Of course they were.

They were just utterly clueless about boys.

Holly was sure that Meghan, with her dirty-blonde,

pixie-ish haircut and little-girl smile, and Jess, with her long ballerina's neck and dark brown bun atop her head, could both get boyfriends if they really wanted them. But both girls were so involved in sports and schoolwork that guys ranked low on their priority lists. Though Jess had briefly gone out with Marc, the cocaptain of the lacrosse team, and Meghan had once hooked up with Jeff, Oakridge High's soccer star, neither girl had ever had a real relationship.

Not too long ago, Holly had been as innocent as her friends, if not more so. But now that she was having some very real drama with her very real boyfriend, she suddenly felt like she was in a *very* different place than Meghan and Jess.

Holly took a fortifying sip of ale. The alcohol was making her feel warm; she unzipped her light green Kangol hoodie. Really, what could be the harm in confiding in her friends? It might be therapeutic to get all that worrying off her chest.

"Okay, here goes," Holly began, drawing a big breath and huddling in close to the girls.

"Jeez, you make it sound so serious," Meghan giggled.

"It *is* serious," Holly snapped — but then felt bad. She never got testy with her friends.

"Wait," Jess said, her voice hushed. "Don't tell me.

Your parents. They're making you keep the cell on you at all times."

Holly shook her head, annoyed at how off the mark Jess's guess was. Her parents *had* been checking in every day, but surprisingly, they'd been pretty mellow. "We're sure Coach Graham is keeping you busy," her dad had said when he'd called on Sunday night. "So we won't bug you." Clearly, Holly's parents found the idea of a school-supervised trip reassuring — and she hoped they *would* keep to their word. She hadn't yet called to tell them about her ankle, because she knew they'd freak.

"Okay, then . . . are you waiting for someone to call?" Meghan offered, pouring herself more ale.

Holly tried not to roll her eyes. *Pulling teeth.* "It's Tyler," she burst out in frustration. "On the way to the airport on Friday, we had this — this thing happen — It was pretty intense. . . ."

"Ooh, you were making out?" Meghan teased, wiggling her eyebrows at Holly. The gesture used to crack Holly up when they were freshmen, but now, she was not in the mood.

"We were about to have sex," she replied flatly.

"Oh," Meghan said, her eyebrows going still and her cheeks coloring.

"Ew, on the way to the *airport?*" Jess asked, looking

flat-out disgusted. "Like, in his car or something?" She shook her head, her tight bun not budging an inch. "You told us last month that you guys had this whole perfect moment planned or whatever —"

"Well, we *didn't* — you know — *finish* what we started," Holly managed to reply, her face growing warm. She hated how the subject of sex instantly made her uncomfortable. And Meghan and Jess were clearly so unable to imagine the situation Holly was describing that she wondered if it was even worth elaborating.

"It's probably for the best," Meghan said consolingly, patting Holly's shoulder. "You shouldn't let him pressure you into doing anything you don't want to —"

"Actually," Holly cut in, feeling a flash of irritation. "It was . . . the other way around." She bit her lip and glanced down at her hands as she heard Meghan let out a small gasp.

"Wait. . . . Holly, *you* initiated it?" Jess asked, sounding bewildered. "That's — that's so not like you."

Maybe you don't know me that well anymore, Holly thought, caught off guard by her own sentiment. Holly didn't doubt that her friends understood her — but just maybe not the her that had a boyfriend.

Instead of getting into all that, Holly simply shrugged, still studying her lap. "I just . . . really wanted to right then," she offered, unsure how else to explain.

"But," Meghan began, her voice low and uncertain, "aren't you . . . you know . . . *scared?*"

Holly tilted her head to one side, considering this notion. *Scared* wasn't quite the right word. Whenever she thought about sex, Holly experienced a mixture of nervousness and excitement and curiosity that felt like a distant cousin of fear — only somehow more pleasant.

"Of course, a little bit," Holly replied, choosing her words carefully. She traced a circle on the dewy pitcher of ale, thinking of how at ease Tyler put her. "But with Tyler, it feels — or at least it *felt* — right." Then she lifted her eyes to meet her friends' gazes. They were regarding her with blank expressions, as if she were a three-headed alien who had materialized at their table.

God, I wish Alexa were here. The thought sprang into Holly's mind, surprising her. Yes, Alexa was a big part of Holly's conflicted feelings toward Tyler. But that was also why Alexa would get where Holly was coming from — and could probably provide some helpful insight. She had *dated* Tyler, after all. If anyone had vast reserves of boy experience to draw from, it was the bold, adventurous Alexa St. Laurent. Holly knew, from the week they had spent together in South Beach, that Alexa didn't think *anything* was scary.

"Anyway, it doesn't matter," Holly muttered. She accepted her cell phone from a shaky-looking Meghan and rolled her eyes. "Let's talk about something . . . else." *Like sports or school or* American Idol *or whatever it is we usually talk about,* she added silently. Holly was aware that the vibe she was giving off might be a little condescending — a first for her — but she couldn't help her aggravation toward her friends.

"We're just trying to help," Meghan insisted, putting one arm around Holly. "Keep going about Tyler — we want to know."

"But she doesn't think we *can* help," Jess observed accurately, frowning at Holly across the table. "Because, you forget, *we* don't have boyfriends, Meghan. We wouldn't *understand.*"

"I never said that," Holly protested weakly, unable to meet Jess's laser-beam stare. "But it *is* kind of different. . . . You guys will see. . . ." Holly trailed off, practically visualizing the hole she was digging for herself.

"Thanks a lot, H," Jess snapped, huffily taking a sip of ale. "Way to make us feel good about ourselves."

Holly felt her chest clench. "Sorry," she mumbled. "I didn't mean it that way." The last thing Holly wanted to do was argue with her friends. But she also didn't think she could remain with them a second longer. Between Jess's glare, Meghan's arm around her shoulder, the laughing Guinness boys, the groping couples at the bar, and the close, sweaty quarters of the noisy pub, she felt like she was choking.

"I'm gonna get some air," Holly announced, shifting away from Meghan and swinging her legs over the side of the bench. She stood carefully, testing her ankle. It was a little tender, but not too achy. Still, she knew she'd never be able to convince her coach to let her run tomorrow.

"We have to head back to the hostel soon," Meghan pointed out, looking up at Holly.

Holly checked the time on her cell phone. Curfew was nine sharp, and it was now eight forty-five. Coach Graham was already at the hostel, no doubt waiting in the dank lobby with a checklist of names. Since the girls had to be up and at 'em at five every morning, going to bed super early made sense.

But sucked.

"Meet me outside and we'll walk back together," Holly sighed, lifting her tote. She was sick of all the boot camp rules, the way Coach Graham treated them like infants. Didn't Holly get enough of that at home? What was the point of spring break if not to have at least a *little* fun?

Holly elbowed her way through the crowd, cell phone in hand. She was so focused on making it to the door that she skidded on a puddle of beer and, losing her footing, tumbled forward in an oh-so-graceful repeat performance of that morning. Gasping, she threw out her hands and grabbed on to the nearest solid object — the arm of the Prince William lookalike.

He turned slowly, a smile lighting up his chiseled, aristocratic face.

Holly froze, forgetting about her ankle. *Wait. Was it . . . could it be?* There were no bodyguards around . . . no photographers . . . it seemed impossible . . . but that *face* . . .

She might have to apologize to Meghan later.

"All right, there?" the possible-prince asked in a smooth, sexy British accent.

"Um, me? I'm, um, I'm awesome," Holly stammered. Her face flaming, she righted herself and gave him a quick thumbs-up sign. The boy nodded, flashed her another royally gorgeous grin, and turned back to his friends at the bar.

Oh my God, Holly realized in horror, her Adidas glued to the floor. *Did I just give the thumbs-up sign to the future king of England?* It seemed that her list of embarrassing moments was growing by leaps and bounds. *I really* am *a mess,* Holly thought, making her way outside.

Rain was falling in slow, heavy drops, like tears. Shivering, Holly zipped up her hoodie and gazed down the Broadway, Wimbledon's main drag. *Ugh.*

Despite the pubs, restaurants, and quaint little "shoppes," the area still felt kind of lackluster to Holly. She'd dreamed of traveling abroad her whole life, but so far, England had let her down. She wondered if another country, another city, might suit her better.

And that was when Holly's cell phone rang.

Glancing down at the T-Mobile in her hand, her heart thrummed with hope. Could it be Tyler? Was he finally, finally calling to say that the car-tastrophe didn't matter, that he adored her, and that he couldn't wait to jump her the minute she got back? Holly squinted at the weird number flashing on the small screen: a plus sign followed by a series of digits. *Huh?* New Jersey was five hours behind England; maybe Tyler had been driving home from volunteering and, in a fit of passion, pulled over to a pay phone. Who else could it be?

"Tyler?" Holly finally answered, her teeth chattering. "Where are you calling from?"

There was a moment of buzzing silence, and then, like a dim echo from very far away, Holly heard the distinct sound of sobbing.

Her throat tightened in horror. Tyler was *crying*? Did he really feel that bad about what had happened? Or was something else wrong? "Tyler?" Holly demanded once more. "Are you okay?"

"It's — it's not Tyler," a girl finally sobbed on the other end, startling Holly. The line crackled angrily.

Holly felt shivers all down her spine. Despite the heinous reception, she recognized that voice. Of course. She'd known it since she was seven years old.

"Alexa?" Holly whispered.

"It's me," Alexa confirmed, sniffling.

Holly felt a stab of worry. Back on Thursday, she'd told Alexa to call her, but considering her friend's blasé response in the cafeteria, Holly hadn't expected to hear from her. And since Paris was one hour ahead of London, it was about ten o'clock over there. Why would Alexa be calling so late on a random Monday night — in tears, no less?

"Alexa, what's going on?" Holly asked, almost too frightened to hear the answer. She looked over her shoulder and saw Meghan and Jess emerging from the pub.

"Hol, I need you," Alexa sobbed. "Can you talk? I'm in really, really big trouble. . . ."

CHAPTER FIVE
Au Revoir

I can't believe I'm here, Alexa fumed as she rose up through the star-sprinkled night sky. It was eight o'clock on Monday, and she and Diego were squeezed into a tiny, glassed-in elevator that was gliding toward the very tip-top of the Eiffel Tower.

Over the past two days, Alexa had tried to remain firm. But whether they were holding hands in the Jardin du Luxembourg or strolling across the wide Pont des Arts, Diego had sulked and sighed and whined about the Eiffel Tower until Alexa wanted to go up there just so she could push her broken-record boyfriend *off* it.

That morning, at the Louvre, she'd finally surrendered for real. Standing on her tiptoes in her Lanvin zebra-print pumps, Alexa had peered through the hordes at the serenely smiling Mona Lisa. Even though Alexa had seen the painting in person about fifty-seven times, she still secretly loved it. There was something so mysterious and independent about the Italian *grande dame* that it never failed to give Alexa shivers.

"Careful," Diego teased, squeezing her waist. "Someone might mistake you for a tourist."

Alexa laughed, turning to stick her tongue out at him. "Never."

"Speaking of which . . ." Diego began, clearly about to launch into another Eiffel Tower soliloquy, but Alexa shut him up by placing her hand over his mouth. Maybe it was being in the huge sun-drenched gallery, surrounded by so many incredible works of art, but she suddenly felt light and airy and gracious. What would Mona Lisa do?

"I'll go," Alexa whispered.

So here she was in her new Zac Posen golden flapper dress and sparkly white Cesare Paciotti mules, her pale golden hair rippling down her back. In an attempt to make the best of this little visit, Alexa had dressed to outdo the tower itself, which — though lit up all night — shimmered from top to bottom for ten minutes on the hour, every hour, like a long-necked jewel.

Stepping out of the elevator, her fingers laced through Diego's, Alexa suddenly regretted wearing the flimsy Zac Posen confection — it was bitterly cold on the third level. The wind gusting through the tall wire barrier rattled Alexa's topaz teardrop earrings. Trembling, she let go of Diego's hand so she could wrap her arms around her slender frame. She wished Diego would get a clue and slip his J. Lindeberg suit jacket around her bare shoulders, but he was clearly too distracted by the dizzying view.

"Wow," he whispered, stepping closer to the edge, his long-lashed black eyes shining. "Alexa, come see — it really *is* the City of Light."

Alexa rolled her eyes as she teetered over in her spiky heels. Hadn't her boyfriend — whom she'd always considered worldly — ever seen a nighttime panorama before? Granted, Alexa realized as she joined Diego, that view from last year's South Beach rooftop hadn't been anything quite like this. In spite of herself, she caught her breath as she scanned the dazzling cityscape. A thousand feet below, the whole of Paris sprawled, elegant and glittery as a strand of emerald-cut diamonds. Alexa had been to the top of the tower before, but never at night. She rested one hand on the wire netting, drinking in the spectacular sight and feeling — okay, yeah — grateful that Diego had dragged her up here. She wished she'd brought her camera but it hadn't fit into the Miu Miu clutch she was carrying.

Alexa reached for her *amant*, aching to slide her arms around him, but, from behind her, there suddenly came raucous laughter. "What the hell *is* this?" someone guffawed, and Alexa and Diego both turned around.

A guy and girl, each weighed down by monstrous backpacks, were cracking up in front of the wax figures of Gustave Eiffel (the architect who'd designed the tower) and Thomas Edison. Alexa had always found those wax models random, but they weren't cause for such commotion. Alexa raised a disdainful eyebrow as the girl — who was petite, with long brown hair and a lip ring — clapped her hands to her cheeks and shrieked, "They're aliiive!" while the guy — backwards white baseball cap, tan shell necklace — laughed even harder.

Alexa shook her head and turned her attention back to Diego, but, to her astonishment, her boyfriend was watching the couple with a wide smile.

"What's up?" Diego called to the rowdy strangers. He raised his arm to wave to them as if they were long-lost siblings.

"Waddup," White Hat Boy called back, lifting his chin by way of greeting while the girl continued to convulse with giggles.

"You know them?" Alexa whispered, instinctively reaching up to jerk Diego's arm down.

Diego ignored her. "Hey, where are you guys from?" he shouted over the wind, indirectly answering Alexa's question.

Ugh, Alexa thought furiously. If Diego *didn't* know these people, why was he chatting them up? He could easily befriend these types back in New Jersey.

Crossing her arms over her chest, Alexa noticed another couple cuddled together in front of the wire barrier, murmuring in what she guessed was Japanese. They were observing Diego's conversation with White Hat Boy closely, clearly intrigued by the antics of crazy Americans.

"Florida," the guy replied, adjusting his backwards cap on his small head. "Orlando."

"Proud home of Disney World," the girl chimed in drily, curling her lip, and Alexa thought that, under different circumstances, she might almost like her.

"No shit — I'm from Miami!" Diego laughed, his eyes dancing, as if this were the happiest coincidence of his life. The couple started laughing, too, loudly commenting on how dope South Beach was.

"I guess it really *is* a small world after all," Alexa muttered, eager to put an end to Diego's insta-love affair with the Disney World Duo. She tugged on her boyfriend's arm again, hoping he'd get the hint: She was cold, hungry, and absolutely ready to head back down.

But, apparently, Diego and his new best friends had other plans.

"Have you guys seen this freakiness?" Lip Ring Girl was asking, gesturing to the wax models, while her partner in crime dug around in his mammoth backpack. "I don't get the French at all."

"Nuts," Diego agreed, and then pointed to the view beyond the wire barrier. "But *that* is something else, huh? It's too bad it's not completely open." Diego made a pouty face, as if, Alexa thought, the people of France had personally betrayed him by not making the Eiffel Tower open-air.

"You know you can stick your face outside, right?" White Hat Boy exclaimed, still wrestling with his backpack. He finally pulled out what looked like a train schedule. "I'm serious, it's so cool — you should try it."

"Really?" Diego replied, grinning, and Alexa's stomach sank; she could just see Diego and Mr. All-American bonding over silly Eiffel Tower stunts all night. But, fortunately, the next thing White Hat Boy said was that he and his girlfriend had to make a late train to Amsterdam — "Dude, we can't wait to blow Paris" — so they needed to take off.

After Diego had bid a hearty farewell to his new-found buddies — Alexa was surprised they all didn't exchange e-mail addresses — he promptly turned around and walked back up to the wire barrier.

Her irritation mounting, Alexa watched as her boyfriend, acting on the instructions of White Hat Boy, poked his face through one of the diamond-shaped openings. *"Bonjour,* Paris!" Diego shouted, his atrocious accent echoing through the night sky. The Japanese couple stared at him unabashedly, and the smattering of other people up there — a sleepy guard, and a few chatty Italian twelve-year-old girls in cashmere capelets — all glanced Diego's way as well, clearly wondering where this lunatic had come from.

Alexa went rigid with shock. *Forget throwing* him *off,* she decided. Now *she* was the one who wanted to jump. Plunging onto the Champ de Mars, her filmy golden skirt flying over her head, would put an appro-priately dramatic end to her humiliation.

"Stop . . . embarrassing . . . me," Alexa said through gritted teeth, marching over to Diego and yanking on his arm. "Everybody's looking."

Diego pulled his head back inside. Alexa expected him to apologize, but instead he angrily set his jaw. "Alexa, give it a rest," he snapped. "Why are you always so hung up on what other people think?"

Alexa recoiled, pressing a palm to her bare col-larbone. What was Diego babbling about? "That's not true —" she began, ready to point out that *any-one* would have been mortified by his display of dorkiness.

"Oh, please," Diego cut in. "From the minute we've arrived in Paris, you've been totally paranoid that everything I do might make you look like a fool — or God forbid — a *foreigner!*" He crossed his arms over his chest, staring her down. "You're a snob, Alexa — I don't know why I didn't see that before."

Alexa narrowed her eyes at Diego. How dare he? *Nobody* reamed out Alexa St. Laurent and got away with it. She opened her mouth to tell Diego just that, but then stopped herself. The top of the Eiffel Tower was *so* not the place to have this kind of argument. "This can wait until later, sweetie," Alexa hissed, glancing over her shoulder to see if the Japanese couple were listening in on their lovers' spat. Why did her boyfriend have to make such a *scene?*

"There you go again," Diego pointed out smugly, apparently pleased to be catching Alexa red-handed.

That did it. Infuriated, Alexa spun around to face him, fists on hips.

"I'm only paranoid," she spat, not bothering to lower her voice this time, "because you, Diego, have been acting like — a jackass." Her boyfriend's dark eyes widened, but Alexa forged ahead, her frustrations spilling out in a torrent. "You've been completely loud and obnoxious — like with those American back-packers —"

"It was nice to talk to someone from back home," Diego mumbled defensively, shoving his hands into his pockets.

"Well, you haven't been making an effort to talk to anyone from *here*," Alexa retorted, remembering an incident from that morning. "Hey, just a news flash for you? Spanish isn't French! You can't say *por favor* to the ticket guy in the Métro and expect him to understand you!"

"Sucks for him," Diego muttered, frowning down at his shoes. "You know I don't speak French. And I don't *want* to."

Typical. Alexa rolled her eyes. "Plus, there's *that.* Your whole immature schoolboy act."

"Schoolboy?" Diego repeated, looking miffed. "In case you've forgotten, Alexa, I took important time off from *college* for *you* — for this trip." He shot her an accusatory glare.

"So what are you implying?" Alexa challenged, taking a step closer to him. "That college is more important to you than . . . *us?*"

Slowly, Alexa sized up her boyfriend — his conservative suit and neat tie, his shiny hair and shinier shoes, his clean-shaven face, now twisted in an angry — and unattractive — grimace. . . . In that instant, Alexa realized that, for all his fiery passion,

Diego Mendieta was, well, boring. She'd found him exciting and even dangerous when they'd first met in South Beach, but now, a year later, here in Paris, Alexa saw how ordinary her boyfriend truly was.

Diego sighed, glancing away from Alexa and back toward the sparkling lights of the city. "Alexa, you're still in high school. You don't know what it's like —"

Bad move, Diego.

"Don't you belittle me," Alexa shot back, her hot temper now sizzling. She saw the Italian girls gawking at them, but Alexa no longer cared.

Diego looked at her, steely-eyed. "Come on, Alexa. Admit it. We have different lives back home. I mean, look at your friends. Portia and Maeve — they're so small-minded and shallow." He shrugged matter-of-factly.

Fresh fury swept over Alexa. Diego *knew* she had recently ditched said shallow friends. How could he lump her with them? "If you think I'm so immature," she snapped over the roaring wind, "then maybe we shouldn't even be together! Maybe you should be dating a *college* girl!"

There was a long moment of silence as she and Diego studied each other, and Alexa wished with all her might that she could take that last remark and rewind it back into her mouth.

Then the corner of Diego's lips curled up in a cruel smirk. "I've had opportunities, Alexa," he said softly. "*Plenty* of opportunities."

Alexa swallowed as Diego's words cut into her skin, sharp as a blade. She thought of Cynthia, the curvy brunette who lived in Diego's dorm at Princeton and was always wiggling around in low-cut Victoria's Secret slips, knocking on Diego's door to "borrow index cards," and shooting Alexa dirty looks in the bathroom. Diego was *surrounded* by girls in college. Girls who probably all wanted him.

And, though the possibility had never occurred to Alexa before, it hit her then: Had Diego . . . *cheated* on her? Maybe, on some weekend when she'd slept over at Portia's mansion instead of Diego's dorm, he'd gone out to a party and stumbled home trashed, only to find one of his sultry hallmates outside his door. Maybe they'd started kissing drunkenly, and. . . .

Impossible, Alexa decided in the next heartbeat. What college girl could compete with *her*? Alexa might still be in high school, but she gave Diego everything he wanted — and then some. No boy — and Alexa had dated an impressive number — had ever been unfaithful to Alexa St. Laurent. It simply wasn't done.

But Diego had planted a seed of doubt in her head. And that was enough to drive Alexa to the brink.

"Opportunities?" she repeated, her voice strangely calm. "How interesting. Here's another opportunity for you."

And there, on the top of the Eiffel Tower — in full view of the Japanese couple, the Italians girls, and the now wide-awake security guard — Alexa raised her hand and slapped Diego Mendieta square across his flawless face.

Talk about making a scene.

Steaming, Alexa stalked out of the Eiffel Tower's entrance, her high-heeled mules slapping the pavement. Diego ran up behind her, grabbing her arm. When she twisted around to confront him, she saw the red handprint on his high cheekbone and felt a tiny pang of remorse.

Diego's own eyes were full of regret. "Alexa, look . . . maybe I shouldn't have said that," he mumbled. "We need to talk. . . ."

"You know what?"Alexa replied icily. "I think what we need is some serious time apart from each other. Because, as far as *I'm* concerned, I am done with you, Diego."

And she was, Alexa realized as Diego held her gaze. Diego clearly wasn't cut out for Paris — and he wasn't cut out for *her*.

Wordlessly, the two of them caught the Métro at Trocadéro and rode it back to their hotel, remaining on opposite sides of the car like strangers. Tonight was supposed to be their last in the hotel, but Alexa knew that she couldn't stay another minute. Right there on the train, she decided that when she got back to their room, she'd pack, check out, and call her cousins, whose number she had stashed on a slip of paper in her wallet. Alexa wasn't positive they were back from Avignon yet, but she'd take a chance. Let Diego sit and stew in the soulless Hôtel Rive Gauche alone for one more night.

But after they'd walked into their hotel room, Diego immediately took off his suit jacket, loosened his tie, and retrieved his suitcase from under the bed. Alexa, who'd started pulling huge handfuls of clothes from the armoire, raised a curious eyebrow. Was Mr. Princeton — homesick for college — catching a flight back to New Jersey tonight?

"You're leaving?" she demanded, a Richard Chai satin tube top dangling from one finger.

"What, did you expect me to stay and subject Paris to my rudeness?" Diego asked quietly. "I think I'd be better off elsewhere." Diego paused to refer to his trusty Frommer's guide, which he'd been keeping on the bedside table. "Like Barcelona," he offered curtly, avoiding Alexa's gaze. "Or any Spanish-speaking place. Barcelona's only an overnight train ride from Gare Austerlitz."

Alexa knelt to unclasp one of her bags, a little unsteady. So Diego, too, had formulated a plan on the Métro. She'd been half-hoping that he would follow her to her cousins', begging for forgiveness.

Since Diego was a meticulous packer (or, in Alexa's opinion, simply anal), and Alexa had practically the whole of Bloomingdale's SoHo to stuff into her six bags, the two of them finished packing at the exact same time. They locked the door, took the elevator down to the lobby in hostile silence, checked out, and exited through the hotel's sliding doors for the last time. Holding their respective bags, they stood on the boulevard St-Germain, regarding each other . . . perhaps also for the last time.

"I guess this is good-bye?" Diego asked gruffly, looking down.

Alexa nodded, feeling a tug of sorrow. How had things fallen apart so abruptly? That morning, she and Diego had been cuddling in the Louvre. Now, their glorious vacation was over, ruined. So much for having the best week of their lives.

For one crazy moment, Alexa wondered if she should follow Diego to Barcelona. It would be easy — she'd trail him to Gare Austerlitz, hop on his train and, in the middle of the night, sneak over to his seat and start kissing him. By morning, they'd have made up and arrived in sunny Barcelona; Alexa had been to Barci before, and though the city wasn't as romantic as Paris, it would do in a pinch.

But no, she realized. She didn't want to go to Barcelona. And she certainly didn't want to follow some *boy* there.

After all, Alexa was fiercely independent.

Wasn't she?

So she reached up, touched Diego's cheek — her fingers caressing the very spot she had smacked — and, her throat thick with tears, whispered, "*Au revoir.*"

In French, the expression literally meant "until we see each other again." Alexa wasn't sure if she and Diego ever would. But who knew?

Then they turned and headed in different directions — he for the Métro, she for the nearest pay phone to call her cousins. Unfortunately, the closest phone was several blocks down, and Alexa, lugging her heavy bags down the empty boulevard, was cursing the mules that pinched her feet. When she made it to the phone booth, Alexa dropped her bags in relief, but then realized she'd never bought one of those little phone cards that were needed to place a call — that was why she'd never gotten around to calling her dad.

Crap.

Alexa drew a deep breath. She'd work it out; she always did. She was nothing if not resourceful. Miraculously, she spotted a tall man with a trim moustache, wearing a double-breasted coat and a cockeyed black beret, striding down the boulevard toward her. *A real Frenchman,* Alexa thought, catching his eye and feeling a warm rush of familiarity. He reminded her of her father's brother, Uncle Julien. He'd definitely be able to help her.

"*Pardon, monsieur,*" Alexa called, waving him over.

He stopped before her with a ready smile. "*Oui, mademoiselle?*"

In her fluent, fabulous French, Alexa explained the phone card sitch, asked if she could borrow his card, and — gesturing to her Miu Miu clutch — promised to repay him.

Alexa noticed that the Frenchman's eyes lingered a beat too long on her clutch — and on her Coach bags — and she felt a flicker of hesitation. But then he shot her another smile, reached into his pocket, and said, "*Pour une belle jeune fille? Mais bien sûr.*"

Alexa grinned and fluttered her eyelashes, accepting the phone card he was extending. She was a sucker for being called a beautiful girl, especially when she'd just broken up with her boyfriend. Then, the instant the phone card touched her hand, the Frenchman reached over and snatched her clutch out from under her arm, scooped up four of her Coach bags and took off down the boulevard in a flash.

"*No!*" Alexa screamed after him. In her blind panic, she found herself shrieking in English. "Come back here, you asshole! Give me back my bags! Somebody stop him! Thief!" Of course, there wasn't another soul on the boulevard, so Alexa grabbed her remaining two bags and started off after him. But it was impossible to run in her mules, and by now, the nimble thief was a mere spot in the distance. Alexa let out a helpless sob. She'd never catch him.

Her whole body shaking, Alexa quickly assessed her bags to confirm that — *whew* — the thief hadn't made off with the one that contained her passport. But since he had taken her clutch — and with it, her wallet — she now had no money, and no scrap of paper with her cousins' phone number, which she'd never bothered to memorize.

And by far the *worst* news of all was that the bastard had snatched the precious suitcase that contained her new lilac-colored piqué Behnaz Sarafpour strapless dress — and most of her best outfits.

She was screwed.

Clutching the phone card and her bags, Alexa limped into the phone booth. With wildly trembling fingers, she dialed her dad in New Jersey; she knew he'd calm her down *and* give her the cousins' number. But the answering machine picked up, so Alexa, craving emotional support, tried her mom in New York. No luck there, either — Alexa was left sniffling to the sound of her mother's "Kiss, kiss, dahling" voice mail prompt.

Who was left? Alexa knew Portia's and Maeve's cell numbers by heart, but calling them now, in this sorry condition, would be a disaster. Alexa could all too vividly imagine the girls gloating over her split with Diego. Some support *that* would be.

Resting her head against the cool glass pane of the phone booth, Alexa finally broke down crying. This was a nightmare. She was boyfriendless, friendless, parentless, penniless, starving — and *freezing* in her silly spaghetti-strap dress. Couldn't she have at least changed back at the hotel? Alexa wished, not for the first time, that she were a more practical sort of person. Someone like, say, Holly Jacobson would have surely slipped into jeans, sneakers, and a hoodie before taking on the streets of Paris by night.

Oh, my God, Alexa realized, catching her breath. That was it.

Holly Jacobson!

Of course. Hadn't Holly said Alexa could call her cell while she was in London? And Alexa was positive she remembered Holly's number, since she'd known it since junior high. Alexa wasn't entirely sure how Holly Jacobson could bail her out of this mess, but all that mattered now was hearing her old friend's reassuring voice.

When Holly answered her phone with the adorably out-of-it "Tyler? Where are you calling from?" Alexa burst into fresh tears — but, through her sobs and the static, managed to convince Holly that it was her, and not Tyler Davis, calling.

"I'm in really, really big trouble," Alexa hiccuped, relieved to have a sympathetic ear at last. "I broke up with Diego and got mugged and now I'm homeless. . . ."

"Are you *serious?*" Holly gasped. Alexa heard her move the phone away from her mouth.

"You guys?" Holly said — Alexa guessed she was addressing Meghan and Jess — "I'll meet you back at the hostel. Tell Ms. Graham I had to — oh, forget it. I'll just deal with her when I get there." There was a pause, and then Alexa distinctly heard Holly say, "No, it's *not* Tyler." She sounded uncharacteristically brusque, and Alexa couldn't help but grin through her tears. A second later, Holly was back. "Okay, tell me exactly what happened," she said calmly.

Alexa started to, but the line kept crackling noisily, and Holly had to constantly interrupt her with "Alexa, I can't *hear* you!"

"This is ridiculous," Alexa moaned. Suddenly, she didn't want to be on the phone with Holly. She wanted to be sitting across from her in a café, watching her friend's green-gray eyes widen at Alexa's tales of woe. With a rush of nostalgia, Alexa remembered all the insane fiascos she and Holly had survived — *together* — in South Beach. Maybe it was because Holly was a childhood friend, but Alexa found her presence unfailingly comforting. Alexa knew that the two of them weren't the best of buddies anymore, but somehow she sensed that having Holly Jacobson with her in Paris would make everything better.

Besides, she was only a Chunnel ride away.

"Hol, just come to Paris," Alexa blurted, gripping the phone. "Please? I'm so alone here." Normally, Alexa never admitted to being helpless, but around Holly, she'd mostly learned to swallow her pride. "You don't need to stay the whole week — maybe, like, a day or two?" She wiped her streaming eyes with the heel of her hand, hoping Holly would agree to the last-minute plan.

"Paris? Now?" Holly cried. "Alexa, are you nuts? I can't! I'm in the middle of my track meet and my coach will *kill* me if I leave and what if my parents found out and —"

"All right, all right," Alexa cut off her friend's rambling. She should have known responsible Holly wouldn't take off on an impromptu trip. "Don't worry about it. Honest."

There was a moment of staticky silence, and then Holly whispered, "Should I try to get there tonight, or is tomorrow morning okay?"

CHAPTER SIX

On the Run

It was somewhere under the English Channel, on the thundering Eurostar train, that Holly realized the enormity of what she'd just pulled off.

Holy shit, she thought, scrunching down in her seat and pulling the hood of her sweatshirt up over her head. Holly glanced at the passenger beside her — a silver-haired woman in a massive mink stole who'd been shooting Holly suspicious looks the whole ride — and her heart started hammering wildly. *I'm a fugitive.*

Trying not to hyperventilate, Holly hugged her knees to her chest, gazed out at the dark tunnel, and replayed the insane chain of events that had led her to where she was that Tuesday morning.

The night before, after talking to Alexa, Holly had made curfew by a hair and, nervous but exhilarated, went up to her room to confer with Meghan and Jess. At first, Holly hadn't wanted to let her friends in on the news, but she knew this stunt would be far too risky to carry off alone. And she didn't want them thinking she'd been kidnapped or something if she suddenly disappeared.

"Why are you letting Alexa boss you around?" Meghan had exclaimed as Holly jammed socks and underwear into her duffel bag. Neither Meghan nor Jess ever bothered to disguise their disdain for Alexa, who they considered snotty and superficial. Holly's newfound closeness with her had been a sore point among the girls all year.

Holly refolded her sea-green Forever 21 halter top, which she'd packed in the vain hope that Wimbledon might have some fun dance clubs. She remained silent for a minute. It would be impossible to tell her friends that there'd been no bossing involved: Holly *was* eager to escape England and, more important, primed to indulge in serious boy analysis with Alexa — and not *them*.

So instead, she explained, truthfully, that Alexa was in dire straits and needed Holly's help, at least for a couple of days. Holly figured she'd only stay in Paris until Alexa was back on her stilettos and return to England in time for the final meet on Friday.

"It won't be too awful," she assured the girls, trying

to convince herself as well. "I mean, I can't even practice or compete with you guys, right? And Wednesday's supposed to be the team's free day in London. Coach Graham won't even notice I'm missing then!"

Jess groaned, flopping back on her pillow. "But Holly, we need you here for moral support. And Coach Graham expects you to be at the meets. You're our freaking *captain*!"

Holly swallowed her guilt. She knew that bailing on her teammates during their big international meet was terrible. But Holly also felt like Alexa's call had been a sign from the heavens. In a way, the choice was no longer hers; she simply had to get on that Chunnel train tomorrow morning — no matter what it took.

Swearing to walk dogs, babysit siblings, and do laundry, she begged Meghan and Jess to cover for her. As Holly packed, she and the girls invented a slew of excuses — from her ankle swelling up to food poisoning, from migraines to anxiety attacks — for when Coach Graham would ask where Holly was. The girls *could* whip out the classic "problems back home" sob story, but that might be dicey; Holly was worried Ms. Graham might decide to call the Jacobsons herself — there was no way in hell Holly was telling her parents about this little excursion to Paris.

"If Coach Graham finds out," Jess warned, turning off the light a mere two hours before their 4:30 A.M.

alarm, "you're toast, Holly." She took a deep breath. "We all are."

Jess's ominous words rang in Holly's head all night and well into the morning. After Meghan and Jess headed off for practice, Holly, clammy-palmed, hurriedly changed into carpenter cords, a long-sleeved waffle shirt and her Kangol hoodie, holding her breath the whole time.

Then — consulting the Fodor's guide to London her parents had given her before her trip — she crept outside (everyone was at the track by then, so the coast was more than clear) and caught the commuter rail, which took her into London proper, and Waterloo station. There, Alexa had told her, Holly could catch the Eurostar train into Paris.

For a second, as Holly entered the enormous station, every single particle of her being screamed at her to turn around and go back to Wimbledon, like the sane, levelheaded, good girl she was. But whether it was her trouble with Tyler (who still hadn't called back, and thus had no clue about Paris) or the frustration she was feeling about her best friends (whom she was now indebted to for life), Holly was also sort of enjoying the thrill that came with breaking so many rules.

Holly Jacobson may have been a good girl, but she was always up for a challenge.

So, her ankle throbbing only slightly, she strode

across the station and bought a round-trip ticket with her Amex. The charge on the credit card, Holly realized as she signed, would be yet another lie she'd have to cook up — this time for her parents, when she was back home and the bill came. But it didn't matter: full steam ahead now.

In a daze, Holly boarded the train and sank into the first window seat she could find. When the fur-draped woman plunked down beside her — after shrieking at the conductor because, apparently, she was supposed to be in first class — Holly hardly glanced up. Her surreal, out-of-body sensation lasted during the aboveground ride through England, but when they entered the Chunnel, she started to seriously freak out about being on the lam.

Suddenly Holly's cell phone rang, jerking her out of her worries. She noticed that the train had come up out of the tunnel and was now speeding through coastal France.

Oh, no, she thought, frantically pawing through her Vans tote for the ringing phone. What if it was Coach Graham calling? Or her parents?

Or . . . Tyler?

Once again, the screen on her T-Mobile showed an unfamiliar series of digits after a plus sign.

"Who — who is it?" Holly whispered into the phone, her entire body tensing up.

"Breathe, Hol," Alexa said, laughing. "Where are you?"

Relief flooded through Holly. "On the train to Paris," she whispered.

"Holly Rebecca Jacobson, you *rock*!" Alexa squealed, and Holly could hear the admiration in her voice. She felt herself start to relax; what she was doing was definitely crazy — but maybe kind of cool, too.

That is, if she didn't get caught.

As the train hurtled on, Alexa filled Holly in on her status since last night; apparently, she'd finally reached her dad, who'd wired her money *and* put her in touch with her cousins, who had, thankfully, just returned from the long weekend with their parents. So Alexa was now staying with Pierre and Raphaëlle, as she'd planned to do anyway — only now it was *sans* Diego.

"Do you still want me to come?" Holly asked, nibbling on her thumbnail. She was starting to worry that her risky rescue mission might now be semipointless.

"Of course I do!" Alexa groaned. "I'm completely traumatized from everything that happened, and my cousins are, like, never around. I need to see you, Hol, so I can, I don't know, be *myself* again." She let out a long sigh.

Satisfied that she still had a purpose in Paris, Holly

told Alexa that her train got in around three that afternoon, and they agreed that Alexa would meet her at the Gare du Nord.

Clicking off, Holly leaned back against her seat with a sigh. For the first time that day, she forgot her fears and felt a tingle of anticipation; she suspected that, in addition to helping Alexa, she might also have a pretty good time in Paris. She was closing her eyes — she hadn't slept at all last night — when the woman next to her tapped her shoulder.

"Excuse me," she said snidely. "Don't I know you from somewhere?"

Holly opened her eyes, seized by terror again. The woman *had* been watching her! Was she in cahoots with Coach Graham? "I — I don't think so," Holly stammered, trying to avoid her gaze.

"It's been bothering me the entire trip," the woman whined, toying with the flashy diamond choker around her neck. "I have an impeccable memory for faces, and I know I've seen yours before. Were you vacationing in Belize this past summer?"

Try sports camp in Massachusetts, Holly wanted to reply, but she bit her tongue.

"Then you were skiing in Whistler this winter," the woman insisted.

Holly blinked at the woman and considered telling

her that, despite the fact that she was Paris-bound, she wasn't at all accustomed to visiting glamorous locales.

"Or . . ." The woman went on, tapping a finger to her chin. "Have you ever spent time in South Beach, Miami?"

Except for that one.

Holly's stomach sank in recognition as she took in the woman's haughty face. *Oh . . . my . . . God,* she thought. *It's Henrietta von Malhoffer!*

Holly and Alexa had encountered the formidable Henrietta von Malhoffer exactly a year ago, when they'd pretended to be guests at a ritzy South Beach hotel. Overhearing the wealthy woman's name and room number in the lobby, the girls had claimed she was their generous aunt in order to get served yummy drinks and nibbles — but had run away before their cover was blown. Back then, Holly remembered, Henrietta had kept her silver mane hidden by a silk head wrap — and apparently hadn't had as many Botox injections — so she'd looked different.

But Holly *hadn't* changed all that much since last year — which explained why the woman had been studying her so intently.

Holly shook her head. What were the chances? She only hoped that Henrietta wouldn't put two and two together and ID Holly as one of the girls who'd charged food to her hotel room.

"Nope," she lied. "I've never been to South Beach in my life." Turning back to the window, Holly tried her best not to burst out laughing. She couldn't wait to tell Alexa.

"Guess who was on my train!" Holly cried as soon as she spotted Alexa in the busy Gare du Nord. Alexa was pacing in front of a ticket window on her cork-wedge espadrilles, looking impatiently at her watch, but she glanced up at the sound of Holly's voice. Holly grinned, feeling a burst of fondness toward her old friend; after the harrowing journey, seeing her was an instant comfort.

"You made it!" Alexa exclaimed, dashing toward Holly. Alexa may have been comfortably ensconced at her cousins' place, but she was still shaky from her mugging, fuming over Diego, and *dying* to bitch and moan to her old friend. Watching Holly approach, a smile blooming on her freckled face, Alexa immediately felt her heart lighten. But she couldn't help choking up a little, too; Holly had traveled all this way for *her*!

The girls reached each other, their arms outstretched, but in the moment before they embraced, there was a sudden awkwardness. After all, it wasn't like Alexa and Holly spent all their time in Oakridge hugging. They hadn't even really said good-bye before their respective trips abroad. Both girls had to admit that, despite their affection for each other, their friendship was still tinged with a bit of tension.

It was Alexa who dispelled any discomfort by throwing her arms around Holly. "Hol, thank you, thank you, *thank you!*" she gushed, wondering how she could ever repay her friend for this major favor. "I hope the trip wasn't a *complete* pain in the ass," she added.

The girls hugged tight, Holly's duffel knocking against Alexa's leg and Alexa's wooden bangles getting tangled in Holly's hair. They giggled as they separated.

"Well, it definitely wasn't easy. . . ." Holly began with a shrug.

"Wait, so *who* was on your train?" Alexa was asking at the exact same instant.

The girls broke into giggles again, and Holly thought about how acting silly with Alexa felt somehow acceptable — as opposed to how immature she felt around Meghan and Jess's clowning.

Holly linked her arm through Alexa's as they began walking. "Henrietta von Malhoffer," she whispered, looking around to make sure the woman wasn't behind them.

Alexa's big blue eyes widened. "Get out!" she cried. "That bitch from the hotel last year?" As she and Holly started laughing, a wild thought occurred to Alexa. "Hol, listen!" she exclaimed, stopping in the middle of the station. "I think it's a sign."

"A sign?" Holly asked. Alexa was forever thinking everything was a sign or an omen. Growing up, she'd been the one who believed in ghosts, and Holly had been the cynic who'd scoffed at their Ouija board games.

"Yes," Alexa said firmly. Now she knew for sure: Getting Holly to come to Paris had been the smartest thing she'd ever done. "The last time we saw her was in South Beach, right?" she explained. "So that means we're going to have just as much — if not *more* — fun than we did *last* spring break." Alexa grinned, leading Holly in the direction of the Métro. "Hol, it's official — Paris is South Beach, part *deux*!"

The girls took the Métro to Le Marais, rehashing Holly's great escape the whole ride. But when they emerged onto the sun-dappled street, Holly stopped her storytelling to gaze around in awe. *Whoa.* The red-and-gold Art Nouveau Métro sign, the elegant pedestrians trotting past, the corner violinist playing a version of "La Vie en Rose" . . . *I am in* Paris! she thought. All Holly knew of Paris she'd picked up from movies, books, or Alexa. It was breathtaking to see the mythical city brought to life, even more beautiful than she'd imagined it.

And then Holly wished that Tyler were there to share in the magic with her. He would lace his fingers through hers as they walked down one of the winding side streets and kiss her softly beneath one of the slender lampposts. Paris, Holly realized with a pang of sorrow, was best enjoyed with a boy.

But now that she was here, she still planned to have the time of her life — *without* Tyler Davis.

"Let's celebrate your arrival over drinks," Alexa declared, slipping an arm around Holly's waist. "We can drop your stuff at my cousins' later, but I thought you'd want to see the neighborhood first." Even though Holly was staring all starry-eyed at the streets of Le Marais, her touristy enthusiasm didn't irk Alexa as much as Diego's had. Maybe, in part, it was because Alexa had expected Diego to be as sophisticated as she was, but she knew that sheltered Holly couldn't help her naïveté.

The girls walked beneath the lovely stone arches of the place des Vosges and past a row of chichi art galleries until they arrived at a corner café that over-looked the trees and fountains of the Louis Treize park. The weather was unseasonably warm —"Hol, you brought the sunshine!" Alexa exclaimed as Holly wriggled out of her hoodie — so the girls sat outside. A dark-eyed waiter materialized with a nod and a low "*Mesdemoiselles?*" leaving both girls momentarily tongue-tied. But Alexa quickly recovered and ordered two kirs, and then they leaned back in their straw chairs, soaking up the afternoon sun and grinning at each other.

"I'm just loving having you in Paris," Alexa said truthfully, giving her friend a grateful look across the small table. She noticed that while Holly also seemed psyched, a mysterious sadness darkened her gray-green eyes. *She's probably still stressed about ditching out on her team,* Alexa reasoned, lazily twining her hair up on her head. *A sparkling night on the town will perk her right up.* Alexa already had plans for the two of them — along with her cousins — to check out some sizzling discothèques that evening.

Meanwhile, Holly was studying Alexa, who, of course, looked stunning in a white wrap top, a necklace of chunky wooden beads, and a low-slung apple-red peasant skirt. Holly shook her head in wonder; only raging clothes horse Alexa would have most of her luggage stolen and still have the perfect trendy outfit to wear the next day. But despite Alexa's put-together exterior, Holly could sense that her normally composed friend was just a tad more vulnerable than usual.

"How are you feeling about, um, Diego?" Holly asked carefully as their drinks arrived, along with a sly wink from their waiter. Holly smiled back shyly. Diego, she recalled vividly, also knew how to turn on the charm. Though Diego *was* a hottie, Holly had eventually realized that he wasn't the right guy for her. Now she was curious to hear how Alexa had come to realize the same thing.

"Pissed," Alexa replied promptly, reaching for her kir. After a night away from Diego, Alexa's simmering anger toward her ex had only boiled hotter. And when Alexa St. Laurent got pissed, she also got defiant. Alexa had already decided that, when she and Holly went clubbing that night, she would grab the most beautiful guy on the dance floor and indulge in the steamiest, sultriest, screw-you-Diego hookup she could possibly have, Mr. Princeton and his "opportunities" be damned. Her impending makeout session — or hey, maybe even more — wouldn't be so much *rebound,* Alexa reasoned, as *revenge.*

"Hol, you wouldn't believe the things that asshole said to me on our last night together," Alexa continued passionately, leaning toward her friend. "And then he just up and left for stupid Barcelona, completely destroying our anniversary trip and —" Suddenly, Alexa paused, studying Holly's serious expression. Now that she wasn't weeping hysterically on the phone, Alexa had the clarity to realize that Holly might *resent* this situation. Alexa sincerely hoped that Holly wouldn't feel like Alexa had stolen Diego away from her only to dump him a year later.

Which . . . hmm . . . was actually sort of what had happened.

But Holly, who seemed intrigued, urged Alexa to continue. And, as the girls sipped their cool, sweet kirs and Alexa explained the whole sordid ordeal, Holly was all understanding and insight.

"You know," she observed, sipping her smooth, delicious drink, which Alexa had said was dry white wine mixed with black-currant liqueur, "Diego comes from a family of doctors — both his parents are surgeons and his uncles, too, I think. I can see how being premed in college might make him a little more uptight, since he's got all these expectations to deal with now."

Alexa stared into her blush-colored kir. She felt a momentary prickle of annoyance that Holly was taking Diego's side, until Alexa realized that her friend had a point. When Alexa and Diego had been together, they were usually too busy *getting* busy to discuss their respective families. But Holly had known Diego's family when she was younger, so she'd probably paid more attention. Alexa felt a surge of gratitude toward calm, thoughtful Holly; Portia and Maeve would have *never* been this helpful in a boy-related crisis.

Alexa reached across the table to squeeze her friend's hand. "You're so wise, Hol," she said softly. "I never stopped to wonder why Diego was getting on my nerves. Mostly, I think the problem was that we just didn't travel well together — we were bickering the entire time." Alexa remembered the grand conclusion she'd reached that morning, over coffee and croissants at her cousins'. "I have this theory," she added. "The couple that travels well together . . ."

"Stays together?" Holly offered with a grin, squeezing Alexa's hand back. "If that's the case, Alexa, maybe we should be dating each *other*!" Holly had always marveled at how famously she and Alexa got along when they *weren't* at home.

Alexa laughed, finishing her kir. "Break it to Tyler gently, okay?" she teased.

There it was again — the fleeting distraction in Holly's eyes.

"Holly," Alexa began softly. "Is everything . . . okay with you and Tyler?" Alexa realized that, throughout her Diego rant, Holly hadn't once mentioned the boy in *her* life.

Holly stared at the green square and spraying fountains across the street. She'd been so ready to dish about Tyler with Alexa, but now, faced with the opportunity, she found herself hesitating. Maybe it was that Alexa had so candidly spilled her guts about Diego, and Holly felt that her own issues were somehow trivial in comparison. Maybe it was Holly's good old natural shyness swallowing her words. Or maybe it was that Alexa herself was at the center of Holly's Tyler heartache. In any case, she knew she couldn't open up just yet. So she shook her head and assured Alexa that everything was cool.

Then Holly glanced at her watch, yawning. Lounging in the café was so mellow that she was finally feeling her fatigue from that morning's escapade; she'd been running on pure adrenaline before. She hoped she'd be able to turn in early that night, or maybe nap a little. "Do you mind if we head to your cousins' place?" she asked Alexa, glad to have a reason to change the subject.

Alexa clapped a hand to her mouth. "*Merde!* We *do* need to go back and change — we're having dinner at my uncle's before we go clubbing!" Alexa had been so focused on going out dancing that the gathering at her aunt and uncle's sumptuous townhouse had slipped her mind. *Plus, we'll have to get Holly Paris-ready,* Alexa decided, eyeing her friend's sloppy ponytail, boring waffle shirt, and makeup-free face.

Clubbing — tonight? Holly sighed as the bill for

their drinks arrived. She should have known an early night would be impossible with Alexa.

Leaving the café, the girls walked the short distance to rue de Sévigné, where Raphaëlle and Pierre lived. Holly was immediately enchanted by the narrow street, with its cluster of slightly crooked houses and funky storefronts. Alexa pulled a brass key out of her lizard handbag and opened a tall, dark wooden door that creaked loudly. Holly was surprised that the musty stairwell they entered didn't have an overhead light, but she followed Alexa carefully up the winding staircase until they reached the third floor.

"Alexa?" Holly asked, her polite instincts kicking in as they stepped onto the landing. "Are you sure I'm not imposing? Your cousins don't even know me —"

"Please," Alexa cut in, rolling her eyes. "Diego was supposed to stay here, too, remember? There's plenty of room, and they'll totally love you." She stopped in front of a dark green apartment door — Holly noticed ST. LAURENT printed above the keyhole — and was fishing in her bag for another key, when the door swung open from the inside and a boy wearing jeans and a white T-shirt stepped out.

The most gorgeous boy Holly had seen . . . in *any* country.

He had smooth olive skin — even darker than

Diego Mendieta's — and thick curly dark hair that spilled messily into his eyes, which — by contrast — were a bright, startling blue. His face wasn't perfect, the way Tyler's was; his nose was prominent, his forehead was high, and his upper lip was fuller than his bottom . . . but somehow it all worked.

Brilliantly.

"Alexa, *mon amour*!" he exclaimed. "*Pardon — je vais acheter une bouteille de vin pour Maman . . .*" Holly was just wishing she understood French when the boy trailed off, turned away from Alexa, and looked right at her. His face broke into a slow, devastatingly sexy smile.

"*Ah.* You are 'Olly, *non*?" he asked, taking a step toward her.

"Ollie?" Holly repeated, unconsciously taking a step back.

Alexa burst out laughing at this cute moment of cross-cultural crossed wires. "He means Holly," she clarified, jabbing her cousin's toned arm. "The French always make the 'H' silent at the beginning of words or names. Anyway," she added, putting her other hand on Holly's shoulder. "Yes, Pierre, this is *mon amie,* Holly, and Holly, this is my favorite cousin in the world, Pierre."

"*Enchanté,*" Pierre murmured, and then, as Holly's heart pounded like mad, he came even closer to her, leaned in, and kissed her once on each cheek. His lips were soft, and she could smell his cologne — sharp and sweet, like some exotic spice. Holly stood stock still, her pulse tapping from his unexpected closeness. She'd never been kissed by someone when meeting them for the first time — especially not a boy.

"Um — nice to meet you," she finally managed, her cheeks burning. She stuck out her hand, but instead of shaking it, Pierre simply took it in both of his for a moment, a smile tugging at his lips as his blue eyes held hers.

"Wait!" Alexa exclaimed, and both Pierre and Holly gave a start, looking her way. "Duh," she went on, shaking back her long hair. "I forgot. You guys *know* each other."

"We do?" Holly asked, her heartbeat still a little erratic even as Pierre released her hand. She certainly would have recalled meeting *this* guy before.

Alexa's eyes were dancing. "Don't you remember, Hol?" she asked. This was one of her most beloved childhood memories. "We crank-called Pierre when we were little! We were playing Truth or Dare and —"

"I pretended to be you on the phone, so we could trick your twelve-year-old cousin in Paris. . . ." Holly finished, and glanced at Pierre. "That was *you*?" she asked in disbelief.

Holly remembered herself at ten — skinny, gawky,

and even frecklier, her hair in two light-brown plaits —
on the phone with a boy she'd never met before. Alexa
had whispered French phrases into her ear, and Holly
had dutifully repeated them into the phone, trying
not to giggle. A boy's voice — just making the transi-
tion to deepness — on the other end had responded
with a confused "Alexa? *C'est toi?*" but Holly had hung
up before he could ask any more questions.

Pierre grinned, lifting one shoulder in a casual
shrug. "We meet again."

Holly nodded slowly. If Pierre had been twelve
when they'd talked on the phone, he was about nineteen now. She had no idea what Pierre had looked
like all those years ago . . . but he certainly seemed to
have matured *very* nicely.

And suddenly, Holly wasn't feeling all that tired
anymore.

CHAPTER SEVEN

Eurotrash

Deliciously steamy and refreshed, Alexa adjusted the teeny pink towel around her body and flitted out of her cousins' bathroom into the small, cozy guest room across the hall. It was where she and Diego would have stayed had their vacation not gone awry. Two narrow twin beds were positioned across from each other — she and Diego would have had to make do with pushing them together again — and a full-length mirror was propped crookedly in one corner. The yellow shutters were flung wide open, allowing the rosy light of a Paris evening to spill inside.

"Shower's all yours, babe," Alexa told Holly, who was sitting on her designated bed and staring into space. "Earth to Holly," Alexa added teasingly, taking out her tube of Frédéric Fekkai styling gel from the makeup bag on her bed. "We need to be all primped and beautiful by the time Raphaëlle gets back from closing up shop."

Alexa's *other* cousin — Pierre's twenty-four-year-old big sis — owned Frou-Frou, an über-hip handbag boutique in the neighborhood. During Alexa's visit to the store that morning, the ever-generous Raphaëlle had said Alexa was welcome to anything that caught her fancy — including the new line of pink-polka-dot drawstring purses. Alexa had declined, thinking she'd check out Dior first; Raphi's stuff, while adorable, wasn't *quite* her style.

"Oops — sorry!" Holly exclaimed, turning to Alexa, her eyes very big. "I zoned out for a second." She'd been thinking of Tyler and — for no apparent reason — feeling guilty. Hurriedly, she rooted around in her duffel, pulling out a towel, soap, and shampoo. "If Raphaëlle's at work, where did Pierre go?" Holly asked casually. "Does he have a job, too?" She'd been wondering that ever since he'd sprinted on down the stairs after they'd met.

Hmm, Alexa thought, a juicy suspicion sprouting in her mind. "He went to pick up wine for dinner tonight," she replied, scrunching product into her wet hair. "And, no — he's a student at the Sorbonne. This is technically Raphi's place, but she lets him crash here."

As Holly headed to the shower, Alexa smiled to

herself. She'd totally picked up on an energy between Holly and her cousin, and now wondered if *something* might be brewing there. Though with Tyler Davis in the picture, probably not.

"Hey . . . Alexa?" she heard Holly call from the bathroom. Her voice was hesitant. "Can I ask you a completely stupid question?"

"Let me guess," Alexa said with a laugh, peeking out into the hall to see Holly's face sticking out from the bathroom door. "The toilet?"

Holly nodded, looking mortified. "Where *is* it? I really have to pee."

"Next door," Alexa replied, pointing. "That's how it works here. They have one room for the shower and sink, and another just for the toilet." She shrugged. "Welcome to France."

Holly sighed, heading for the other room. She'd *never* figure out this country. First there'd been Pierre and his surprising two-cheek kiss. Then there was the apartment itself; all slanted ceilings, uneven wooden floors, and old-fashioned moldings, it seemed straight out of the nineteenth century. But the walls were painted with giant black and white polka dots, and orange shag rugs, bright lava lamps, and retro French movie posters took up every inch of space. Holly, who was accustomed to the simple symmetry of her suburban split-level in Oakridge, had never seen anything quite like this.

The shower, too, proved to be a mystery. Once inside, Holly had to struggle with the odd handheld nozzle; there was no ledge to rest it on, so while Holly shaved her legs, the stream of water kept spraying her in the face. It was the least relaxing shower of her life.

When she finally emerged, a little winded, Holly wrapped her yellow towel tight around herself, gave her wet hair a shake, and padded out of the bathroom. She was hardly thinking as she turned the knob on a closed door across the hall, but when she stepped into the room, Holly's heart leaped; this wasn't the guest room where she and Alexa were staying, but a boy's bedroom. The navy blue quilt on the single bed and a poster of the French soccer team above the desk were dead giveaways.

So was Pierre, who was standing next to the bed, wearing absolutely nothing but white boxer shorts.

"Oh, my God, I'm so sorry," Holly gasped, her face catching fire, as her eyes — almost without her own volition — swept over Pierre's broad shoulders and smooth, olive-skinned chest. Holly felt her stomach somersault but she found herself unable to turn away. "You're, um — you're back from getting wine," she added unnecessarily, her voice shaky.

"'Olly," Pierre said warmly, without a trace of embarrassment or surprise. He flashed her a grin, his teeth very white against his dark complexion.

Something about him briefly reminded Holly of a pirate — in the best possible way. "I am just . . . how you say, changing?" Pierre added casually. He gestured to the pair of jeans in his left hand, which he'd clearly just stepped out of, and tilted his head to one side, his blue eyes sparkling.

"Changing," Holly affirmed tremblingly, as the blush in her face made its way down her neck to her damp collarbone. Suddenly, she realized that — in her short towel — she wasn't all that covered up, either, and, felt a fresh wave of shyness. "I — I should go," she mumbled, ducking her head and hurrying back out into the hall, taking care to close the door firmly behind her. As she headed over to the *real* guest room, Holly couldn't help thinking that, if Tyler, or any boy she knew from back home, had been in the same position as Pierre — walked in on by a girl they'd just met — they'd have acted as fidgety and flustered as she was now feeling. Pierre's matter-of-fact cool had been refreshingly different.

And, okay, yeah. Pretty damn sexy.

Trying to banish images of Pierre's sculpted upper body from her mind, Holly slipped into the guest room, where Alexa stood in front of the full-length mirror, wearing a simple black tube dress, champagne-colored strappy sandals, and a miserable frown. In a heartbeat, Holly decided not to mention the random encounter with Pierre. It wasn't *that* big a deal after all, and calling attention to it would somehow give it more weight.

"I hate it, hate it, hate it," Alexa declared, hands on hips. "I'm capital-B boring."

Holly glanced over, grateful for the distraction. She saw nothing wrong with Alexa's outfit but knew better than to argue with her stubborn friend. "So wear something else," she suggested, unzipping her duffel and pulling out the halter top that had been wasted on Wimbledon. Thankfully, Alexa seemed too wrapped up in her clothes to notice Holly's crimson face. Sometimes, Alexa's self-absorption could be a good thing.

"I don't *have* anything else!" Alexa wailed, spinning around and sorting through the surviving clothes that she'd dumped onto her bed. The thief had left her with very slim pickings. "At least," she added, tossing a tank top over her shoulder. "Nothing that's right for Eurotrash."

"For *what?*" Holly asked, running her fingers through her wet bangs.

"Eurotrash," Alexa repeated, returning to the mirror. "*The* hottest new discothèque in Paris, and where we'll be going with the cousins right after dinner."

Despite the dissatisfaction with her outfit, Alexa felt a shiver of excitement; she'd never been to Eurotrash, but considering its spicy reputation, she was sure it would provide a most scintillating evening. As she reached for her LaLicious body butter to smooth over her arms, Alexa imagined dirty dancing with some European sex god to the rhythmic beats of house music, and her pulse quickened. *Take that, Diego Mendieta.*

Meanwhile, Holly's pulse was also racing — for an entirely different reason. *The cousins.* So Pierre would be coming, too. Drawing a deep breath, Holly held up her halter. "Would *this* be okay for — for Eurotrash?" she asked, wanting to giggle at the ridiculous name.

Alexa turned to assess. Holly's top was clearly a designer knockoff, but its bright sea-green color and crystal beading along the V-neck were *très* chic. Plus, lucky Holly — who was much more well-endowed than A-cup Alexa — would fill it out nicely. "It's perfect," Alexa assured her friend with a grin. She was impressed; it seemed Holly didn't need a major Paris overhaul after all.

The girls were slipping on their dinner-party cover-ups — a sparkly shrug for Alexa, a black cardigan for Holly — when a knock sounded on their door.

"*Allô?*" Pierre called. "You are, *euh* . . . how you say . . . *decent?*"

Holly had been reaching for the doorknob but she pulled back, her heart thudding. She wasn't quite ready to see Pierre again. And she wondered if his "decent" comment was a private joke meant for her.

"More or less," Alexa teased, scooting by Holly to open the door. "Look at you, hot stuff!" she added when she saw Pierre standing there, holding a bottle of wine and wearing a sky-blue shirt that matched his eyes. Having a cute cousin, Alexa had decided, was both a blessing and a curse; he made for fun eye candy but was also the one boy she could never have.

"And *you*," Pierre replied, giving Alexa a wide smile. "It is, perhaps, in the genes?"

"Definitely," Alexa laughed, stepping out into the hall and revealing Holly, who'd been standing paralyzed behind her.

This time, Holly realized as she and Pierre regarded each other, she had no excuse to turn and hurry away from him. So she watched, holding her breath, as Pierre's eyes moved with agonizing slowness up from her skinny-heeled black sling-backs to her distressed denim miniskirt to the sea-green halter to, finally, her lips and face, which makeup guru Alexa had done up with berry-stain gloss, subtle blusher, and smoky eye-liner. Holly knew she looked mighty different from the two times Pierre had seen her before. As his lips parted in surprise, something dangerously close to pleasure flushed Holly's skin. She wasn't used to boys — not even Tyler — staring at her in this way. And suddenly,

Holly felt the opposite of how Tyler had made her feel back in the car in Oakridge: *desirable.*

"'Olly," Pierre finally whispered, as if overcome. "You are . . . you look . . ."

Then they all heard the front door slam.

"*Mon Dieu!*" a girl's voice cried in panic. "I'm *late!*" What followed was a stream of furious French words that Holly could only guess were curses.

Alexa and Pierre glanced at each other, grinned, and, at the same time, said, "Raphi."

Still unsteady, Holly followed Pierre and Alexa into the living room, where a curvaceous twenty-something girl was sitting on the sofa, frantically tugging off one of her super-high platform boots. She wore a thick polka-dot headband, a sleeveless orange tunic cinched in the middle with a bronze-buckled belt, and cropped tuxedo trousers. Her wild halo of black curls and tan complexion instantly gave her away as Pierre's sister; only her eyes — dark brown, slightly almond-shaped, but just as mischievous — were different from his. Holly wondered how fair-skinned, flaxen-haired Alexa could have such exotic-looking cousins.

"The American!" Raphaëlle exclaimed when she looked up. She bounded off the sofa and hopped over to Holly on her shoeless foot. "Wow, *c'est* cool that you're here," she gushed, with hardly a hint of an accent. "I *love* speaking the English, and Alexa won't let me with her, but now I can practice!" This time, Holly was prepared for the effusive one-two kiss Raphaëlle bestowed on her and was pleasantly surprised that Alexa's fashion-forward cousin — who Holly had been imagining as some prissy diva — was so warm and bubbly.

After Raphaëlle had changed into what she deemed more parent-appropriate shoes — vintage, round-toed orange pumps that Alexa was completely jealous of — the foursome tumbled out of the apartment into the warm Paris night. After a short Métro ride, they were hurrying down the impossibly fancy rue du Faubourg St-Honoré. As Raphaëlle and Pierre led the way to their parents' home, Alexa gazed dreamily at the various designer houses: Givenchy, Hermès, Christian Lacroix, Hervé Léger. . . . Haute couture heaven.

"We'll go shopping here tomorrow, Hol," Alexa declared, linking her arm through Holly's. "And we'll hit up avenue Montaigne, too." Alexa felt sort of bad tossing Daddy's money around in boutiques, but after all, her *luggage* had been stolen. Destiny was practically begging her to shop, right?

"Uh . . . sure," Holly replied, thinking *You shop, I'll watch.* There was no *way* she'd be able to afford even a pair of earrings from any of the deluxe stores lining the long, narrow street. But she did like the idea of her and Alexa spending a girly day around Paris together.

The St. Laurents' townhouse was a deep creamy color, with gargoyles jutting out from the roof and a lion's head knocker on the heavy wooden double doors. Holly remembered Alexa saying that her uncle was an important diplomat, and Holly suddenly felt intimidated. When the door opened, though, she — along with the others — was swept up in the arms of a voluptuous, olive-skinned woman with luxurious black curls and flashing dark eyes. She wore a flowing ruby-red caftan, harem-style pants, and furry kitten-heeled red slippers.

When the woman released them, Holly noticed that dangling from her neck was an elaborately designed gold hand with an eye painted in the middle of it; Holly recognized the cool pendant from a charm bracelet her second cousin — who lived in Israel — had sent her last year.

"*Bienvenue!* Welcome!" the woman gushed, managing to double-kiss Alexa, Pierre, Raphaëlle, and Holly in two seconds flat. "I am Aziza," she told Holly, putting out her hand and beaming. "Alexandria's aunt. Please do come in, savor my home, and eat."

Aziza's accent, Holly noticed, was not only French, but a little bit of something else, too. "Alexa, where is your aunt *from?*" Holly whispered as they all stepped into the foyer, which was decorated with vibrant Middle Eastern tapestries and a plush Oriental rug on the marble floor.

"Tunisia," Alexa whispered, thrilled to be back at her aunt and uncle's welcoming, fun place. She'd spent a lot of time here when she was little and had always felt like Aziza was more of a mom than, well, her real mom. "In North Africa, you know?" Alexa explained. "But she lived in Israel when she was young, before her family moved to Paris."

Wow, Holly thought. Having spent her whole life in Oakridge, she was fascinated by such cosmopolitan people. And now she knew where Raphaëlle and Pierre got their striking looks.

Alexa's uncle, by contrast, had pale blue eyes, a shock of silver hair, and a dignified demeanor. He was sitting in the living room, reading a newspaper and smoking a pipe. In his impeccable three-piece suit, he instantly reminded Holly of Alexa's father. After Julien had politely greeted everyone, they all trooped over to the dining room. The long, candelit table was overflowing with tantalizing platters of food and an array of champagnes and wines, to which Pierre gamely added his bottle. Holly looked on, speechless, as Julien uncorked Pierre's contribution and poured his son a glass of Burgundy; she couldn't for the life of her imagine drinking with her parents. Or *anybody's* parents, for that matter.

Alexa, sitting beside Holly, was sipping her flute of fizzy Veuve Clicquot without a second thought. The drinking age in France was technically sixteen, but Alexa's dad — like most French parents — had *always* been fine with her imbibing at the dinner table, so by now, Alexa was a seasoned drinker.

"*Tiens, chérie*," Aziza said to Holly, handing her two serving plates at once. "Take, dear — they are delicious." On one plate were clusters of small, dark coils shimmering in garlic sauce; on the other were soft beige cubes on a bed of olives and tomatoes.

Holly glanced questioningly at Alexa, but her friend was busy enjoying her champagne. So Holly, not wanting to be rude, smiled and helped herself to both mysterious dishes. *I always give Tyler grief for not being adventurous with food,* she reminded herself, as she sampled one of the dark coiled shapes. Its texture was rubbery, but the combination of garlic and butter tasted heavenly. She was trying one of the odd beige cubes — it was kind of mushy, if also tasty — when Alexa poked her in the side and murmured, "Enjoying some authentic French cuisine?"

"What *is* this stuff?" Holly whispered. Glancing across the table, she saw that Pierre and Raphaëlle were eagerly digging into the same dishes.

Alexa bit her lip, wishing she hadn't said anything. Holly would probably throw up or pass out when Alexa told her what she was eating. "Don't freak," she whispered, touching Holly's elbow. "But those —" she indicated the dark coiled shapes —"are *escargots*."

"You mean — *snails*?" Holly choked out, her mouth still half-full. Her face slowly drained of color. "What — what about these —" She pointed to the beige cubes.

Alexa cringed. *Even worse.* "*Cervelles provençales*," she whispered reluctantly. "Or, um, calf brains."

Holly dropped her fork with a loud clatter as horror welled up inside her. *Snails and brains?!* What was *wrong* with the French? Instinctively she grabbed for her napkin to spit out the *cervelles*, but as Pierre caught her eye across the table, Holly knew she had to get it together. She couldn't humiliate herself in front of this boy again. *Chew, swallow, don't die,* she told herself firmly. She managed to do just that, and then finished off with a huge gulp of champagne — which Alexa had thoughtfully poured into her glass after breaking the bad food news.

Alexa patted Holly's shoulder, proud that her friend hadn't entirely lost it, and then turned her attention to her own *escargots*, and the questions Julien was asking her about her dad.

"You are okay?" Pierre asked Holly quietly. Clearly, he'd noticed that her face matched her green halter, but though his voice was concerned, there was amusement in his blue eyes. The others at the table were chatting and thankfully seemed to have missed Holly's gag attack.

"I think so," Holly managed, her head spinning. But *was* she? How had she ended up here, at this unfamiliar table, with this sophisticated French family, eating the weirdest stuff imaginable? Just that morning — a lifetime ago — she'd been in her Wimbledon hostel. Suddenly, with a flash of worry, Holly wondered if her disappearance had been discovered by Coach Graham. But as Pierre continued to smile at her, Holly pushed all thoughts of Wimbledon aside. She didn't want to go back to that other life anytime soon. And as bizarre as France felt to her, Holly realized that she also sort of liked it — snails, brains, and all.

Several heady hours later, after a salad, a cheese tray, glasses of dessert wine, and slices of luscious chocolate cake, the very stuffed and slightly tipsy St. Laurent cousins and Holly bid Aziza and Julien adieu and headed straight to Eurotrash. It was near midnight, and even on a Tuesday, the trendy Right Bank club boasted a mile-long line outside. But because Raphaëlle was buddies with the bouncer — she'd recently designed a handbag for his pop singer girlfriend — he kissed her cheeks and lifted the velvet rope for her and her entourage.

Alexa felt a flutter of admiration for Raphaëlle as she followed her into the dark, pulsing night-club. As a rule, Alexa wasn't easily bowled over by anyone, but she'd always been a little in awe of her eldest cousin, who — with her boho style and vivid personality — was the essence of individuality. Sometimes, around Raphaëlle, Alexa felt very much her mere eighteen years, and she couldn't help but wonder if — in her name-brand clothes and carefully applied makeup — she came off as just another high-maintenance, glossy American girl.

It wasn't a thought Alexa liked to dwell on.

Inside Eurotrash, Raphi flounced off to join her hipster friends, who were smoking at the serpentine chrome bar, leaving Alexa, Pierre, and Holly on the ele-vated platform above the dance floor. Alexa shed her sparkly shrug, soaking everything in: the strobe lights coloring the dance floor, the metallic silver couches strewn with kissing couples, and the floor-to-ceiling tinted windows that allowed clubgoers to stare out at the moonlit Champs-Elysées.

Alexa scanned the crowd and caught sight of a tall, lanky guy with a shaved head, wearing aviator shades and a ripped tee, amid swarms of other potential boy toys. She felt the delectable thrill of possibility. Sure,

Alexa *had* been madly in love with Diego, but, God, she'd forgotten how fun it was to be single. And, since she was conveniently in Paris — land of the *liaison* and home of the hottie — what better place was there to savor her new status?

Alexa was more than ready for her rebound revenge.

Grabbing Holly's elbow, Alexa hollered over the pounding music: "Let's get two Stoli on the rocks and sandwich some cutie, okay?" She hoped poor Pierre wouldn't mind hanging alone. *Or,* she thought with a devilish smile, *he can come and dance with Holly.*

Holly pulled back, unsure. The dance floor was swarming with high-cheekboned, trendily outfitted club kids, and Holly suddenly felt very young, even in her halter. Not to mention that she'd much rather dance to eighties songs — like pre-Kabbalah Madonna — than the house music blaring here. Although she'd had a blast clubbing in South Beach, now that Holly had a boyfriend back home, she wouldn't feel too comfortable grinding with some anonymous European guy.

Shaking her head, Holly apologetically offered her still-sore ankle as an excuse. So Alexa shrugged, blew her and Pierre a kiss, and started off toward the bar, clearly on a boy-finding mission. Holly hoped Alexa knew what she was doing; she didn't think delving into a hookup right after a breakup was necessarily the best plan. But what did she know about boy stuff, really?

"Would you like to sit down?" Pierre asked. His hand on Holly's bare arm made her stomach jump. He gestured to the closest metallic couch, where two lanky boys lounged, sharing a cigarette. Holly agreed, and she and Pierre sat down on the opposite end from the boys. Since the couch wasn't that big, they had to sit sort of close together. Holly tried not to focus on the fact that Pierre's knee was kind of rubbing against hers as he leaned in and asked if she wanted a drink.

"No," Holly replied, too quickly. Then, as Pierre nodded and casually draped his arm over the back of the sofa, she understood that he hadn't been asking in a sketchy, I-want-to-get-you-drunk way — he'd simply noticed Holly's discomfort and was trying to break the ice. Holly glanced at Pierre and gave him a sheepish smile.

Pierre returned her smile, holding her gaze for a beat. "Your eyes," he said softly, still leaning close, his knee still touching hers, "they are a very nice green."

Holly shifted on the sofa, fighting down the beginnings of a deep blush. "Well, I think they're more gray-green," she replied, her tongue feeling clumsy in her mouth. Holly wasn't used to talking about her looks with anyone. When they were kissing, Tyler would sometimes pull back to study her face and whisper that she was pretty, but he'd never wax poetic on the exact shade of her eyes. "I mean, I guess their color depends on the weather," Holly rambled on, fiddling with her silver ring. "Or on my mood, or what I'm wearing, or . . ."

"This — how you say — shirt?" Pierre interjected, gently taking the hem of Holly's halter top and slowly rubbing it between his thumb and forefinger. "*Oui.* This shirt, it turns your eyes green."

"Um, yeah," Holly managed, acutely aware of Pierre's touch. She made a mental note to wear green for the rest of her stay in Paris; fortunately, Holly had added lots of that color to her wardrobe after a lime bikini had brought her very good luck last year.

Pierre removed his hand from her shirt and ran it through his dark curls. But his own beautiful eyes remained on Holly, almost as if — Holly barely dared entertain the thought — he couldn't get enough of looking at her. Holly wondered if it was possible to spontaneously combust from too much blushing in one night. *Must . . . change . . . the . . . subject,* she thought, her mind casting around wildly for something bland and basic to bring up. Something like . . . school.

"Pierre, what are you majoring in at the Sorbonne?" Holly blurted, not even bothering to try for a natural segue. Like any high school senior, Holly got borderline obsessed with anything college-related, so she *was* genuinely interested in Pierre's answer — especially if it took her mind off the fact that their arms were now pressing together. She leaned back against the sofa, willing herself to relax.

"Well, I think our system is a bit different from American universities," Pierre explained, his warm breath tickling her ear, "but I am studying law. It was my father's idea — I do not like it much." He rolled his eyes, and Holly grinned, fully understanding that particular issue.

"Say no more," she replied, feeling her blush start to fade. "My parents want me to go to law school after college, too." She drew her finger across her throat in a kill-me-now motion, and Pierre cracked up. Holly felt a rush of warmth; she'd made him laugh. It was funny how a shared sense of humor could translate regardless of language boundaries.

"Talking about school," Pierre said (Holly wanted to correct him by saying "speaking of," but she held back; his malapropisms were too adorable), "I have no classes tomorrow." Pierre's hand, resting on the back of the couch, very lightly brushed the nape of Holly's neck. Though Holly tried to fight the feeling, tingles raced down her body. "Alexa tells me that this is your first time in Paris," he went on, his voice low. "So perhaps, 'Olly, you would enjoy it if I took you on a tour?"

Holly bit her lip, her heart pounding hard enough to be heard over the music. There were so many reasons for her to say no: She didn't know Pierre that well, she'd promised Alexa they would go shopping tomorrow, and, most important: Tyler, Tyler, and . . . Tyler. Holly felt bad enough as it was, sitting so close to a guy whose slightest touch turned her skin hot, who'd complimented her eyes, and who spoke her name so charmingly. Spending an entire day with him in the world's most romantic city might feel like mere heartbeats away from . . . *cheating*.

But Holly was frustrated with Tyler, who *still* hadn't called. And it wasn't like Pierre was a random sleaze who'd picked her up at Eurotrash; he was Alexa's sweet, smart cousin — and, Holly felt, a new friend. She'd be sorry to miss his take on Paris — which would surely prove more interesting than Alexa's overpriced shopping spree. So, without giving it another guilt-ridden thought, Holly turned to Pierre and smiled, watching as his blue eyes lit up hopefully.

And *that* felt like reason enough to tell him yes.

Stoli on the rocks in one hand, hips slowly swiveling to the music, Alexa was right where she wanted to be — smack in the middle of the throbbing Eurotrash dance floor. She'd just danced to Daft Punk's "One More Time" (the music that was hot in Europe was pretty much always played out in the States) with Aviator Boy, whose name, he'd whispered to her, was Jean-Claude. But before Jean-Claude could start kissing her, Alexa had decided there were tastier options to explore — shaved heads didn't really do it for her — and waved him off. Her first post-Diego hookup *had* to be a memorable one.

A sudden pair of hands on her waist didn't surprise Alexa too much. Even in her plain black dress, she was confident she looked as sultry as any of the international supermodels working it on the dance floor.

And when Alexa turned around, a supermodel was what she saw.

He had lush, white-blond hair that swept sexily over one eye and fell in waves to his square chin. The eye not hidden by the sweep of hair was a deep midnight blue, and fringed with the darkest, longest lashes Alexa had ever seen on a guy. His jaw-dropping body looked familiar, and Alexa whirred through the boy-Rolodex in her mind — *Did he kiss me in Cannes when I was fifteen? Hit on me in an Amsterdam bar two summers ago? Walk the runway at Fashion Week in New York last year?* — until she realized she'd seen him that very afternoon. While Alexa was on her way to meet Holly, he'd pouted at her — shirtless — from a billboard above the Métro station.

But glimpsing Model Boy in the flesh was much, much nicer.

They started dancing, his hands on her waist, her free hand on his shoulder as she held on to her drink. Their bodies moved sinuously together. Alexa threw her head back, her hair rippling down to her waist, and she laughed as Model Boy leaned in to touch his lips to her neck. Diego could take his Princeton girls and *move* to Barcelona for all she cared. She'd done it — she'd snagged the most beautiful guy in all of Eurotrash.

Model Boy took Alexa's head in his hands and tilted her back up so they were eye to eye. "I'm Sven," he whispered, giving her a big-toothed smile. "*Parlez-vous* — uh, *anglais?*" Over the music, Alexa could make out a trace of a Swedish accent.

Alexa's heart leaped; so Sven assumed she was French! Who said male models were dumb? Beaming, Alexa slid her arms around Sven's neck, slipping her free hand beneath the collar of his sheer, fitted black shirt. Alexa reflected that, in the States, no straight boy would be caught dead in what Sven was wearing. But she knew, from the way he was gripping her hips, that Sven couldn't be gay — he was just European. By now, Alexa had learned to spot the difference.

"Alexa," she whispered, standing on her tiptoes so

her lips touched Sven's perfect earlobe. "And I do speak English. But we won't be talking much, will we?"

Taking her cue — *he's practically a genius!* Alexa thought — Sven lowered his face and kissed her, soft and deep. Delighting in the feel of his lips on hers, Alexa moved her hand to the back of Sven's head, intensifying the kiss. A second later, though, some of Sven's hair got into her mouth, so Alexa pulled back, giggling and wiping her lips. *The perils of kissing a long-haired boy.* Normally, when fooling around, *Alexa* liked to be the one with the hair dramatically spilling everywhere. Maybe a guy with a shaved head would actually have been better.

"Watch it," Sven chided her, shaking his luscious locks back into place.

Alexa couldn't tell if he was joking or not, but, more turned off by the second, she watched as Sven reached into the back pocket of his jeans and pulled out a handheld mirror. Frowning into it, he fussed with his hair, making sure each golden strand was back in place. Then Sven ran a discerning finger over one of his arched eyebrows and puckered his lips at the mirror, as if he'd rather be kissing *it* than Alexa.

Oh my God, Alexa realized, her stomach plummeting in disbelief. *He's even more vain than . . . me.*

When Sven was finally finished examining his

stunning self, he tucked the mirror away and pulled Alexa in for another long kiss. But this time, Alexa didn't move her lips in response, so Sven pulled back and flashed her a pinup-worthy grin.

"Oh, *I* get it, Vanessa," he said, tossing his hair as if he were in a shampoo commercial. "You are, ah, afraid you'll get too carried away by kissing me."

"It's Alexa," Alexa replied, through gritted teeth.

"So come back to my place," Sven continued obliviously. "I'm staying at the Ritz-Carlton. I have a photo shoot in the Bois du Boulogne early tomorrow morning, but we can still party all night." Then he fluttered his lashes at her — which, Alexa realized, was *her* signature come-hither move. This was all wrong.

Alexa wasn't sure if it was all the champagne she'd had at dinner, the vodka she was drinking now, or the fact that Sven was Narcissus come to life, but suddenly she felt sick to her stomach. A year ago, Alexa knew she would have *jumped* at the chance to spend the night at the Ritz-Carlton with a Swedish supermodel. But now, the thought of a one-night stand with Sven wasn't sitting right with her at all. *Maybe I'm more mature than I was back then,* Alexa thought, removing her arms from around Sven's neck and rattling the cubes in her glass of Stoli.

Or maybe she just couldn't bring herself to hook up with a boy who was prettier than she was.

Alexa told Sven she had other plans, flipped *her* blonde hair over one shoulder, and sauntered off into the crowd. As she made her way to where Holly and Pierre were sitting, Alexa imagined Holly's reaction to the ridiculous Sven story. Knowing levelheaded Holly, she'd probably tell Alexa that a "revenge" hookup was pointless anyway, and that Alexa should take a time-out from all boys until she'd healed completely from Diego.

And she'd be absolutely correct, Alexa realized with a resigned sigh. Alexa had many times before tried to swear off boys for a spell, but she'd always wound up surrendering to someone seductive; last year, for instance, it had been Diego. This week, though, she'd have to stand strong. She would simply shop and hang out with Holly, not seek out boys, and *not* let herself be tempted. In the middle of Eurotrash, with the strobe lights swirling around her, Alexa made up her mind: There wasn't a single guy in Paris who'd be able to seduce her. After all, if she could turn down an actual male model, then she could turn down anyone.

Right?

CHAPTER EIGHT
X Marks the Spot

"Are you sure you're not mad at me?" Holly asked Alexa as they were getting dressed the next morning. Outside their shuttered windows, the day had dawned sunny but brisk, and white-aproned men from the *pâtisserie* next door were whistling as they washed the cobblestone street with buckets of soapy water.

"Whatever, Hol," Alexa sighed, tugging on her hip-hugging Chip & Peppers. "If you want to go traipsing around the city like some tacky tourist, I certainly can't stop you." She buttoned the jeans over her flat belly and rolled her eyes. She hadn't *believed* it when Holly had told her that she was blowing off their shopping trip to prance around with Pierre. Hadn't Holly busted out of Wimbledon so the two of them could have quality bonding time?

139

Plus, Alexa's head hurt from the toxic champagne-and-vodka combination she'd drunk last night, she was miffed that Sven's hair had looked better than hers at Eurotrash, and deciding to take a breather from boys *always* put her in a grouchy mood.

"I know you think sightseeing is lame," Holly spoke quietly from her bed, lacing her Adidas. It was a point Alexa had been bringing up all morning, despite the fact that Holly had never been to Paris before and was well within her rights to act like a tacky tourist. "But Pierre offered, and —"

"And because you have a huge crush on him, you couldn't say no," Alexa snapped, regretting her words a second later. When she'd come upon them at Eurotrash last night, Holly and Pierre had been cuddled so close on the sofa they'd practically been making out. But it was clear that Holly was also in major denial over their chemistry.

"Hold up." Holly got to her feet, her cheeks hot. "Alexa, I do *not* have a crush on Pierre." Her voice came out trembly when she spoke his name, which killed Holly. She was glad the door was closed; she knew Pierre was making coffee in the kitchen. "I'm with Tyler, remember?" Holly added defensively. "My boyfriend?" *Who you haven't heard from in four days,* a little voice singsonged in her head.

"Are you?" Alexa retorted, turning to face Holly.

"Then why have you not talked about him even *once* since you've been here?" Alexa couldn't shake the nagging suspicion that Holly had some drama going down with Tyler and, for no good reason, was keeping it from her. Holly could be annoyingly secretive sometimes.

Holly averted her eyes, scooping up her tote bag. Here, again, was her chance to spill the Tyler saga to Alexa. But Holly wasn't about to bare her soul now, *especially* after Alexa had flung that ludicrous Pierre accusation at her. Plus, Holly herself was on edge that morning; her parents had awoken her at six A.M. with a chirpy call, wanting to know how the running was going. Holly, who detested lying — and sucked at it — had hurriedly rattled off an unconvincing "Oh-Mom-and-Dad-England's-great-but-I'm-*so*-busy" speech before clicking off. Now, she was plagued by the fear that her parents might discover the truth before she made it back to Wimbledon.

"Pierre's waiting," she told Alexa, straightening the hem of her forest-green sweater. "So . . . I guess we'll meet up with you at some point?" she added softly. As miffed as she was, Holly hated to leave with things so sour between herself and Alexa.

"I suppose," Alexa sighed, slicking her hair back into a long ponytail. She'd call Holly's cell later that afternoon, once she'd cooled off.

Holly nodded and, without looking back, strode

out of the guest room. Alexa heard Holly and Pierre exchanging flirtatious good mornings — *God,* she thought, *would those two just get it over with and hook up already?* — and then the creak and slam of the front door as they headed out.

In a way, it was peaceful to be alone in the apartment; Raphaëlle had long since left for work. As Alexa slid on her burgundy Lia Sophia ring, a crisp breeze, smelling of hyacinths, blew into the room. She shivered in her chocolate-colored tank, realizing she'd be cold going out in just that. But besides her sparkly shrug — which was so wrong for daytime — all her cover-ups had been stolen. She *could* probably pilfer something from Holly's duffel bag, but Alexa was still feeling sore toward her friend and didn't want to be seen on the ritzy avenue Montaigne in one of Holly's fleeces.

Then Alexa remembered that when she'd arrived on her cousins' doorstep in tears Monday night, Raphaëlle had said she could borrow whatever she might need from her closet without even asking. Free handbags, free clothes . . . Alexa realized she'd been a fool to turn down her cousin's generosity.

Besides, Raphi's hippie-retro style was starting to grow on her.

Feeling like a naughty little sister, Alexa sneaked into Raphaëlle's bedroom, which smelled of incense and patchouli and was strewn with wrinkled baby-doll dresses, white patent-leather boots, slouchy metallic clutches, and piles of French magazines. The walls were covered in framed snapshots of Raphi with various hot guys. Alexa knew, from their conversation over dinner last night, that her cousin was juggling about twenty different boys at once — a feat Alexa had always aspired to. As Alexa flung open the doors to Raphi's bursting closet, she was wowed by her cousin's effortless Parisian cool. *If I'd stayed in France, and never moved to New Jersey,* Alexa wondered, reaching for a turquoise-studded belt on the top shelf, *would I have ended up more like Raphi? Would I be less into labels and more into vintage?*

She wasn't sure.

But she *was* sure that she loved the baby-blue sweater with the shiny round buttons that was staring out at her from the messy closet. When Alexa slipped it on, the fabric seemed to soothe her skin, so she admired herself in Raphi's mirror, scrawled her cousin a *Merci!* note, and returned to her room to grab her Chloé bag. Alexa was starting for the door when, at the last minute, she remembered her camera. What with the Diego disaster and Holly's arrival, Alexa hadn't had a free moment for her beloved photography. She figured she could snap some shots of the city today, in between boutique-hopping.

Maybe all that couture would inspire her.

However, after Alexa had shimmied into dozens of Lolita Lempicka slip dresses, strapped on a slew of Louis Vuitton sandals, and even auditioned a spangly Gaultier bustier, she was feeling more drained than inspired. She did buy a yellow silk Lucien Pellat-Finet shift at Colette — how could she resist? — and a pale pink Chanel wallet to replace her stolen one. But as she ambled down the rue de Rivoli with her shiny shopping bags, Alexa felt — for possibly the first time in her eighteen trendsetting years — designered out. She guessed it had to do with her eye-opening experience in Raphaëlle's bedroom; suddenly, Alexa felt that there might be more to fashion than name-dropping. Maybe she could even check out the vintage shops Raphi frequented in Le Marais instead.

Besides, Alexa reasoned as she wandered along the quai du Louvre, her mother was a buyer for Henri Bendel in New York, so Alexa could get her share of designer goodies back home.

The satiny waves of the Seine glinted in the afternoon sun. Forgetting about clothes entirely, Alexa-the-*artiste* reached spellbound into her bag, taking out the professional Nikon camera her dad had given her for Christmas. Aiming the lens at the river, she zoomed in on the glorious bridges that arched, like a graceful row of dancers' arms, across the water.

The nearest bridge was the romantic Pont-Neuf, which stretched to the Ile de la Cité. Alexa had had her first kiss on that bridge, when she was seven, with a green-eyed classmate named Henri. One afternoon, she and Henri had been throwing pebbles into the water when Henri had suddenly leaned in and kissed Alexa clumsily on the lips. She, of course, had kissed him right back. Alexa smiled at the sweet memory as she focused her camera on the Pont-Neuf.

Through her lens, she made out a lone figure leaning against a lamppost in the middle of the bridge: A pale, thin guy in a dark sweater and jeans, smoking a cigarette and brooding, as the wind whipped his auburn hair. It was such the perfect Parisian shot that Alexa decided to get closer; she liked to sneak candid photos of people. It made her feel like the great French photographer Robert Doisneau — one of Alexa's idols.

Alexa walked onto the bridge with her camera in hand, grateful now that she had the day to herself; Holly thought snapping artsy pictures was completely boring. And though Diego had once admired Alexa's passion for photography, his interest in it had dwindled after a year. Alexa's throat tightened as she zoomed in on Cigarette Boy. *No one understands me,* she thought, feeling tragically poetic.

As the camera clicked, the guy — who'd been

gazing out at the river — turned abruptly toward Alexa. She froze when she saw the look on his face — pure, scorching anger. His lips were curled into a snarl, and his hands were balled into fists.

As an aspiring photographer, Alexa knew that some people despised being caught off guard by a camera. But she'd never seen someone get *this* furious. Monsieur Bastard flung his cigarette into the water and, scowling, stormed over to her, muttering French curses under his breath. Instinctively, Alexa hugged her camera to her chest and took a fearful step back, bumping into one of the round stone benches that curved out of the bridge.

"*Casse-toi,*" Cigarette Boy spat and, to Alexa's horror, clamped his hand around her wrist and wrested the camera out of her grasp. She noticed, in the brief moment that their hands touched, that his fingers were stained with paint.

"What do you think you're doing?" she demanded in French, grabbing for her camera, but he fended her off. Was she getting mugged *again*? Her palms were clammy and her heart was hammering; she and Cigarette Boy were the only people on the bridge. Beneath them, a Bateau-Mouche tour boat slid across the glittering water, but Alexa knew no one on board would hear her if she screamed. "I'm going to call the police!" Alexa threatened, her voice cracking, as she looked around helplessly for a pay phone. Why did she keep running into psychotic French guys whenever she was alone?

"Go ahead — they're as *sick* of you stupid paparazzi as the rest of us," Cigarette Boy retorted, in machine-gun-fire French. He was opening the camera and yanking out her precious strips of amber-colored film. "If I end up in the tabloids once more —"

"Oh my God — stop!" Alexa cried in French, swiping at his hand, which now contained the crumpled roll of film. She couldn't believe it. This first-class ass was going to pay — big-time. "First of all, I'm *not* with the paparazzi," she hissed, narrowing her eyes at him. Insulting much? Alexa had always imagined that *she* would one day have her photograph snapped on the red carpet — *never* the other way around. "And you'd better reimburse me for that film," she added. *If you can,* she thought, sizing up his scuffed boots, paint-splattered jeans, and stubbly jawline. Clearly, Cigarette Boy was some broke slacker.

Slowly, his eyes swept over Alexa's face, and his features softened. "So you don't — you *don't* know who I am?" he asked quietly. Then, after a moment, he held the camera for Alexa to take back, but kept the film.

Alexa accepted the camera, confused. Something else Cigarette Boy had said now registered: *If I end up in the tabloids once more.* Alexa felt a chill rake through her. Could this scruffy young guy be . . . *famous?* No way. Alexa read French *Vogue* every month and considered herself very plugged in to Parisian pop culture. If Cigarette Boy was truly *someone,* she'd have recognized him, right?

Alexa studied his face: the cat-shaped, slate-gray eyes that were the same color as the water below the bridge; the tousled reddish-brown hair; the small jagged scar above his upper lip. He did seem achingly familiar, though, unlike Sven, he wasn't model-gorgeous enough to be on a billboard. *But he's definitely sexy,* Alexa thought, before she could stop herself. A rare blush warmed her cheeks.

"Who *are* you?" Alexa finally asked, still in French, her voice barely above a whisper.

Cigarette Boy looked down modestly, kicking a pebble with the toe of his dirty boot, sticking his hands in the front pockets of his jeans. "Xavier Pascal," he murmured in his deep, slightly raspy voice. "You know . . . the painter?"

Alexa shook her head as her blush spread along her neck. She *didn't* know. It was true that in Europe, an up-and-coming young painter could garner as much flashbulb attention as a hot actor, but since Alexa no longer *lived* in Paris, she wasn't aware of any new art-world stars. Alexa felt a pang of humility; so much for fancying herself an expert on all things French. *Xavier Pascal.* She made a mental note of the name and decided to Google him at an Internet café or check his credentials with Raphi that evening.

Xavier glanced back up at her, the corner of his mouth lifting in a half-smile. "You are American, *oui*?" he asked, suddenly switching to heavily accented, but undeniably charming, English.

Alexa gasped, almost dropping her camera. How had he *guessed*? She was confident that her French was more or less as flawless as it had been when she'd lived here. Was it only because she hadn't recognized his name? Talk about arrogant.

"What makes you say *that*?" Alexa demanded in stubborn French, tossing her blonde ponytail over one shoulder.

Xavier leveled her with his cool gray gaze, a smile still tugging at his lips. "Something about you," he said, in a soft, lilting English. He lifted his hand and, as if it contained an invisible paintbrush, waved it around Alexa. "Something about you told me: 'This is an American girl pretending to be a Frenchwoman.'"

Alexa felt her blush deepen and she glanced down, hating that this mysterious stranger had somehow pierced her surface. But, even if Xavier was a super-famous artist, she wasn't about to let him condescend to her like that.

"Go to hell," she snapped, sticking to French, and turned on her heel, but Xavier's warm hand on her arm stopped her.

"Wait a minute," he said, switching back to French. "Your film." When Alexa faced Xavier, he was gesturing to the crumpled roll in his hand, looking apologetic. "Let me fix it?" he offered softly, his tilted cat's eyes sparkling.

"You know that's impossible," Alexa protested. She snatched the film from his grip — noticing the feel of his fingers against hers — and dropped the ruined roll into her Chloé bag, along with her camera.

"You won't even let me try?" Xavier teased, giving Alexa a slow, suggestive smile. "I'm an artist, you know. I'm good with my hands."

I bet you are, Alexa thought, suppressing her own smile. She reminded herself that she was on a strict boy diet, but a tingling started low in her belly. Suddenly faint, she swayed on her cork-soled espadrilles, realizing she hadn't eaten anything that day except for a *pain au chocolat* after leaving the apartment. Backing up, Alexa sank down onto the curved bench behind her and took a deep breath.

"Are you all right?" Xavier asked carelessly. Without waiting for a response, he eased his lithe frame onto the same bench. Lazily, he stretched out his long legs, crossing them at the ankles, and reached into the front pocket of his jeans, pulling out a ragged pack of Gauloises. "I've been rude," he added, as he tapped two cigarettes into his palm. "You know *my* name, but yours remains a mystery." He placed one cigarette in his mouth, his eyes never leaving Alexa's face.

"It's Alexandria — Alexa," she replied, fiddling with the buttons on Raphi's sweater. Last night, telling Sven her name hadn't been a big deal, but with Xavier, it felt almost sensual, as if she'd revealed a sliver of skin to him.

"The pleasure is all mine," Xavier murmured and, instead of extending his hand, held out the other cigarette toward her. Alexa hesitated, but then found herself bending her head down and allowing Xavier to place the cigarette between her lips. That, too, felt incredibly sensual. Xavier lit his cigarette first, then hers, cupping the flame against the wind. Alexa took a quick drag of the Gauloise, tasting the burn. Unlike Portia, she'd never been an accomplished smoker.

As Alexa fought down a cough, she thought she saw Xavier's lips twitch with laughter; he seemed to notice everything. *A true artist,* Alexa thought. And it was in that moment, as Xavier regarded her with his laughing cat's eyes, that Alexa suddenly realized why he seemed familiar to her. She *had* seen Xavier once before — that Saturday afternoon when she and Diego had gone to Montmartre, and she'd made serious eye contact with a scruffy sketcher. Yes, he looked different in a dark raggedy sweater, as opposed to the black T-shirt and disguising hat he'd worn then, but he was without a doubt the same intriguing stranger.

Was it kismet that they'd reconnected today? Alexa's stomach jumped at the thought.

"I'm curious, Alexa," Xavier was musing aloud in French, resting one elbow on the back of the bench and pinching a flake of tobacco off his tongue. "If you didn't know who I was, why were you taking my picture?"

Alexa took another drag, realizing that Xavier, of all people, *would* understand what she'd been doing that afternoon. So, as they sat smoking on the intimate bench on the lamp-lined bridge — with only the occasional car driving past or couple strolling by — Alexa explained her love of photography, and Xavier in turn talked about painting. Feeling reckless, Alexa told Xavier about seeing him in Montmartre, and he, half-smiling, said he did remember a beautiful blonde girl crossing his path. But since he spent a lot of time sketching there — soaking up the gritty vibe and getting back in touch with his struggling-artist roots — it was hard to keep track of the passersby.

"But I won't forget you now," Xavier murmured,

slowly tracing the pad of his thumb along Alexa's cheek. Her breath catching, Alexa turned toward him, wondering if — hoping that — he would kiss her. She knew she was supposed to be resisting all boys, and that she'd only just met Xavier, but Alexa was suddenly dying to feel his mouth on hers. Normally, she might have even made the first move, but somehow, she felt that Xavier had the upper hand here.

There was no kissing *yet*, but their talking on the bridge flowed into their walking across it, to the Ile de la Cité, where the ancient spires of the Notre Dame cathedral rose overhead. Xavier insisted on treating Alexa to lunch to make up for the film (which Alexa no longer gave a damn about). Over steaming bowls of bouillabaisse and icy bottles of beer at a tucked-away *brasserie* — where their waitress kept shooting shy, admiring glances at Xavier — they finished Xavier's pack of Gauloises and covered the basics. Alexa confessed to being American — but Paris-born — and college-bound. Xavier, smirking behind a haze of smoke, told Alexa he was twenty-one, had been a wild child growing up on the French Riviera, and dropped out of high school to paint full time. Fresh off her Mr. Princeton experience, Alexa found the idea of a high school dropout exceedingly hot.

After lunch, she and Xavier strolled languidly through a nearby leafy-green park, the backs of their hands touching. Alexa was wondering how they could extend their dreamlike afternoon when Xavier's cell phone rang. As he removed it from the back pocket of his jeans, Alexa — with a jolt — remembered Holly.

I was supposed to call her! she realized, glancing guiltily down at her watch. It was after five o'clock; by now, Pierre must have met up with some friends, and poor Holly was probably alone in the apartment, weepily waiting for Alexa to show up. Alexa noticed a Métro sign up ahead and figured she should hop on a train to go home. But one glance into Xavier's striking face as he frowned down at the caller ID expelled all thoughts of Holly. Alexa didn't care how bad a friend she was being — she couldn't even *consider* leaving this boy just yet.

Xavier answered with a gruff "*Allô?*" and then muttered a series of brusque *oui*s and *non*s before clicking off.

"Who was that?" Alexa asked, intrigued. *Another artist? A gallery owner?* She had to admit she *was* a little starstruck by Xavier; many people they'd passed today had gawked at him, or pointed and whispered.

"Just bullshit," Xavier replied in English — they'd been switching back and forth all afternoon. Then he stopped walking, let out a sigh, and regarded Alexa seriously. "But I'm afraid I do need to run. Stupid obligations . . ."

Alexa bit her lip, trying not to show her disappointment. So this was it. She'd get on that Métro and go back to Le Marais, the painter on the bridge remaining only a surreal memory. But then, before she knew it, Xavier was moving closer to her, hooking his thumbs through the belt loops of her jeans, and drawing Alexa in. *Finally,* Alexa thought, melting at his nearness. She ran her hands down his sinewy arms, breathing in his scent — a musky mix of cigarettes and paint. The fact that the guy who was pressing her to his chest was the same one who'd viciously yanked the camera from her grip earlier that day gave Alexa a twisted little thrill; she liked knowing Xavier had a bad-boy streak in him even as his lips were caressing her neck.

"I have to see you again," he murmured in French, his breath hot against her ear. "Tomorrow night." It wasn't a question.

"Tomorrow night," Alexa echoed, wondering how she'd be able to live until then.

"Give me a pen," Xavier instructed softly. He didn't even bother to ask if Alexa *had* one, but fortunately she did — though she had to reluctantly pull back from Xavier's embrace to fish the ballpoint out of her Chloé bag. Handing the pen to Xavier, she watched, mesmerized, as he turned her hand over in his — making her shiver at his touch — and wrote into her fair skin, like a tattoo, the bold letter *X*, followed by what

Alexa guessed was his cell phone number. Alexa reflected that there couldn't be a more tantalizing boy's name than Xavier; though it was pronounced "zahv-YAY" — with a *Z* — having the secret *X* in there made it all the, well, se*x*ier.

When Xavier was finished writing, he gave the pen back to Alexa with a teasing grin. Then, ever so slowly, he slid his hands down from Alexa's waist and into the back pockets of her jeans, a move that made Alexa's whole body tingle. "I'm very glad you took my picture today," Xavier told her softly in French. Then, at long last, he slanted his mouth down over hers in a hot, ravenous kiss.

Alexa closed her eyes, wonderfully dizzy, as their tongues met. It was funny that she'd had her first kiss in Paris at seven; now it seemed she was *truly* being kissed for the first time, as if none of her other experiences with boys — not even Diego — counted. Alexa clung tighter to Xavier, relishing the feel of his lean, ropy body against hers.

And his lips — as she'd predicted the first time she'd seen him — tasted of Gauloises and cheap beer.

Later, when Alexa floated into the apartment — her lips swollen and her legs shaky — she was surprised, and disappointed, not to find Holly there; Alexa had been dying to dish about Xavier with her friend. *She's probably still out with Pierre*, Alexa thought, mildly miffed.

But really, too delirious to care.

She was heading down the hall toward the guest room, thinking about the fact that she'd never wash her hand again, when she bumped into Raphaëlle, who'd just emerged from the bathroom. Raphi was wearing plastic hoop earrings, a flowy yellow blouse over low-rise dark pink bell-bottoms, and flat, strappy silver Grecian sandals. Naturally, since it was Raphi, the insane outfit looked smashing.

"Alexa, you scared me!" Raphi gasped in English, shaking out her thick black curls. "But hey, you look great in my top," she added, giving an approving nod toward Alexa's ensemble.

"Thanks," Alexa mumbled, glancing down at herself. She'd forgotten she'd even borrowed the sweater. And now that it smelled like Xavier, she didn't ever want to return it.

"I thought you'd be with Pierre and Holly," Raphi added, studying Alexa curiously.

"I don't know *where* they are," Alexa replied, with a note of bitterness. She still felt wobbly, so she leaned against the wall for support.

"Ooh, they're alone?" Raphi giggled, her dark eyes

dancing. "*Mais c'est* cool! I think my brother has a crush," she added, echoing Alexa's sentiment from that morning.

Typically, Alexa would have been all over Holly-and-Pierre gossip, but now she had other things on her mind.

"*I* have a crush," she whispered, grinning. "On Xavier Pascal."

Raphi snorted, rolling her eyes. "Join the club. You and every other girl in France. Ever since *Le Figaro* did that piece on him last month, when he exhibited at the Centre Pompidou, everyone's been *drooling* —"

"So he *is* famous?" Alexa interrupted. Even though people on the street and in the café had stared at Xavier today, she still hadn't fully believed his celeb status.

Raphaëlle squinted at Alexa, clearly confused. "Of course. Didn't you say — how else do you know him, then?"

"I spent the day with him," Alexa burst out, her cheeks coloring as she flashed the back of her hand to Raphi. "And he gave me his number." She giggled in a very un-Alexa-ish manner.

Raphi's mouth dropped open. "Alexandria St. Laurent, are you lying to me?" She grabbed Alexa's hand and studied it, her almond-shaped eyes widening in shock. "You're — *dating* Xavier Pascal?"

"I guess," Alexa laughed, realizing that her time-out from boys had fallen by the wayside. It seemed she'd actually met the one guy she *couldn't* turn down.

Minutes later, Alexa had described the whole magical encounter, and she and her cousin were curled up in Raphaëlle's bedroom like a couple of teeny-boppers, going through Raphi's stack of magazines and squealing over each new discovery of Xavier. Raphi showed Alexa the article in *Le Figaro* that came complete with a spread of Xavier's paintings — abstract geometric shapes — and a blown-up photo of Xavier himself, in all his smoldering glory.

"I can't believe it's really him," Alexa sighed, falling back on Raphi's bed and clutching the magazine to her chest.

"And look at this," Raphi said, flopping down beside Alexa with a copy of the latest *Pariscope*, which listed all the city's film, music, and arts events for the coming week. She tapped a page on the arts section. "He's having a big fancy gallery opening on the place des Vosges this Friday."

Alexa propped her chin in her hands and stared dazedly down at the information on the opening. Xavier hadn't mentioned the splashy party to her, but maybe he planned to invite her to it when they met up tomorrow — Thursday — night.

With a sigh of longing, Alexa wondered what she and Xavier would do tomorrow — and thought about that kiss in the park again. Anticipation warmed her skin; if Xavier Pascal could reduce Alexa St. Laurent to molten lava with just one kiss, she couldn't *imagine* what several more kisses might lead to.

But she also couldn't wait to find out.

CHAPTER NINE
Between Two Boys

"Tell the truth, 'Olly," Pierre instructed as he handed Holly a hunk of fresh bread topped with Camembert cheese. "You are having fun with me today?"

Holly set her cup of sparkling water down on the park bench, returning Pierre's grin as she accepted his treat. "You can say that," she answered, biting into the crusty-warm bread and buttery-soft cheese. Then she closed her eyes and tilted her face up toward the mild afternoon sun, breathing in the scent of tulips that filled the Tuileries gardens.

Of course, the *real* truth was that Holly Jacobson was in bliss.

That morning, she and Pierre had kicked off their grand tour of Paris in the Latin Quarter. Pierre, looking adorably studious in wire-frame glasses, had had to drop off a paper at the Sorbonne, so afterward, he'd given Holly a tour of the funky, student-centric neighborhood. The place de la Sorbonne — the tree-lined square where cooler-than-thou college kids chilled over coffee and cigarettes — instantly captivated Holly. She pictured herself as a French university student — clad in a black turtleneck, miniskirt, and flats, à la Audrey Hepburn — scurrying down the rue des Ecoles with her books in her arms, shopping for flirty little dresses at Naf-Naf, or meeting Pierre for a study date at a cozy bar on the cute rue Mignon.

Somehow, sporty Tyler Davis did not fit into the bohemian picture.

In a café hung with red-fringed lamps on the rue St-André-des-Arts, Holly and Pierre met some of Pierre's friends — brilliant, bespectacled Christophe; wisecracking, red-haired Sebastien; and friendly, willowy Nathalie — for crêpes. It was Holly's first time trying the paper-thin pancakes, and at Nathalie's urging, she ordered hers smeared with Nutella and sprinkled with powdered sugar. Holly decided it was the most ambrosial snack she'd ever had, and she could have stayed in that café all morning, munching crêpes and answering Pierre's friends' enthusiastic questions about teenage life in America ("What is this thing — *'omecoming?*" Sebastian had demanded, cracking Holly up).

But their next activity was even better: a

Bateau-Mouche ride along the Seine. Their elbows lightly brushing, Holly and Pierre stood side by side on the open sundeck, the wind at their backs, the banks of Paris on either side of them. As they glided past the flying buttresses of Notre Dame, Pierre sweetly explained the layout of the city.

"I know that you dislike snails," he began, flashing her a quick grin (Holly, blushing over her dinnertime blunder, swatted his arm in response). "But Paris, she is *like* a snail," Pierre continued, making a circular shape with his hand. "Everything starts from the first *arrondissement* — neighborhood — and, how you say, spirals out from there." He then described how the Seine split the city into Left and Right banks, and how the bridges connected each side. Holly nodded, fascinated both by Pierre's descriptions and the way his black curls kept falling into his eyes.

When they sailed under the Pont-Neuf —"Paris's oldest bridge," Pierre-the-tour-guide pointed out, putting his hand on Holly's shoulder — Holly, for one crazy instant, could have sworn that she saw Alexa up on that bridge, arguing with some guy. The girl's long golden ponytail certainly looked like it belonged to Alexa, although, Holly reasoned, her friend would probably never wear that baby-blue sweater. As the boat slid onward, Holly felt a pinch of remorse over breaking her plans with Alexa that day.

Holly managed to forget all about Alexa — and her lingering Wimbledon worries — when she and Pierre arrived at their next destination: the Arc de Triomphe. In full-on tourist mode, Holly threw her head back, admiring the soaring, moon-colored arch, and Pierre waited patiently while she snapped photos with her disposable camera.

"'Olly, if you please, I will take one of you?" Pierre offered, motioning for her to hand him the camera.

Whenever she posed for pictures, Holly became supremely self-conscious. Standing on the Champs-Elysées, with the arch behind her, she put her hands behind her back and tried to smile naturally as Pierre aimed the camera at her. Holly fleetingly imagined showing Tyler the photo when she was back in Oakridge, and her boyfriend asking her who had taken it.

Oh, no one. Just some guy I spent a perfect day with.

Slowly, Pierre lowered the camera, suddenly serious as he regarded Holly. "*Comme tu es belle,*" he said quietly.

Holly wasn't sure what it was Pierre had said, but she did know that *belle* meant, well, *beautiful*. Trying to ignore the fluttering in her belly, Holly took the camera back from Pierre and they started down the wide, sweeping Champs-Elysées. They strolled past the avenue's shops and outdoor cafés until they reached the breathtaking place de la Concorde. This time, Holly asked *Pierre* to pose for a photo in front of the tall Egyptian obelisk, figuring she'd hide that picture from Tyler if she had to.

By then, their stomachs were rumbling, so Pierre suggested putting together a picnic. They bought two baguettes, a variety of cheeses, juicy tomatoes, and a bottle of sparkling water from Monoprix and carried everything to the manicured gardens of the Tuileries, where they now lounged on a bench.

"*Alors,* what do you think of Paris so far?" Pierre asked Holly, once they'd established that she was having fun. He shaded his eyes from the sun as he turned to look at her.

Holly brushed her bangs off her forehead, gazing across the park at the huge palace that was the Louvre. "It's not what I expected," she replied thoughtfully. "I mean, the whole stereotype of the French being rude — that's not true. Your friends are so great —"

"*Merci,*" Pierre said graciously, pouring himself more Perrier.

"But then there's the dog poo," Holly added, shooting Pierre a mischievous grin.

"*Quoi?*" Pierre asked, the bottle pausing in midair. He shook his head and laughed.

"You know," Holly giggled, feeling strangely carefree. She leaped off the bench and began pantomiming the frantic side-stepping they had been doing all day.

Holly had quickly realized that *everybody* in this city seemed to have dogs but nobody seemed to clean up after their pets. As a result, one had to walk around Paris with a careful eye toward the ground. Back home, Holly was obsessive about picking up after her yellow Lab, Mia.

"'Olly, you are so funny," Pierre said. Holly tried not to notice the tenderness in his voice — or in the way he was studying her. Then, to her surprise, Pierre put down his plastic cup and also jumped to his feet. He came close to her, and for a crazy split second Holly wondered — *no! yes!* — if he was going to kiss her.

Instead, Pierre poked her in the ribs, his naughty smile once again reminding her of a rakish pirate. Holly shoved him away; she was insanely ticklish, and once she'd been attacked, she couldn't stop laughing. Pierre, clearly picking up on that weakness, jabbed Holly in her side again, so she shrieked, darting away.

"Don't — you dare!" she told him, scurrying across the grass. Leaving their food for the time being, Pierre chased her, but even with a semi-injured ankle, Holly Jacobson was not an easy girl to catch.

Hair flying behind her, she sprinted through the Tuileries, down the long walkway that was flanked by trees, with Pierre on her heels, as an old woman reading a book on a bench shot them a scowl. The pain in her ankle seemed to disappear entirely — had she really been in Wimbledon at all? — as Holly raced past the tinkling fountains and ornate statues and then doubled back toward their picnic bench. Suddenly, she felt Pierre's arms encircle her waist from behind. He tackled her, and they tumbled backward onto the grass, eliciting glares from buttoned-up, well-behaved passersby.

"*Ah, maintenant* I have you," Pierre declared, tickling Holly's ribs as she collapsed with helpless laughter. They were so close, Holly could feel the heat radiating from Pierre's body and smell his spicy-clean scent. Even though she was struggling against him, Holly was also loving the feel of Pierre's fingers running up and down her sides. She wasn't used to tussling with a boy like this — with Tyler, it was all gentle cuddling — and she enjoyed the challenge.

"Stop — stop!" Holly finally gasped, and Pierre did stop, releasing her and rolling onto his back. Holly inadvertently fell forward, landing on his chest, and Pierre's arms went around her, keeping her there.

Oh . . . my . . . God, Holly thought, as she and Pierre grew silent, their faces inches apart. She studied the pure blueness of Pierre's eyes, the fullness of his upper lip, and was unable to beat down the desire building within her. To make matters worse, Pierre slowly moved one hand up her back, and over to her face, where he carefully traced the shape of her lips with one finger.

The ringing of her cell phone from deep inside her Vans tote jerked Holly back to reality. Abruptly, she she pulled away from Pierre, her cheeks flaming.

"I — um, I need to get that," she muttered, lunging like mad for her bag on the bench.

Could it be Tyler? Holly wondered, her stomach tightening with dread. *Did he somehow* know *that I just almost kissed another guy?* Squeezing her eyes shut, she put the phone to her ear without even checking the caller ID.

"Holly Jacobson, why aren't you *back* yet?" Meghan cried, over the blare of car horns on the other end.

Holly sat down shakily on the bench, trying to come to her senses. Hearing her best friend's voice in the middle of the Tuileries, moments after play-wrestling with Pierre — *and* when she'd been expecting Tyler — defined disorienting.

"Oh, Meggie — it's — you," Holly stammered, watching as Pierre got to his feet, brushed off his jeans, and grinned at her. Suddenly, realizing why Meghan might be calling, Holly felt a surge of panic. "Did — did something happen?" she whispered, pressing the phone hard against her ear. "Did Coach

Graham find out?" On cue, she felt a sharp stab in her left ankle, as if her body were reminding her that, yes, Wimbledon had happened all right.

A burst of static on the line left Holly in tortured suspense for a second, and then she heard Meghan's hesitant "No." Holly let out the breath she'd been holding, but Meghan continued, her voice tense. "Not yet, anyway. Jess and I have used every excuse in the book —"

"Including problems at home?" Holly whispered, thinking back to her cheery conversation with her parents that morning.

"Yup," Meghan said grimly. "So now Coach Graham thinks you've got food poisoning from bad shepherd's pie, chronic headaches, and, like, clinical depression or something." Meghan paused for effect, while Holly's stomach twisted. "Obviously she's getting a little suspicious."

"*Merde*," Holly whispered, using her favorite new French curse word, as Pierre sat back down on the bench and cast her an amused glance.

"Huh?" Meghan asked.

"Nothing," Holly replied.

"Anyway," Meghan went on in a rush. "Thank God today's our free day, so Jess and I have been hiding out in London. We're totally paranoid, though — I'm calling you from a phone booth in Leicester Square, and Jess is standing guard outside in case Coach Graham happens to be around somewhere." She sighed. "I don't know *what* we're going to tell her tomorrow, and if you're not here for the final meet on Friday . . ." Meghan trailed off threateningly.

Holly looked at Pierre, who was carefully slicing into one of the ripe tomatoes with a plastic knife, his dark hair tumbling over his forehead. He looked up briefly and smiled at her. The rational part of Holly — the part that usually dominated her every move in life — told her she should go back to the apartment, pack, and catch a Eurostar train to England *today*. But really, how could she leave Paris so soon? She'd only just gotten to know this wondrous city. And how could she leave Alexa now, when they hadn't even spent a full day together?

And, okay, *maybe* — just maybe — she couldn't leave the French boy at her side.

"I need to stick around for at least another day — Alexa's still in terrible shape," Holly fudged. She pictured her friend twirling around in some designer dressing room, and bit her lip.

"I hope she isn't, like, making you sleep out on the street with her," Meghan said bitterly, clearly assuming that evil Alexa had dragged Holly into Paris's dark underbelly. "I can just see her doing that."

"Meggie, Alexa's not stranded anymore," Holly replied, rolling her eyes. "We're staying with her cousin Raphaëlle." Even though she felt Pierre's eyes on her, Holly deliberately didn't mention him to Meghan. She was worried that her voice might crack on his name again, and Meghan would guess that something was up.

Not that anything *was*.

"But I promise I'll be back by Friday," Holly added firmly. "Didn't I say I would before I left? There's no way I would miss our final meet, Meggie."

Holly took a deep breath, trying not to get too nervous. It would be okay. She'd catch a train to England tomorrow evening, arrive in Wimbledon by night, and be there to cheer her team on at the ten A.M. meet on Friday. Coach Graham would be none the wiser.

As long as Meghan and Jess could keep up the charade until then.

After thanking her friend over and over, Holly clicked off and turned to face Pierre, who was regarding her with unabashed curiosity. *He doesn't know I'm an outlaw*, Holly realized with a shiver. Hoping to keep her Wimbledon breakout as quiet as possible, Holly had begged Alexa not to tell her cousins about it. So Pierre and Raphi assumed that Holly had just hopped over from England for the heck of it.

"Everything is fine?" Pierre asked, passing her a slice of tomato and, to Holly's relief, not mentioning their tickle fight. "I did not intend to listen to what you were saying, but I could not help hear that, perhaps, you will leave tomorrow?" There was an unmistakable flash of disappointment in Pierre's eyes, and Holly glanced away from him, biting into the tomato.

"Um, yeah," she mumbled, not wanting to elaborate. "There's just . . . some stuff I need to . . . I can't really . . ."

"*Ça va,*" Pierre interrupted, resting a hand on her shoulder — which, of course, gave Holly heart palpitations. "I understand." Holly glanced back at him, and his smile was too tempting for words. "You are a . . . how you say? A woman of mystery."

I am a woman of mystery, Holly thought, her pulse quickening, as she and Pierre cleaned up the picnic and made their way toward the big glass pyramid in front of the Louvre. She continued to savor this new idea for the rest of the afternoon, while she and Pierre swept through the Louvre in a whirlwind — Holly, unlike Alexa, wasn't much for museums, but a peek at the Mona Lisa and the Venus de Milo made her feel extremely cultured — and then swung by the Eiffel Tower.

Holly snapped shots of the tower from the Champ

de Mars but told Pierre she had no desire to visit the very top, because she was terrified of heights. So after Pierre had bought Holly a miniature Eiffel Tower from a street vendor — he insisted that she needed a cheesy souvenir to commemorate their touristy day — they rode the Métro back to Le Marais. As Holly, drained but content, resisted the urge to drop her head on Pierre's shoulder, she reflected that she'd *always* remember this day — and Pierre — with or without a souvenir.

But their adventure wasn't over just yet. When she and Pierre emerged from the St-Paul station into the softly falling twilight, Pierre asked Holly if she'd be up for a quick dinner at his favorite neighborhood spot. "If you are not tired of me," he added, laughing.

Like a date? Holly thought, gulping. No — it couldn't be. Despite that almost-maybe-kiss in the park, Holly was sure that Pierre only saw her as a friend. Holly generally assumed that most boys did. Which was the opposite of how Alexa operated.

At the thought of Alexa, Holly wondered if her friend had wanted the two of *them* to have dinner. But Alexa hadn't called all day — probably because she was still holding a grudge. *Figures.* Holly pictured Alexa holed up in the apartment, sullenly waiting for Holly to return. Normally, Holly would have been psyched to spend the evening with Alexa, but she knew that tonight, her friend's prickliness would only ruin her sublime mood.

And that made up Holly's mind.

She looked back at Pierre. "No," she told him truthfully, with a bashful smile. "I'm not tired of you at all."

As they chatted easily about the events of the day, Pierre led her down a series of intricately winding streets until they reached one very long, very narrow street that, according to a small, dark blue sign Holly spotted on the corner, was called rue des Rosiers. "The street of the rosebushes," Pierre translated, gently taking her arm and steering her toward the right. "Even though we will not see any here today."

The rue des Rosiers was unlike any street Holly had been on. It was packed tightly with food shops that overflowed with pita, falafel, hummus, and other Middle Eastern treats. A bustling deli was on one corner across from a chic shoe boutique. Many of the stores, Holly noticed, had bright neon signs that were written in Hebrew; she recognized some of the letters from her Hebrew school days, when she was twelve. The people spilling out of the shops and cafés were a mix of trendy Parisian teens and bearded old men in black hats who looked as if they'd stepped out of the past.

"Where *are* we?" Holly asked Pierre, as she accidentally slipped off the thin sidewalk into the street.

"This was the old Jewish quarter," Pierre explained, helpfully guiding Holly back up on the sidewalk as a man on a moped roared past. "It's interesting, *non*? In the Middle Ages, most of the Jewish people in Paris, they lived here. But today, it is all these different shops and restaurants." He gestured down the length of the street, his smile tinged with nostalgia. "My mother, she used to always bring Raphi and me here to buy sweets before Rosh Hashana."

"Wait, you're Jewish?" Holly asked, almost stumbling again. Alexa wasn't Jewish, so Holly hadn't expected any of her extended family to be.

"*Oui.* Well, my father, Alexa's uncle, he is Catholic, like most Frenchmen," Pierre explained, stopping in front of a restaurant whose window was emblazoned with a genie's lamp and the name Ali Baba. "But my mother, who is from Tunisia, she is Jewish, and so — how you say — technically, I am as well."

"I'm Jewish, too," Holly said, as Pierre pushed back the heavy drapes — the restaurant didn't have an actual door — and motioned for her to enter. Holly felt a smile playing on her lips as she thought of her parents, who — despite adoring Tyler — were always saying that Holly should find, as her mother put it, "a nice Jewish boy." *So they'd certainly approve of Pierre,* Holly realized as she ducked through the drapes. Then, her cheeks flaming, she dismissed the notion. Why was she even thinking that way? It wasn't like she and Pierre were going to get married or something.

Right?

Stop it! Holly ordered herself, as she stepped inside the restaurant, which, Pierre explained, was Tunisian as well. Holly admired the dazzlingly exotic space; instead of tables, there were low, candelit banquettes with overstuffed pillows as seats. Lush velvet tapestries hung from the ceiling, and a sultry belly dancer performed on the opposite end of the room from where Holly and Pierre stood.

Well, Holly decided, as she and Pierre settled down on pillows at one of the banquettes, *this sure isn't Applebee's.*

Ever since her traumatizing meal at the St. Laurents', Holly had been a little wary of the food in Paris. But, she reasoned, as a waitress set a bowl of shiny black olives on their table, Pierre hadn't let her down so far today, and the scents streaming from the kitchen were fragrant and rich. Pierre recommended the couscous with meatballs, and when the steaming dish arrived, Holly discovered that the fluffy white couscous — mixed in with chickpeas, carrots, and pumpkin — and the spicy-smoky meatballs were mouthwatering. She and Pierre, famished from their full day, dug in with gusto.

"I wish Tyler liked this kind of food," Holly mused aloud between bites of couscous.

"Who is this Tyler?" Pierre asked casually, reaching for his water glass.

Oh, no. Holly's stomach tightened as a coldness washed over her. Although Tyler had flitted in and out of her thoughts all day, Holly hadn't ever brought him up in conversation. It wasn't like Holly had gone out of her *way* to avoid talking about her boyfriend with Pierre; it just hadn't felt necessary. And since Holly hadn't been gabbing to Alexa about Tyler, either, she was sure her friend hadn't mentioned him to her cousins.

So, for all Pierre St. Laurent knew, Holly Jacobson was absolutely and completely single. And for some bizarre reason Holly wasn't yet able to articulate, she didn't *want* him thinking otherwise.

Grateful for the darkness of the restaurant, Holly glanced down and twisted the napkin in her lap. "Tyler? I — um — well, he's . . . nobody," she whispered, feeling her gut wrench at the lie. "Nobody important." *Only my boyfriend of a full year.* She lifted her burning face to see that Pierre was studying her, his blue eyes bright with intrigue.

"*Ah, oui?*" he murmured, giving her a slow smile. "More secrets from the mysterious woman?"

Holly shook her head, sighing. Between Wimbledon and Tyler and Alexa and Pierre, she was sick of all the secrets she had to keep track of. But then, as Pierre moved his plate aside and slid his hand across the table toward her, Holly wondered if Pierre found her secretiveness . . . kind of hot.

Confirming her suspicions, Pierre took her hand in his, and then slowly, ever so slowly, traced one finger up and down Holly's open palm.

Holly closed her eyes, shivers of pleasure rippling through her body. She didn't want Pierre to stop touching her. When she opened her eyes again, her breath caught as she met his gaze. *Okay*, Holly realized. *Maybe he* does *see me as more than a friend.* And maybe Alexa *had* been right that morning when she'd said that Holly was crushing on Pierre. Holly couldn't ignore it anymore: The attraction between her and Pierre was mutual — palpable.

In the weirdest way, Holly realized that she was only able to flirt with Pierre . . . *because* of Tyler. Holly had never before considered that ironic bonus of having a boyfriend: It gave her a new self-assurance that allowed her to loosen up around guys she might normally feel intimidated by. Why did life have to work that way?

Suddenly, with Pierre holding her hand, but Tyler on her mind, Holly felt as if she were on a crazy seesaw — literally caught between two boys. Caught between the familiar and the new, between Oakridge and Paris, between a guy who'd recently rejected her advances and a guy who — if Holly was totally honest with herself — made her feel like the sexiest girl alive.

Did she have to choose?

As if he intended to make up her mind for her, Pierre leaned across the small table, coming so dangerously close that, had Holly leaned in, their lips would have surely met. "'Olly," he murmured, his frustratingly kissable mouth mere inches from hers. This felt ten times more intimate than that moment in the Tuileries. "Perhaps you have not noticed this, but I think that you are . . . *merveilleuse.*"

"You do?" Holly whispered back, her eyes widening. "I mean, I am?" *Merveilleuse.* If some guy had called Holly "marvelous" in English, she'd want to giggle. But, in French, and in Pierre's low, passionate voice, the word sent the blood straight to Holly's face. "Um, you're not so bad yourself," she began haltingly, already mortified, but then was cut off by a faint ringing sound.

At first, Holly assumed the noise was only in her spinning head. In the next second, she realized that it was coming from her Vans tote under the table. It was her cell phone.

"Pierre — sorry," she stammered, reluctantly pulling her hand out from under his and reaching down for her bag. "Give me one second?"

Every other time Holly's phone had rung on this trip, she'd immediately thought it was Tyler. But now, Holly was so overcome by the scents of foreign spices and so absorbed in her exchange with Pierre that she didn't even stop to wonder who might be calling — she just wanted the person on the other end to go away.

I'll check who it is, and then turn off the phone, she decided.

Holly lifted her T-Mobile out of her bag and glanced down at the caller ID.

As her heart froze, she wondered if, in some crazy way, speaking his name out loud had summoned him from across the ocean.

Because this time, it *was* Tyler.

CHAPTER TEN
Truth and Consequences

"And then what happened?" Alexa asked Holly eagerly, examining an orange corduroy handbag before placing it back on the shelf. "He leaned over the couscous and . . . *what*?"

"You know," Holly stalled, fiddling with an actually-pretty-cute mint-green clutch. She swallowed the lump in her throat and said no more.

It was Thursday afternoon; after sleeping in and eating a leisurely lunch at their favorite corner café on the place des Vosges, Alexa and Holly were browsing in Raphi's tiny-but-trendy boutique, Frou-Frou. Because Alexa had been rambling on nonstop about her dreamy day with the painter, Holly had only just described *her* day with Pierre — except she was trying to downplay the dreaminess. Plus, Holly had now arrived at Tyler's phone call, and she really didn't want to get into that. In part because Holly *still* hadn't fessed up to Alexa about Tyler.

But mostly because she didn't want to start crying in the middle of Frou-Frou.

Last night, in Ali Baba, Holly had stared in horror at Tyler's name as it flashed on her cell screen until, panicked and conflicted, she'd switched the phone off without answering — as she'd planned to do, anyway. But by then, the charged moment between her and Pierre had passed, and though Pierre tried to engage her in conversation, Holly had been distracted and jittery, obsessively wondering if Tyler had left a voice mail. Soon, Pierre gave up on his attempts, so they finished the meal and walked back to the apartment in awkward silence. After they'd bid each other a terse good night outside the guest room, Holly turned her cell phone back on — only to see that there were *no* new messages.

Which meant that she'd passed up her big chance to finally talk to Tyler — and maybe salvage what was left of their relationship.

But do I even want to? Holly agonized, clutching the purse and avoiding Alexa's gaze. Even though Tyler's missed call nagged at her like crazy, the thought of Pierre still made Holly jelly-kneed. By the time she'd gotten up that morning, he had already left for his classes at the Sorbonne, so there hadn't been a chance to resolve their awkwardness from the night before. And since Holly had to catch an eight o'clock train out of Gare du Nord that very night, she wondered if she might have to leave Paris without ever saying good-bye to Pierre at all. At this thought, Holly let out a long, sorrowful sigh.

"No, I *don't* know, but let me guess," Alexa spoke up, bringing Holly back to the present and the bright, pink-and-black boutique. "Pierre kissed you, and you liked it, and now you're all freaked because of Tyler and —"

"He didn't *kiss* me," Holly hissed, warmth flooding her cheeks. She glanced around the crowded store to see if anyone had overheard. She wanted to kill Alexa — first for hitting so close to the mark, and second for filling Holly's head with vivid images of actually kissing Pierre: his full lips against hers, her hands buried in his thick curls — so different from Tyler's silken waves — their breaths meeting. . . . *What would it be like to French-kiss a French boy?* Holly wondered, unable to suppress the naughty thought. She was sure her face was even darker than the slouchy burgundy tote Alexa was now turning in her hands.

Alexa shot Holly a knowing look and opened

her mouth — to say something about Tyler, Holly guessed — but then, to Holly's great relief, Raphaëlle came hurrying over from the back of the store, curls flying and dark eyes shining. Raphi had greeted Alexa and Holly briefly when they'd first come into the shop, but then she'd had to tend to some customers.

"My girls!" Raphi exclaimed in English, looping one arm around Alexa's waist and the other around Holly's. "A million apologies for abandoning you. Did you find anything you like?"

"Okay, fabulous much?" Alexa cooed, fingering the fabric of Raphi's empire-waist blue dress, which her cousin wore over a long-sleeved black shirt, striped tights, and combat boots. Alexa felt plain by comparison in her white wrap top and red peasant skirt (yes, the unthinkable had occurred — Alexa St. Laurent was repeating outfits).

"Raphi, I *need* you," Alexa added, suddenly remembering what she'd wanted to ask her cousin ever since yesterday's not-so-successful shopping venture. "*S'il te plaît,* find me a purse I can take on my date with Xavier Pascal — *and* tell me where I can get some fun vintage-y stuff?" She widened her blue eyes at her cousin, whose own eyes had grown enormous.

"So you're definitely seeing him tonight?" Raphi asked in a stage whisper, giving Alexa's waist a fast squeeze and releasing Holly — who, Alexa noticed, was now totally spacing out. "Oh, *c'est* cool, Alexa!"

"*C'est* very cool," Alexa affirmed breathlessly, brimming with excitement — and nerves. Every time Alexa thought about her impending night with Xavier, her belly performed a series of backflips. No wonder she'd only been able to take two bites of her *salade niçoise* at lunch. Alexa had never been so anxious about seeing a guy before — though, to give herself some credit, she wasn't exactly used to dating a bona fide celebrity.

Over lunch with Holly, Alexa had also been uncharacteristically nervous about calling Xavier. Whenever she'd been single back in Oakridge, Alexa had phoned, IM'ed, and e-mailed boys she was interested in without hesitation. But this time, sitting at the outdoor café, she'd had to embarrassingly hold Holly's *hand* while punching the numbers into her friend's cell (in the past, Alexa had always done the hand-holding for Holly) *and* had lost all powers of speech as soon as she heard Xavier's low, throaty voice in her ear. Thankfully, she hadn't had to say much; Xavier took charge right away.

"French-American girl," he'd murmured teasingly in French. "I knew I'd hear from you. I'll pick you up with my Vespa around seven tonight, and we'll see where the evening takes us, *non*?"

Oui, oui.

"Let me see what I have for you in my storeroom downstairs," Raphi was saying. She winked at Alexa and headed off again. "And for you, too, Holly," she added over her shoulder, smiling mischievously. "In case you also have a date tonight."

Holly gulped, wondering if Raphi might be hinting at something with Pierre. Could it be? Holly brushed the idea — and her wild surge of hope — aside, and shot Raphi a weak smile. "No date for me," she replied. "Not unless it's with the conductor of the Eurostar train."

Chuckling, Raphi hurried away, and then Holly felt herself attacked from the side by Alexa, who flung her arms around Holly and practically knocked her over into a display of fringed leather satchels. Alexa may have looked delicate, but her hugs often had the force of gale winds.

"I keep blocking out the fact that you're *leaving* tonight!" Alexa cried, clinging to her friend. "What am I going to do without you?" She was missing Holly already.

"Uh, I think you'll have enough to keep you busy, Vespa Girl." Holly giggled while a woman in an expensive-looking houndstooth trench coat frowned at their loudness from across the store. "You so don't need me," Holly added, returning Alexa's hug.

Actually, Holly wasn't sure resilient Alexa had really needed her in the first place, but Holly had had too much fun in Paris to really mind.

"Don't go yet, Hol," Alexa declared, pulling back and regarding Holly seriously. "My flight back isn't until Sunday, and we haven't even gone out dancing at Les Bains *or* Favela Chic, and — oh, my God — don't you want to see Versailles?" Needless to say, *Alexa* didn't want to see Versailles for the umpteenth time, but she figured that classic tourist option might pique Holly's interest.

Holly felt a pang of sadness, wishing there was some way she could prolong her stay. "Alexa, you know I have to be at that meet tomorrow," she explained, setting down the green clutch on the shelf. "But,"she added, nudging Alexa in the side. "Promise to call me first thing in the morning to fill me in on your scandalous date?"

Holly had to admit that the Xavier situation intrigued her — and not only because it gave her a mental break from her *own* boy dilemmas. She'd been curious ever since last night, when she'd come into the guest room, cell phone in shaky hand, only to have Alexa jump on her, squealing incoherently about a camera, a kiss, and a phone number. Holly had realized, as Alexa finally sat down and spilled the yummy details, that her friend *hadn't* spent her afternoon brooding after all. And when Alexa showed Holly the photos of Xavier in the stack of magazines she was keeping next to her bed (but probably would have preferred to put under her pillow), Holly hoped she'd get to meet the famous artist.

Standing in Frou-Frou and studying Alexa's radiant face, Holly felt a tickle of concern over how quickly and recklessly Alexa was falling for this new guy. Though the passionate painter did sound just right for Alexa, Holly wondered, as she had before, if her friend wasn't plunging into something too soon post-Diego. But Holly, not wanting to puncture her friend's euphoria, decided against mentioning that issue.

"I only wish I knew what we were *doing,*" Alexa sighed, sinking down onto one of the many pink beanbag chairs scattered throughout the store. The whole surprise element of their date *was* sexy, but the constant guesswork was stressing Alexa out much more than she was accustomed to. "Hol, why can't you be psychic and tell me what's going to happen?" she pleaded, smiling up hopefully at her friend.

"Hmm," Holly said, feeling playful now that she wasn't dwelling on the Pierre–Tyler conundrum. "I predict . . . that by the end of the night Xavier will be asking you something." Holly grinned and, despite the fact that she was in the middle of a chic boutique, wiggled her hips and softly sang, *"Voulez-vous coucher avec moi ce soir?"* in an uncannily good imitation of that cheesy "Lady Marmalade" song — which had, incidentally, taught Holly her only complete French phrase. Then she blushed and ducked her head, hoping none of the chichi customers had witnessed her impromptu performance.

From her perch on the beanbag chair, Alexa burst out laughing. She loved it whenever her normally buttoned-up friend got her silliness on, which seemed to be happening more often lately. If only Holly, the poster girl for self-consciousness, knew how charming and funny she could be when she loosened up a little. Then, as the words to the song sank in, Alexa felt her cheeks color. She imagined Xavier *actually* asking her to sleep over that night, and a bolt of anticipation shot through her.

Before Alexa could swoon, however, Raphi returned bearing a purple satin clutch with a shimmery silver clasp, and a paisley bag that were both clearly meant for Alexa. She also held the mint-green bag Holly had been admiring earlier. Urging the girls to put their euros away, Raphi sent them off, along with instructions on where to find the best vintage shopping spots.

By the time a happily exhausted Alexa and Holly made it back to the apartment around six, they were laden with bursting shopping bags and had to scramble to take care of their respective duties — showering for Alexa and packing for Holly.

An hour later, a towel-clad Alexa was blow-drying her golden hair in front of the guest-room mirror, trying not to feel too antsy, while Holly was stuffing two new purchases — a green safari-print wrap dress and flat-heeled suede beige boots — into her bulging duffel. Holly had just succeeded in zippering the duffel shut when the doorbell buzzed.

"Shit, that's him!" Alexa gasped, her stomach jumping as the blow-dryer slipped out of her grasp. "I'm not even close to ready! Hol, can you —"

"No problem," Holly said, getting to her feet and hurrying out of the room, her own excitement mounting. She ran through the empty apartment — neither Raphi nor Pierre was home yet — and unbolted the door.

"*Bon soir*," the extremely attractive guy leaning in the doorjamb murmured. He was wearing a battered leather jacket over a tight black T-shirt and shredded jeans. He removed his wraparound sunglasses and then slowly ran his gray eyes up and down Holly's body. "You are not Alexa," he pronounced in English, his stubble-darkened face breaking into a grin.

"Um, yeah, I'm not," Holly replied, instinctively

crossing her arms over her chest as her cheeks reddened. She hated how she always shrank into herself whenever guys sized her up — though, considering Xavier's what-do-you-look-like-naked? stare, her shyness felt almost justified. Holly couldn't believe that this was the same Xavier that Alexa had raved about. And though the artist resembled his photographs in the magazine, Holly noticed that in real life, he gave off a vibe that was less *celeb* and more, well, *sketch.*

"You are lovely in a different way," Xavier said, his eyes finally moving up from Holly's chest to her face. Running a paint-stained hand through his unkempt auburn hair, he stepped into the apartment, even though Holly had made no move to invite him in.

"Thanks," Holly muttered, taking a big step back. Normally, a hot guy like Xavier calling her lovely would have given Holly a minor coronary attack, but now she felt kind of . . . annoyed. Wasn't he supposed to be all smitten with *Alexa*?

Xavier gave a small laugh, reaching into the front pocket of his jeans and pulling out a pack of cigarettes. "And you are more innocent," he observed accurately, placing a cigarette between his lips. "So perhaps it *isn't* true, then, what they say about American girls?" He grinned at Holly again.

"*What* do they say about American girls?" Holly

asked defensively, now putting her hands on her hips. Her timidity was starting to give way to full-on pissiness.

Xavier struck a match against the side of his ratty matchbook, raising one eyebrow. "You know. That you are all willing to . . ."

"Xavier."

Holly turned at the sound of Alexa's voice to see her friend was strutting down the hall as if it were her personal runway. In a matter of minutes, Alexa had managed to change into an off-the-shoulder, plum-colored top with long bell sleeves, a tiny white skirt with a jagged hem, and lace-up, knee-high brown boots. She'd even piled her hair on top of her head in the faux-messy style worn by many chic French girls. Had Holly not been so thrown off-kilter by Xavier, she would have complimented her friend on successfully pulling off the boho-chic look she'd been coveting as of late.

Alexa's heart fluttered as she saw Xavier see her. He removed the lit cigarette from his mouth, his lips curving up in that familiar half-smile she was already half in love with. Then he gave her a slow, appreciative nod. Abandoning her cool, Alexa rushed over to him and draped her arms around his neck; since her boots had sky-high heels, she and Xavier were now almost the same height. Xavier slid his hands down her back and then leaned in close, kissing the soft skin right below her earlobe, which made Alexa's head swim.

"Let's get out of here," she whispered in French, her lips tickling his. Alexa was in such a fog that, as Xavier took her hand to lead her out the open door, she barely heard Holly speak her name.

"Hol, I'm sorry!" she exclaimed, whirling around to see her friend behind her, hands on hips and mouth set in a firm line. Letting go of Xavier's hand, Alexa asked if he wouldn't mind waiting while she and Holly had their good-bye moment. Xavier agreed to hang out downstairs, and, shooting Holly a fast wink, turned and left.

"So I guess I couldn't convince you to stay," Alexa sighed, wrapping Holly in a bear hug. Though she *was* bummed about Holly's departure, a tiny part of Alexa was also eager to hurry up this fond farewell so she could join Xavier outside.

"Alexa — listen," Holly said, extracting herself from Alexa's embrace. "I need to tell you something." She took a deep breath, feeling the butterflies start in her stomach; Alexa was *not* going to react well to this one. But Holly knew that she had to speak up that instant, before she left Paris. "About Xavier."

"Isn't he *amazing*?" Alexa exclaimed, her face lighting up. She glanced longingly over her shoulder. "I should really get downstairs —"

"I don't like him," Holly cut in.

Alexa turned back to her friend, shocked. Holly rarely made such firm declarative statements — and, like the Pollyanna she was, always gave people the benefit of the doubt. Alexa knew, for example, that Holly wasn't wild about Portia and Maeve, but Holly had never said anything blatantly negative about them. Why would she randomly take issue with *Xavier?*

"What are you *talking* about?" Alexa demanded, putting her hands on her hips in an unintentional imitation of Holly's pose. Facing each other, the girls squared off, the tension already building between them.

"I don't like him," Holly repeated firmly, trying not to crack under Alexa's hard gaze. "I felt like he was being — um — really forward with me, and he seemed, I don't know, almost sleazy. . . ." Holly bit her lip, not sure if she should continue. She felt terrible telling Alexa that Xavier had been semi-hitting on her, but Holly didn't want Alexa to walk out that door without knowing the whole truth. But to her surprise, Alexa looked not upset, but amused.

Alexa laughed, rolling her eyes. Now she got it. *Of course* sheltered little Holly Jacobson would be turned off by suave, worldly Xavier Pascal. She'd probably been appalled by his stubble. "Hello, he's *French,*"

Alexa explained, her impatience mounting. "That's how guys *are* here —"

"Not Pierre," Holly interrupted, blushing. She felt herself start to tremble.

"Oh, please," Alexa snapped. "Grow up, Holly. Pierre is *not* as innocent as he seems." *Or maybe you've failed to notice that he'd like to* voulez-vous *you himself,* she thought venomously.

"Well, neither am I," Holly shot back, feeling a burst of fury as Alexa continued to smirk. Holly thought back to Xavier's earlier assessment of her, and realized she was fed up with being regarded as a five-year-old. And no matter how much she despised confrontations, Holly couldn't *stand* to let Alexa St. Laurent condescend to her for the zillionth time in their friendship.

"I know you think I'm naïve, Alexa, but I'm not stupid," Holly went on, determined to get her point across. "There's just something . . . something about Xavier I don't *trust.*" Holly couldn't pinpoint where this distrust came from, but she'd felt it in her gut, like a stomachache, from the instant she'd seen Xavier on the doorstep. And even though bullheaded Alexa was being infuriating, Holly still wanted more than anything to look out for her oldest friend.

Studying Holly's earnest expression, Alexa felt

the smallest tremor of doubt; maybe she'd been so swept off her espadrilles by Xavier that she hadn't stopped to wonder if he might be playing her. Then Alexa brushed the suspicion away. She knew how to read guys — she was a freaking *expert* on them — and if that kiss from yesterday was any indication, then Xavier was as into her as she was into him. And even if Xavier *could* be sort of sketchy, Alexa realized with a wry smile, that was exactly what made him so irresistible. Alexa was *done* with playing it safe. Who wanted some squeaky-clean Mama's boy like . . . well, like Tyler Davis?

"Thanks for the heads-up, Hol," Alexa said coldly. "But that's why *I'm* with Xavier, and you're with *your* boyfriend — *if* you can call him that," Alexa added. "I mean, have you guys even had sex yet?"Alexa saw Holly's face flush at these words. She knew how intensely private Holly was about that stuff, and felt mildly guilty that she'd gone there.

But she was kind of curious.

Does she know? Holly wondered, her stomach clenching as she stared back at Alexa. *Does she know that Tyler doesn't want me the way he wanted her?* Holly felt the warm, salty threat of tears, and she swallowed hard. "Can we leave Tyler out of this?" she whispered, her bottom lip quivering.

Alexa's knee-jerk reaction was to comfort a clearly

shaken-up Holly — she hadn't meant for this to erupt into a real fight — until she realized something glaringly obvious. How had she not seen it before?

"But, in the end, this is *all* about Tyler, isn't it?" Alexa asked softly, flicking her eyes over her friend's confused face. "It's about Tyler, and Diego, and every other boy that's ever come between us."

"You're not making sense, Alexa," Holly sniffled, dabbing at her eyes. What did she care about Diego anymore?

"Yes, I am," Alexa replied steadily. "You're jealous of me, Holly Jacobson. You always have been. And this time, you're jealous of what I have with Xavier — and *that's* why you're flipping out about him." Satisfied with her logical conclusion, Alexa folded her arms across her chest, waiting for Holly to admit that Alexa was right, that she was terribly sorry, and that Alexa should have an amazing time on her date.

"Okay," Holly burst out, catching Alexa off guard with the force of her response. She no longer looked like she wanted to cry, but like she wanted to kick something — hard. "I admit it — I *was* crazy-jealous of you and Diego last year. And maybe I am currently jealous of what you had with Tyler — whom, by the way, I *tried* to go all the way with, but he turned me down —" She paused for a breath while Alexa felt her jaw drop. "*But,*" Holly continued, jerking her thumb toward the shuttered living room windows, which looked out onto the street below, "you can *elope* with Xavier for all I care. I wouldn't go near him if you paid me a billion euros."

On cue, both girls heard the revving of a moped's engine from the street. Alexa hesitated; she was *dying* to ask Holly to elaborate on her insane Tyler comment, but Xavier was waiting downstairs, and Alexa was too angry right then to have a heart-to-heart with her similarly seething friend.

"I know this may come as a shock," Alexa said coolly, turning to leave. "But I never asked for — and I certainly don't need — your approval, Holly. On *anything.*"

"Then maybe you shouldn't have dragged me here from England!" Holly retorted, taking a step closer to Alexa. Holly knew, deep down, that she'd come to Paris pretty much on her own terms, but suddenly, she felt like laying the blame on Alexa. "Do you even care that I could get kicked off the track team or, I don't know, *expelled,* if they find out what I did?" *Expelled.* As she spoke, Holly's breath caught in fear; how had she not realized the full consequences of her actions before? "I didn't even really *have* to come," she went on shakily. "You just wanted someone here to stroke your ego!" Then Holly paused and put a hand to her mouth, shocked by her own words. She hadn't intended to be so cruel — *or* to admit that truth about Tyler earlier. Something about arguing with Alexa always unleashed Holly's hidden temper.

Alexa rested her hand on the doorknob, feeling her chest tighten with hurt. Was Holly implying that she was a *user*? That was absurd; Holly had been more than ready to leave England herself. And Alexa didn't want to lose another second of her romantic night with Xavier on this immature quarrel. "Then you shouldn't have come," Alexa said simply, turning to go. If her hair hadn't been pinned up, she would have tossed it, for dramatic effect. Instead, she added, over her shoulder, "So now why don't you go back to your safe little world, and have a blast at your fabulous . . . *track meet.*"

With those withering last words, Alexa cast a glance back at Holly's expression — a mix of pain, astonishment, and anger that Alexa knew would bother her all night — and slammed out of the apartment.

CHAPTER ELEVEN
Voulez-Vous?

Trying to regain her composure, Alexa maneuvered carefully down the winding staircase in her high-heeled boots. Her face felt hot and splotchy, so with trembling fingers, she reached into her purple satin clutch and removed her Nars compact. Checking her reflection, Alexa stepped out onto the street — and instantly collided with Pierre, who was drifting toward the entrance. Her cousin's bright blue eyes were hopeful, and he seemed as distracted as Alexa herself was feeling. The two cousins, each clearly in their own worlds, brushed by each other with barely a "Ça va."

The cool evening air felt like balm against Alexa's skin. She sighed, tilting her head back to gaze at the pale mauve sweep of sky, where a few bold, sparkling stars were making their early debut. Then she looked across the street to see Xavier sitting on his sleek, dark blue Vespa, flexing the handlebars and grinning at her in the most inviting way imaginable. Her heels clattering against the cobblestones, Alexa hurried over to him, swung one long leg over the moped, and eased herself onto the small seat. It was her first time on a moped, and she felt a thrill race through her, dispelling any leftover negativity.

"Do you have a helmet for me?" Alexa whispered in Xavier's ear as she wrapped her arms tight around his body, her bare knees squeezing against his sides. Xavier himself wasn't wearing a helmet; his thick auburn hair blew into his eyes as he glanced back at her.

"What would be the fun in that?" Xavier responded, his voice low but his eyes dancing.

Oh, boy. Alexa inhaled sharply, and then returned Xavier's mischievous smile. "You're so bad," she told him softly. Without meaning to, she heard Holly's voice in her head — *there's something I don't trust* — but then flung the thought away.

Xavier leaned in until his forehead touched Alexa's. *"Merci,"* he whispered. Then he faced forward to rev the engine, and the Vespa shot away from the corner, careening down the street.

The wind lashed at Alexa's face, and she hugged her arms as tight as she could around Xavier. *I'm going to die,* Alexa thought as Xavier zipped at breakneck speed around the next corner. *I'm going to die with Holly mad at me and —* A Citroën sped past them, and Xavier narrowly missed swerving into the small car. Alexa screamed, burying her face in his worn leather jacket, but Xavier only laughed, yelling into the wind that she should loosen up and have a good time.

And as they zoomed through the city, with the sky darkening above them and the Eiffel Tower glimmering overhead, Alexa let herself surrender to both the wind that was savaging her hair and the wild sensation of flying forward at a million miles a minute. By the time she and Xavier reached rue Oberkampf, with its brightly lit bar signs and hopping ethnic restaurants, Alexa was wide-eyed and breathless, and her spirits were as high as they'd ever been on a night out in Paris.

After trying in vain to pat her upswept hairdo back into place, Alexa swung her legs off the moped, took Xavier's hand, and let him lead her into a place called Café Mercerie. They stopped at the grungy bar to get two bottles of dark amber beer — from a sullen bartender with an eyebrow ring who asked for Xavier's autograph — and proceeded into a tiny, dimly lit back room lined with long sofas, where a DJ was spinning French hip-hop. There they were greeted by a cluster of artsy guys and girls — all wearing black-framed glasses, vintage band T-shirts, cuffed jeans, and tortured expressions — who, Xavier explained to Alexa, were his closest friends. Alexa felt a dash of disappointment; he hadn't said anything about meeting up with friends, so Alexa, naturally, had assumed they'd be spending some serious time alone.

But, she reminded herself, *the night is still deliciously young.*

As Xavier went over to dole out cheek-kisses, his friends gazed critically up at Alexa through a veil of cigarette smoke — most of them not bothering to hide their smirks. Alexa began fiddling with her hair again, hoping it didn't look *too* awful. Suddenly, even though she'd never had the experience, Alexa felt like a shy girl standing in front of the popular table at lunchtime. Holly popped into her head, but then Alexa dismissed all thoughts of her friend entirely.

When Xavier returned to her side, hooked an arm around her waist and, in his low, laughing voice, introduced Alexa to the group as *"ma copine,"* Alexa felt her usual confidence bloom back up, and she grinned. Even if he'd been joking, Xavier Pascal had still called her his girlfriend — a title Alexa hadn't even dared hope for. Best of all, none of his hipster buddies seemed to guess that Alexa was American — though one of them *did* comment that she resembled Kate

Bosworth (Alexa felt slightly offended; the look she'd been going for was *much* more Sienna Miller).

While his friends resumed their drinking and chatting, Alexa and Xavier nestled close together on one corner of a sofa, holding hands and sipping their beers. Next to them was a beanpole-skinny guy with a chipped front tooth named Etienne who, Xavier whispered to Alexa, was well-known across France for dipping himself in paint and then rolling across blank canvases. Alexa nodded, her pulse quickening at the realization that she was in the *heart* of Paris's sizzling art scene. *This is where I belong,* she thought contentedly, resting her head in the crook of Xavier's musky neck and feeling utterly at peace in this smoky, seedy bar. Alexa knew then, with utmost certainty, that she couldn't fly back to New Jersey on Sunday. Leaving Xavier — and his fascinating world — seemed unfathomable.

As if reading her mind, Xavier glanced down at her, his face breaking into a smile of such tenderness that Alexa wondered how she — or Holly — could have ever second-guessed him.

"My little angel," Xavier murmured in French, and Alexa realized it was the first time she'd ever been called that; after all, apart from her looks, Alexa was anything but angelic. But she relished hearing Xavier speak the words. Then he bent his head and gave her a soft, tantalizing kiss on the lips. Alexa let out a sigh of pleasure, savoring the feel of Xavier's hand as it slid up her knee and along her thigh. Alexa wasn't shy about PDA to begin with, and she adored that Xavier was caressing her in front of all his friends; it made their relationship somehow real — official.

Her head still on Xavier's shoulder, Alexa closed her eyes, feeling light and floaty as the alcohol — and his touch — went to her head all at once. To her delight, Xavier kept his hand on her leg as he began talking to Etienne about some museum or another. The boys' art world banter drifted over Alexa, meaningless, until she heard Etienne ask Xavier about his gallery opening on Friday night. Snapping to attention, Alexa lifted her head off Xavier's shoulder and sat up straighter, assuming now would be when he'd invite her to his big bash.

But before Xavier could do any such thing, a girl with a scarlet-red bob sitting on Etienne's other side announced to the group at large that Café Mercerie was "over" and they needed to move on to Le Scherkhan, another spot on rue Oberkampf. Alexa scowled at the scarlet-haired girl; not only had she unintentionally broken up Alexa's electric moment with Xavier, but she'd usurped what was usually *Alexa's* role — the one who decided when it was time to check out the next happening bar or club.

Before Alexa could protest, everyone — Xavier

included — was polishing off their drinks and standing up. Reminding herself that she *had* always wanted to go on a Parisian bar crawl, Alexa followed suit, and soon the whole pack was heading out of Café Mercerie, with Alexa and Xavier bringing up the rear. The minute she and Xavier stepped out onto the street, two middle-aged men wielding chunky cameras sprang into their path. Certain they were bandits, Alexa shrieked and clung to Xavier's arm. But instead of grabbing her bag, the men began snapping pictures and shouting "Xavier! Monsieur Pascal! *Un photo pour* Le Soleil!"

As Alexa blinked against the pop and glare of the cameras, she finally grasped who the two men were. *Paparazzi!* Real, actual paparazzi, from *Le Soleil,* the French gossip rag masquerading as a newspaper, which Alexa's uncle Julien often made fun of. So Xavier had been right; the tabloids *were* always on his tail. But even as Alexa sensed Xavier tensing up beside her, she couldn't help feeling a rush of raw excitement. So *this* was what it was like to be truly A-list — to have your privacy invaded, to be blinded by camera flashes, to see grown men clamoring like little kids for one precious shot of *you.*

It was fantastic.

And in the split second before Xavier lashed out in fury at the photo snappers, Alexa tossed them her most dazzling smile and posed, one hand on her hip, the other on Xavier's arm. As the cameras clicked away, Alexa felt that this was a moment she'd been traveling toward all her life — she'd always secretly believed that she was destined for *some* sort of fame.

Plus, she couldn't wait for Holly Jacobson, along with Portia, Maeve, and everyone back home, to gnash their teeth in envy when Alexa's face ended up all over international newsstands.

Xavier, though, quickly put an end to Alexa's fantasizing. Muttering an impressive string of curses, he shrugged out of Alexa's grasp and charged toward the two men, jaw set and fists at the ready. Alexa gasped, wondering if she should run over and stop him, but she felt another current of excitement that kept her rooted to the spot. Xavier's friends, on the other hand, started to scatter; Alexa heard one of them groan "Not *again*" and another remark that she wanted to be gone before the cops showed up.

Clearly, Xavier vs. the paparazzi was a ridiculously common occurrence.

"Back off, assholes," Xavier threatened, and gave one of the men a hard shove. Alexa's heart slammed against her ribs, her apprehension mingling with anticipation. Was there going to be a fight? She'd never witnessed a brawl on the street — needless to say, that didn't happen all too often in tree-lined Oakridge, New Jersey. Holding her breath, Alexa watched as the paparazzo staggered backwards, almost dropping his camera. His partner in crime advanced toward Xavier, but Xavier shoved him as well, and the two men, clearly cowed, promptly scampered away into the night.

Xavier spun around to face Alexa, breathing hard, his smoke-colored eyes fiery and his mouth twisted in triumph.

To Alexa, he'd never looked hotter.

They rushed toward each other, and Alexa threw her arms around him in a "my *hero*!" gesture — even though, come to think of it, Xavier hadn't really rescued her from anything. But when the guy in question was this sexy, who *cared*?

Xavier scooped Alexa up, cupping her butt in his hands as she wrapped her legs around his hips, and there, in the middle of rue Oberkampf, they kissed — long and hungry and deep. Everything, *everything* — from the blur of the city lights to the roughness of Xavier's stubble to the memory of that scandalous near-fight — turned Alexa on like crazy.

She wrapped herself tighter around Xavier, aching for even more of him, but he ended the kiss and glanced over Alexa's shoulder, his brow furrowing. "Did my friends leave?" he murmured, sounding only vaguely concerned.

"I think so," Alexa replied, as Xavier slowly released

her and she dropped back to the ground. "They must have gone on to Le Scherkhan." Suddenly, the last thing Alexa wanted to do was follow them; the world seemed to have boiled down to two bare essentials — her and Xavier.

Xavier was right on her wavelength. He fixed his eyes back on Alexa's face, his lips tilting up once again in a half-smile. "Good," he whispered. "Let them go." Then he reached down and grabbed both of Alexa's hands, his expression suddenly serious. "Alexa, come with me. I want you to see my studio," he declared. "It's not far from here." He nodded toward where he'd parked his moped.

"Your studio?" Alexa echoed in giddy disbelief. Her cheeks were still flushed from the kiss, but they now burned even deeper. Though Alexa considered herself rather artistic, she'd never been in a real painter's studio. And now she was being invited to Xavier *Pascal's*. It was almost too much to absorb.

"Yes," Xavier exclaimed, his eyes searching hers. "A girl like you should not have had to witness such violence tonight —"

"Well, it wasn't *too* terrible," Alexa cut in, with a grin.

"No. Your beautiful eyes should only feast on beautiful things," Xavier continued, running his hands up her arms. "So come see my paintings. Please. Let me show you my greatest passion."

And really, all it took was Xavier saying the word *passion* to get Alexa back on his Vespa.

This time, she unpinned her hair and let it fly freely behind her like a golden banner as she and Xavier tore through the nighttime streets. They rode to the nearby Bastille district, which was full of dim, narrow alleyways, all lined with different bars and clubs. Xavier's studio was on one such street — the rue de Lapp — and located right above a humming Cuban salsa club. As Alexa passed the club, she thought briefly of Diego. Her ex-boyfriend hadn't crossed her mind all night, and now she forcefully shook him out of her head as Xavier unlocked the street door and led Alexa up a crooked flight of stairs.

But when Alexa arrived in Xavier's spacious loft, with its floor-to-ceiling windows that showed all of Paris by night, any thoughts of Diego disappeared on their own. "Oh, wow," she murmured, and began to walk in a slow circle, mesmerized by the bright canvases that were everywhere — hanging on the white walls, propped up against the columns, and drying on the floor. Most of the paintings were of stark geometric shapes — indigo circles and citrus squares — but Alexa's eye also fell on a few charcoal sketches of people — a young boy playing in the street, an old woman knitting — as well as an abstract painting of a girl with flowing black hair. Everything was as exquisite as the guy who had created them.

"You like it?" Xavier asked, grinning. He shed his leather jacket and draped it on a crate of paintbrushes, clearly enjoying Alexa's reaction.

"Oh, yes," Alexa sighed, appreciatively eyeing Xavier in his tight black T-shirt. Then she gave a small start when she heard his cell phone ring from the pocket of his jacket.

"*Merde*," Xavier hissed, pulling out the phone. As he had last time, he flipped it open with a brusque greeting, spat out a few monosyllabic words, and then flung the phone shut again, tossing it onto a low table strewn with unlit candles, cigarette butts, and empty wineglasses.

"Do you need to go?" Alexa asked, worried that their time at the studio was over already.

"*Non*," Xavier replied, rolling his eyes. "Just some bullshit." Then he smiled at Alexa, turned, and headed for a small refrigerator in the corner. "Do you want a glass of wine?"

"Um, sure," Alexa replied, studying a painting of a shattered octagon. She didn't need a drink; Xavier's astonishing artwork was enough to make her feel buzzed. And for a second, as Xavier returned with a bottle of white wine, two glasses, and a cigarette for himself, Alexa wondered if she might be in over her head. *I'm still in high school,* she thought, randomly flashing on an image of herself striding down the Oakridge High hallways. How had she ended up here, tonight, with a famous twenty-one-year-old artist?

Not that she was complaining.

Xavier poured them each a glass of wine, and they sat on the long black couch that was flush against the wall. Other than the couch and the table, the refrigerator, a standing lamp, and an artist's stool set up across from the sofa, the studio was devoid of anything but art. And right then, Alexa didn't think anything else was necessary in life.

"Do you live here, too?" she asked Xavier, taking a sip of wine and running her fingers along the couch's soft material; it would be comfortable enough to sleep on, certainly.

Xavier shook his head, glancing away from Alexa and into his wineglass, as if he found some inspiration there. "I have a flat on the Left Bank," he replied distractedly, taking a drag off his cigarette. "And a small country house in Provence."

Provence. Alexa set her wineglass on the floor and collapsed back against the pillows and patterned silk throw. She closed her eyes and thought about the southern French countryside — the vineyards and fields of sunflowers and gentle caress of the sunlight. Suddenly, almost without her own volition, she pictured herself and Xavier in that setting. They lived in a yellow house on a hilltop, surrounded by olive trees. Xavier had a studio in the shed, and she had her own darkroom in the basement. All day, he would paint her, and she would photograph him, and then, at sunset, they would lie in a lazy hammock, kissing. They'd be married in a garden bursting with wildflowers, and they'd have lots of talented babies. . . .

"Alexa? Would you open your eyes?"

Alexa let her eyes flutter open, and she gave Xavier a sheepish smile. She knew it was foolish — almost in a Holly Jacobson way — to actually think she was going to spend the rest of her life with Xavier Pascal. Though, on the other hand, why not? She could withdraw her enrollment from Columbia and move to France over the summer — her dad would definitely be cool with that plan. Alexa studied Xavier to see if he had somehow guessed at her heady thoughts, but instead he was studying *her*. He put his cigarette out in his wineglass and leaned in close, rubbing a hand across his chin, clearly deep in thought.

"Stay just like that," he told her, holding his hands out to indicate she shouldn't move from her reclining position. "Perfect." Xavier's face lit up, as if he'd discovered some secret treasure. "Alexa," he whispered. "*You* are perfect. I must capture your beauty."

"You — you want to draw me?" Alexa asked, going breathless. And to think she'd just been imagining pretty much that exact scenario — well, except with marriage and children thrown in.

"It is not a matter of wanting," Xavier murmured, holding her gaze as he stood up slowly. "I *have* to draw you. Here. Now."

Alexa nodded, trying to remain still on the sofa, but her pulse was racing, and it was all she could do not to start leaping up and down in elation. This night kept unfolding in ways that were ever more thrilling. She watched as Xavier darted, catlike, across the studio to retrieve a sketchpad and a wedge of charcoal from a box of art supplies in the corner. When he returned, he went into professional artist mode: depositing his supplies under the stool, turning off the standing lamp, and lighting the candles on the low table, which filled the studio with a soft, flickering glow that made Alexa feel incredibly alluring. Then, before Xavier began the actual sketching, he came over to the sofa to reposition Alexa a little.

It was divine torture; slowly, Xavier ran his smooth, deft hands all over Alexa's body — uncrossing her legs, moving one of her arms above her head, raking his fingers through her hair, and tugging her top farther down her shoulders. Alexa could feel her skin reaching dangerous temperatures, and her limbs trembled with desire. And although Xavier's expression was all seriousness, his gray eyes blazed with lust, and she saw him quickly lick his bottom lip — again reminding her of a cat — as if Alexa were a tasty dish he was preparing to consume.

"It's warm in here, isn't it?" Xavier suddenly asked, straightening up and stepping back from the sofa, a devilish smile on his lips. As Alexa felt herself melting into the sofa, Xavier reached down and tugged his black T-shirt up over his head, revealing his ripped torso and a dark star tattoo on his left shoulder. Tossing the T-shirt on the floor, he finally returned to his stool, sat down, and took up his sketchpad and charcoal.

Ooh, Alexa thought, her gaze lingering on Xavier's tattoo as he began sketching. She'd never dated a guy with a tattoo before, and the mere sight of it sent shivers through her body. She continued to watch Xavier, rapt, as he scratched the charcoal across the paper in fast, sure strokes, his eyes flicking from Alexa on the sofa and back down to the sketchpad with lightning rapidity.

I feel like I'm in Titanic, Alexa thought wryly, as she reclined there. *Only not naked.* She giggled out loud. *Yet.*

"Shhh." Xavier held a finger to his lips, but his eyes were laughing. When he resumed sketching, Alexa studied the tilt of Xavier's head, the way he bit down on his lower lip in concentration, and how the soft candlelight cast mysterious shadows on his face. Her stomach gave a leap, as if she were suddenly plummeting from a great height. And then Alexa realized that she was, in fact, falling, despite the fact that she was perfectly still on the sofa.

She was falling in love with Xavier.

It felt different from how she'd fallen for Diego — this love felt more definite, more certain, but also, at the same time, scarier. Bottomless. Alexa was reminded of the dizzy, exhilarating sensation she'd had while riding on Xavier's moped — the sensation of losing control.

Alexa heard herself sigh, and Xavier glanced up at her, chuckling.

"Impatient?" he asked, and then, to Alexa's surprise, tore the sheet off the pad and held the finished sketch up for Alexa to admire. She hadn't thought so much time had passed, but clearly she'd been too deep into her lovesickness to notice.

Alexa felt her mouth drop open as she examined the sketch of herself. How had he done it? With a few quick brushes of charcoal, Xavier had managed to harness her spirit: the lively glint in her big eyes, the princessy poutiness of her bow-shaped lips, the lush abandon of her long hair. But there was also something surprisingly vulnerable about the girl in the picture — an unexpected sensitivity that softened her confident expression. Alexa felt as if she were staring into a true, secret mirror, seeing the self only *she* knew existed. *Xavier gets me,* she thought, awestruck. All her life Alexa had felt woefully misunderstood; now, as she stared across the studio at Xavier, she realized she'd finally met someone who could read her soul.

"Do I — I really look like that?" Alexa murmured, her voice catching.

Xavier glanced from the sketch over to Alexa, and then nodded, his lips curving up in a grin. "Yes. You are —" He paused, as if suddenly overcome, and then pushed the stool back, standing up. "Alexa, you are the purest essence of what is beautiful. And your eyes — they contain vast oceans of fire and truth."

Alexa wasn't quite sure what that meant, but she didn't care. And then Xavier was approaching her, the sketch left forgotten on the floor, and he was beside her on the couch, plunging his hands into her hair and pulling her in for kiss after kiss, his mouth hot and urgent on hers. His kisses trailed down to her neck, and he slid his hands along her body — only this time, it was definitely not for the sake of art.

And Alexa discovered that he'd lied on the bridge yesterday — Xavier Pascal wasn't just good with his hands.

He was incredible.

They fell back against the sofa together, their bodies entwining. As she and Xavier continued their feverish kissing, Alexa let her own hands wander over his body. She trailed one hand down the length of Xavier's smooth, muscular back, while letting the other lightly rub the nape of his neck. When they came up for air, Alexa, smiled at him, tracing the jagged scar above his lip with her fingertip.

"How did you get that?" she whispered, curious.

"From a fight, back when I was young and stupid," Xavier explained, leaning in to nip her earlobe.

"And now you're older and wiser?" Alexa laughed, kissing the tattoo on his shoulder and thinking about his scuffle with the photographers that night.

Xavier nodded. "Now I have you," he whispered into her ear. "My muse."

Alexa thought she might pass out. *Hello, Dream? This is Coming True. It's so nice to meet you.*

Xavier began hiking up her short white skirt, his lips still against her ear. "Do you want to stay over here tonight?" he asked, his fingers as smooth as his voice.

Alexa tried as hard as she could not to hear Holly's

voice singing *voulez-vous coucher avec moi?* She knew, though, that this *was* her and Xavier's *voulez-vous* moment: the instant in which they decided just how serious they were going to get. Alexa felt the briefest flicker of hesitation; though she felt so close to Xavier, she *had* only met him yesterday. And hadn't she decided she was too mature for one-night flings when she'd rejected Sven in Eurotrash?

But this isn't just a fling, Alexa thought, wrapping her arms around Xavier. As if to confirm that thought, Xavier spoke into her ear once more — and this time what he said made Alexa's heart swell with joy.

"Je t'aime."

Those were Xavier's words.

The world's most meaningful, wondrous, heart-pounding words — in *any* language.

And though Xavier and Alexa had been speaking to each other in French all night, those words unleashed in Alexa such unblemished happiness that, when she spoke next, her tongue chose the language that, despite everything, came most naturally to her. She spoke English.

"Me, too," Alexa said, arching her back, her mouth seeking his. "I love you, Xavier."

And then they didn't need words anymore.

CHAPTER TWELVE
L'Amour

"I hate her," Holly muttered, dragging her duffel out of the guest room, her cheeks flushed with still-bubbling anger. "Track meet. If you can call him your boyfriend. Like I care. She's such a bitch."

Holly realized that in talking to herself, she probably sounded like a crazy old woman, but it didn't matter. Nobody was around to hear her anyway; seconds ago, Alexa (the bitch in question) had stormed out of the apartment for her date with Sketchmaster Xavier. Then, Holly, too furious to cry, had done some storming of her own, back to the guest room to retrieve her bag.

The fight with Alexa had left Holly a whopping fifteen minutes to get to Gare du Nord, and as she crossed the living room with her duffel bag in tow, she had no idea how she was going to do that. The Métro would probably take too long, but she didn't know *where* she could catch a cab; unlike in New York — the only big city Holly was semi-familiar with — you couldn't just hail a taxi anywhere in Paris. Annoyingly, there were specific stands that — as Holly had discovered when she, Alexa, and the cousins had tried to get home from Eurotrash at three in the morning — seemed to be located as far as possible from any human activity.

Holly stood at the front door of the apartment, feeling the symptoms of what had to be an oncoming anxiety attack, when she heard a key turn in the lock. She gasped — once at the sound, and then again when she saw the person walking in.

"Pierre," Holly said.

"'Olly," Pierre said.

They looked at each other.

"Um, I was just leaving," Holly mumbled, swiftly turning her gaze to the floor. "Like, for good." She pointed unnecessarily to the duffel in her hand, her face reddening. She felt the tension crackle between them — a tension that was very different from the one she'd felt when fighting with Alexa.

"I can see that," Pierre said softly.

Holly bit her lip, studying her Adidas. Now was clearly the time for their good-bye, and Holly wondered how best to handle it. The face-off with Alexa had left Holly feeling edgy and reckless (as face-offs with Alexa often did), and for a second, she considered saying exactly what was on her mind: *Thanks for showing me Paris, Pierre. I'm sorry I was so weird last night. And, oh yeah, I think I might be in love with you, but I have a serious boyfriend back home whom I never told you about. Later!*

Or not.

Opting instead for an abrupt "bye," and a quick wave, Holly tried to walk around Pierre to the door, but to her astonishment, he blocked her way.

"'Olly, I am afraid I cannot let you leave tonight," Pierre announced, crossing his arms over his chest. His voice had a teasing lilt to it, but when Holly lifted her head, she saw that his expression was hopeful. Suddenly, without understanding why, Holly felt a small *ping* of excitement in her chest, as if she somehow sensed that Pierre was about to change her destiny.

Which, of course, he was.

"Why not?" Holly demanded, trying to sound firm, even as she felt her duffel wobble in her hand. "I have to catch a train, Pierre."

"Because." Pierre shot an impish grin at Holly, reached into the pocket of the messenger bag slung across his chest, and, with a flourish, pulled out two blue tickets. "If you leave tonight you will lose your only chance to sit in the front row of the Opéra Garnier and see an incredible performance of *Roméo et Juliette*. It begins at eight, but I believe we will make it if we hurry."

Holly glanced from the tickets to Pierre's beaming face, not fully comprehending. "You mean, the play?" was all she could manage. The slight thrumming in her chest was progressing to actual thumping.

Pierre shook his head and glanced down at the tickets, as if to double-check. "*Non* — the ballet," he replied. He looked back at Holly, a small crease of concern appearing in his smooth olive forehead. "You like ballet, yes?"

Surprisingly, Holly Jacobson *did* like ballet. She almost felt like it was her dirty little secret. Nobody at Oakridge High would ever look beyond Holly's hoodie-and-sneakers exterior and guess that she had a private passion for tights and toe shoes. But Holly's parents had shoved her into ballet lessons when she was six, and despite the pink girliness of it all, she'd loved ballet's rigors and challenges. Though she'd quit when she started running in junior high, Holly still fiercely believed that dance was as much a sport as track or soccer.

But, Holly realized as she nodded at Pierre, *her* interest in ballet was a hell of a lot less surprising than *his*. Back home, Holly didn't know a single boy who would willingly sit through a dance performance. Over winter break, she'd hesitantly broached to Tyler the possibility of taking the train into New York to see *The Nutcracker* at Lincoln Center, but she'd only gotten as far as "*The Nut —*" before Tyler cut her off with exaggerated gagging motions. Holly remembered something Alexa had said to her over lunch that day — that European guys tended to have more interest in cultural stuff than their American counterparts — but then Holly dismissed all thoughts of Alexa entirely.

Still, Holly couldn't resist asking Pierre if he went to the ballet often, and felt kind of relieved when he laughed and shook his head. "These are from my parents," he explained, giving the tickets a tap. "They are, how you say, members? *Oui.* Members of the Opéra Garnier. They go to a ballet or an opera almost every week. But tonight they have to attend an event for my father's work, so *voilà*, they gave me their tickets." Pierre paused and gave Holly a slow, knee-melting smile. "And, 'Olly, you were the first person that I thought of."

Okay. Holly's heart had now achieved full slamming-against-ribcage status. So maybe Raphi *had* known something about this — known that Holly would in fact have a date. Tonight. At eight o'clock. Which, naturally, was when Holly's train was leaving. And she knew, from glancing at the schedule earlier, that it was the last train going to England that night.

"Pierre, I'm so sorry," Holly said, her throat constricting. "It does sound great, but I can't — I really have to get —" Suddenly, Holly paused, and saw her two options branching out before her, like in a "Choose Your Own Adventure" novel. One road led to Puma sweatpants and tight ponytails and the steel-gray sky above Wimbledon. The other led to Holly in her new green safari-print dress and a sumptuous opera house, with Pierre sitting next to her in a dark theater.

Hmm. A toughie.

Holly felt recklessness warming her blood again. The thing was, despite her earlier grumbling, Holly *did* care about what Alexa had said. And the memory of Alexa's derisiveness — over Holly's lack of boy-experience, over the track meet — fueled in Holly the desire to do something *different*. To swerve off her appointed path. Holly's roiling resentment toward her friend, combined with Pierre's delectable nearness and the invitation in his dreamy blue eyes, all came together in one powerful instant.

Holly Jacobson chose her own adventure. For tonight, she chose Paris.

Blushing, Holly smiled back at Pierre and gave him a small, barely perceptible nod. *This feels right,* she realized. Why had she even hesitated? And, more important, why had it not occurred to her before that she could take a *morning* train to England? The track meet wasn't until ten tomorrow, and the ride from Paris took only about three hours. All Holly had to do was set her alarm for dawn and catch the earliest train possible out of Gare du Nord.

Meghan and Jess would understand.

"*Ah*," Pierre said, a huge grin spreading across his face. "You have changed your mind?"

"Well, first I have to change my *clothes*," Holly replied, unable to suppress her own grin as she gestured down to her jeans and waffle shirt. Pierre himself looked very Euro-boy-cute in a tweed blazer with the collar turned up, worn over a plain white T-shirt, pencil-skinny black pants, and black loafers.

"You will thank me for this afterward, I promise," Pierre said. He came up very close to her and, as she had that day in the park, Holly got the stomach-swooping sense that Pierre might kiss her. But instead he spun her around and pointed her in the direction of the guest room. "Go change — quickly!" Pierre urged. "The show will not wait for us."

The show will not wait for us, Holly thought as she hurried back into the guest room with her duffel. Breathless, she tore open her bag and pulled out the new dress and flat-heeled boots she'd been dying for a chance to wear. Shows did not wait and neither did life. And Tyler or no Tyler, track meet or no track meet, Holly Jacobson was sick of walking in on life midway through the opening dance. This time, she wanted to be there when the curtain came up.

"Bravo!" Holly heard herself calling, two glorious hours later, as the heavy velvet curtain came down on the ballet of *Roméo et Juliette.* She and Pierre, along with the rest of the audience, were on their feet, clapping wildly for the dancers, who'd just taken their final bow. Holly had never said the word *bravo* before in her life, but then again, she'd never seen a performance like this one — all lavish costumes, jaw-dropping dancing, heavenly music, and of course, tragically star-crossed lovers. Holly had realized that anybody who thought ballet was boring had clearly never sat in the front row; many times, she'd felt like the dancers were flying right out *at* her. It had been — just as Pierre had promised back in the apartment — incredible.

"So, I was right, yes?" Pierre asked. He and Holly strolled into the marble-and-gilt lobby of the Opéra Garnier amid a swarm of dressed-to-the-nines Parisians — some women in silken gowns and garlands of pearls, some men in crisp black tuxedos — all clucking over the ballet. "This was worth missing your train for?" He gently put a hand on Holly's back to guide her out of the ornate opera house and into the warm, starry night.

"Most definitely," Holly sighed as they drifted across the sweeping plaza. "This was worth everything."

The cobblestone streets were bursting with people — amorous couples on the corners, giggling girls in platform flip-flops racing toward some unknown destination — and Holly breathed it all in. After a solid year of domestic activities like playing on Tyler's Xbox, she was loving being out this late with a handsome boy at her side, the hazy crescent moon overhead, and the very air buzzing with possibility. Holly had decided to leave her cell phone back at the apartment, and without its weight in her new mint-green clutch, she felt as free and untethered as a balloon. "Or maybe I'm just a sucker for Romeo and Juliet," she added with a grin, glancing down at the glossy program in her hand.

"*Ah*, me? I am different," Pierre said, brushing his dark curls out of his eyes — a gesture that Holly had grown accustomed to, but that never failed to make her melt. "I enjoyed the ballet, yes, but I have never understood this Romeo and Juliet business," he explained as they started down the boulevard Haussman. "It is supposed to be the greatest story of *l'amour* — of love — in the world, *n'est-ce-pas?*" he offered with a thoughtful glance at Holly, who nodded. "But they are *teenagers*. Juliet — she has, what? Fourteen years? And Romeo, he has seventeen? Tell me, what do teenagers know about great and true love? I find this . . ." Pierre flicked his thumb and middle finger together. "Crazy."

"Do you mean that?" Holly asked, turning to Pierre in surprise. She'd initially pegged Alexa's soulful cousin as more of a romantic. "But it's *forbidden* love!" Holly argued, gesturing with her hands. The night's energy was loosening her normally more reserved tongue. "And, come on, Pierre," she added, shaking her head. "Of course teenagers can fall totally and completely in love. When you're a teenager, everything becomes so *intense* — so important . . ." Holly let out a sigh, remembering herself at thirteen, when she'd first felt the cruel sting of a crush.

"You take love very seriously, 'Olly," Pierre observed, a teasing smile playing on his lips. "Perhaps too seriously?"

"I do not —" Holly began defensively, but then her heartbeat increased at a dramatic rate. *Forbidden love. Teenagers.* She looked down at her boots, avoiding Pierre's gaze. *Oh, God,* she thought, in a mild panic. *Was I talking about . . . us?*

Thankfully, Pierre chose that moment to suggest

that they grab a late dinner on the Ile St-Louis. Flustered, Holly agreed — with the one request that the meal not run *too* late, since she'd set her travel alarm clock for the ungodly hour of five in the morning. But by the time she and Pierre were splitting a steak frites and a bottle of wine on a terrace overflowing with flowers, Holly's alarm was the last thing on her mind. As she and Pierre ate and drank and continued to debate the ballet, eleven o'clock magically morphed into midnight, and soon they were making their tipsy way over to the nearby Café-Brasserie St. Regis, to pick up some *bière à l'emporter*.

Sipping their cups of cold, bubbly beer, they wandered over to the illuminated Notre Dame cathedral, behind which they came upon a wild array of street performers, from fire-eaters to jugglers to bongo drummers. A DJ was spinning techno and trance, and packs of kids danced, waving glow sticks.

Watching the impromptu party from the periphery, Holly felt both uncomfortable and intrigued; she'd never been to a rave, but she figured the vibe at one would come close to this. She hung back, but an enthusiastic Pierre — "they call this 'the show,'" he explained — talked her into staying. Holly soon felt all her reserve dissolving as she and Pierre finished their beers, danced in fits and starts, and chatted up some Australian backpackers who were still dirty from the

Eurorail. The party was still raging when the two of them decided to cool off with a walk across the river.

"I should really get back to the apartment," Holly said unconvincingly as she and Pierre strolled along a quiet stone quay, their arms brushing against each other. She tossed a glance down at her wristwatch. It was well after two in the morning.

"Yes," Pierre said, with just as much conviction. "You should." Holly felt their elbows bump slightly.

"Mmm," Holly replied, closing her eyes. Her head was pleasantly heavy from the wine and beer, and she was enjoying how the river breeze playfully lifted her hair and kissed the back of her neck.

"Look," Pierre whispered, squeezing Holly's bare arm to get her attention. Holly let her eyes flutter open, and saw that Pierre was motioning to a flight of stone steps that led down from the quay to a narrow little nook right on the water. "These secret places, they are perhaps my favorite in all of Paris," he added quietly.

"Let's check it out," Holly whispered back, feeling a spark of excitement. She wasn't usually one to explore hidden-away corners in cities, but the slim strip of gravel by the water seemed to call to her. She grabbed Pierre's hand and led him down the steep unlit steps until they reached the secluded spot. Wordlessly, Pierre took off his blazer and spread it on the ground, and he and Holly sat down, hugging their knees and gazing out at the water.

"Oh, *Pierre*," Holly sighed, admiring how the river shone glassy-black in the moonlight. Across the way, the lights of the Left Bank shimmered and winked at her, tantalizing and coy. "It's — it's amazing," she added dreamily, resting her chin on her knees. She'd never fully experienced Paris by night before.

"*Oui*," Pierre murmured, and Holly felt his eyes on her profile. "Amazing. This is exactly what I am thinking."

At Pierre's words, Holly felt tingles rush through her limbs. She had grown deliciously accustomed to Pierre tossing off a flirtatious compliment every so often, but tonight, his voice seemed different — deeper, more serious. Her pulse fluttering at her neck and wrists, Holly sat very still as Pierre moved closer to her, and she felt the undeniable energy pulse between them.

And then suddenly, it was no longer the river breeze that was lifting Holly's hair off her neck, but Pierre himself, his hands slipping carefully through her fine, honey-brown strands. *Is he really doing that?* Holly thought dazedly, wondering if she should tell Pierre to stop. But, in the next heartbeat, as Holly's skin flushed hotter and hotter, Pierre leaned in and kissed her neck, his lips soft and warm and slow. And he certainly didn't stop.

"Oh, *Pierre*," Holly repeated, only this time her meaning was completely different — and her words were faint with breathlessness. She had every intention of telling him how wrong this was, but her eyes were closing with pleasure and she was inclining her head to the left, giving Pierre more of her neck to kiss. And, really, Holly knew she was powerless to stop this moment — this natural culmination of everything that had been building since the day Pierre had kissed her hello in the stairwell. What was happening between the two of them felt as certain, as inevitable as the current of the river as it lapped against the bank.

Pierre seemed to be thinking along the same lines. "I have wanted — this — for so long," he whispered into Holly's ear, his breath catching, his lips still brushing her neck. Gently, Pierre tilted Holly's head back up, and turned her face toward his. Holly thought she could see her reflection in Pierre's light blue eyes, and she felt, for the first time in a long time, as beautiful as Alexa. She gave Pierre a small smile, biting her bottom lip, and Pierre swallowed hard, his Adam's apple moving up and down.

As Pierre brought his face in even closer to hers, Holly closed her eyes again, welcoming the wave of desire that engulfed her. She wasn't sure who even started the kiss, but, in the next instant, their mouths were fitted together, and Holly found herself kissing

Pierre with a passion she hadn't even known she was capable of. His tongue tasted like honey, and the feel of his full lips was so deliciously unfamiliar that Holly's whole body quivered. There, on the deserted river-bank, they turned toward each other completely, Holly's arms sliding tight around Pierre's neck, his claiming her waist. Their bodies pressed together and they continued to kiss hungrily as the crescent moon moved across the water.

Kissing while sitting up suddenly seemed like a silly idea; before she knew it, Holly was lying back against Pierre's jacket, and he was above her, his hands tracing the curves of her body, his touch care-ful but confident. As Pierre's fingers floated along the seam of her dress, Holly gave a small start, and Alexa's words from earlier sprung unbidden into her mind: *Pierre is* not *as innocent as he seems.*

No kidding.

"*Ça va?*" Pierre murmured, drawing back a little to smile down at her. His hair was rumpled and his eyes were sparkling.

"*Ça va,*" Holly replied, surprised at how easily the French came to her. She knew the phrase more or less translated to "It's cool." And, even though Holly wasn't used to making out with foreign boys on hidden riverbanks, she *was* cool with this. She was ready.

She'd *been* ready back in Oakridge — perched on the brink, waiting to dive in.

And, from the looks of things, Pierre St. Laurent was there to catch her.

As their kissing and caressing picked up again, Pierre started to stretch out alongside her, but space on his blazer was limited. Holly shifted helpfully to one side, but felt something sharp poke her in the back. A pebble. "Ow," Holly mumbled, pulling back from Pierre to readjust herself on the blazer. As she did so, her palm dug into the scratchy gravel. *What am I doing?* Holly wondered. Clearly, a riverbank wasn't the most convenient place for a hookup, but before Holly could say anything about that, Pierre was kissing her again.

Then, suddenly, as if the cold, hard ground had awoken her, Holly was reminded of that night in the car with Tyler — how, they, too, had tried in vain to get comfortable together. And once she had thought of Tyler, Holly was unable to *stop* thinking of him. Tyler, whose sweet, gentle kisses were as familiar to her as the back roads of her hometown. Tyler, who — tonight, between the ballet and the beer and the walk along the water — had receded in Holly's mind, but now returned, as vivid as if he were beside her on the moonlit bank. What *was* she doing here, lying on the gravel in the middle of Paris, ready to do who-knew-what with a boy she barely even knew?

And, in that instant, even as Pierre was kissing her, Holly realized that there was only one boy with whom she wanted to make out in inconvenient places. And with whom she wanted to go all the way.

So she whispered his name.

Pierre immediately broke off the kiss and pulled back, his brow furrowed, his breathing unsteady. "Tyler?" he repeated, his eyes searching hers. Holly wondered if Pierre remembered the name from the restaurant last night.

"Tyler," Holly affirmed, her voice wavery. Slowly, she struggled to sit up, warm tears gathering in her throat. She hadn't meant for this to happen — none of it. She hadn't meant to blurt out Tyler's name like that, but she also hadn't intended to hook up with Pierre in the first place. Or had she? Everything was a giant, jumbled mess.

Pierre raised one eyebrow, sitting back on his heels and studying Holly. "He is your boyfriend?" he asked quietly. "From New Jersey?"

Holly's stomach lurched. *Right on the money.* Unsteadily, she got to her feet, trembling a little. "How did you — did Alexa tell you?" she asked, preparing for another reason to hate her friend.

Pierre shook his head, smiling wryly as he also

climbed to his feet. "'Olly, I am not a fool," he said, bending down to retrieve his wrinkled blazer. Brushing the gravel off his jacket, he met Holly's gaze and she saw the raw disappointment written on his face.

Holly felt the tears start at the corners of her eyes and she glanced down. Of course, smart, insightful Pierre would be able to guess the truth from her reaction. Holly felt terrible for keeping him in the dark all this time. As all of her various guilts — over Pierre, over Tyler, over Wimbledon — melded together in a blur, Holly was unable to put a stopper on her tumbling emotions. So she did what any normal girl would do in her position.

She burst into tears.

Pierre took a step toward her, and, since Holly had no other place to rest her head, she leaned it against his chest, weeping into his soft white T-shirt. She felt him hesitate for a second and then begin to stroke her tousled hair.

"Pierre, I'm *sorry*," Holly sobbed, her voice muffled. "There's so much I've kept from you. Yes, Tyler is my boyfriend, and we've been together a whole year but he doesn't even *know* I'm in Paris," she rambled, hiccuping. "And neither do my parents because I escaped from my track meet in England, and *that* was why I needed to leave tonight, and if Coach Graham catches me, I might get kicked out of school, and Meghan and

Jess will get in trouble, too, and they're probably so mad at me, and now I'm in this fight with Alexa so I have no friends left and — and . . ." Her breath running out, Holly let herself collapse into sobs once more, burying her face deeper into Pierre's shirt. She felt drained, but not in a terrible way; it was kind of liberating to finally shed all her secrets.

Some woman of mystery.

"'Olly, *écoute-moi* — listen to me," Pierre spoke up, his voice calm and steady. "It is okay." He put one hand under Holly's chin and lifted her tear-streaked face so they were eye to eye. "Well, maybe it is not okay," he amended, a smile flickering across his face. "But it is certainly no reason to cry."

"Please don't be nice to me, Pierre," Holly sniffled, resisting the urge to blow her nose on the hem of his shirt. After her big confession, she'd expected Pierre to despise her, but his kindness was only making her feel worse. "I'm this total liar, and I led you on and —"

"You are not a liar," Pierre insisted, before Holly could go off another diatribe. "It is my fault, too — I never asked. You see, I suspected that you had a boyfriend, but I think perhaps I did not want to know."

"You suspected all along?" Holly whispered, searching Pierre's warm blue eyes in surprise.

"Well, I was wondering always how a girl so beautiful and funny did *not* have a boyfriend," Pierre

238

replied, softly cupping her cheek with his hand. Holly's heart jumped, both from Pierre's touch and his sincere words. But this time the vibe between them felt surprisingly relaxed, less charged with sexual tension. *Maybe we just needed to get it out of our systems*, Holly thought, remembering their earlier kissing — which now seemed sort of surreal.

"This Tyler, he has a lot of luck," Pierre added quietly as his mouth curved up in a thoughtful smile. "And I am sure he is ... how you say? A good — guy?"

In spite of her tears, Holly couldn't help her own smile. She loved it whenever Pierre clumsily tried his hand at American phrases, and it was simultaneously weird and refreshing to hear Tyler's name in Pierre's adorable French accent. *Tie-laire.* Like everything else about Holly's time in Paris, it shed bright new light on something all too familiar. *Tyler* was all tangled emotions. *Tie-laire* was somehow ... manageable.

"He is a good guy," Holly admitted, wiping her eyes with the back of her hand. "But Pierre — so are you." Although her face turned hot, she held Pierre's gaze, knowing she owed him more of an explanation. "You're wonderful — different from any boy I've ever known," Holly whispered, meaning every word. "And I got so caught up in spending time with you that I sort of let myself pretend that I *was* single ... and that we were . . ." Holly trailed off, feeling herself choke up again. *In love*, she wanted to say. But *had* she loved Pierre? Or had it just been lust? Was it possible to love two boys at once?

"I was caught up in you, too," Pierre said, matter-of-factly, tracing a line down Holly's cheek. "Still, 'Olly, you must think about it — we did not do anything so very wrong. So we kissed a little bit." Pierre tilted his head to the side and grinned at Holly. "This does not make a great tragedy."

Holly bit her lip, knowing deep down that Pierre was right. In the end, they *weren't* Romeo and Juliet. And, thankfully, she hadn't let them go any further tonight. Yes, technically, she'd cheated on her boyfriend — something Holly had never thought herself capable of — but Holly also knew that her three-day flirtation with Pierre probably wouldn't be enough to shatter her year-long-relationship with Tyler.

Providing that relationship still existed.

Holly sighed, her head fuzzy. "I guess I agree with you," she finally told Pierre, reluctantly stepping out of the warm circle of his arms. "But I still need to figure stuff out — it's all so complicated."

"*L'amour, c'est compliqué,*" Pierre agreed. He was quiet for a minute, looking out at the water, and then he turned back to Holly. "And, 'Olly, if you cannot figure out things with Tyler," he added with a smile. "You know, I will still be here in Paris."

Holly nodded, her heart racing at Pierre's offer. By way of response, she stood on her tiptoes and kissed him on both cheeks, returning his gesture from the day they'd met. She was shivering a little in the cool night air, so Pierre shook out his blazer once more and then draped it around her shoulders. Then, as wordlessly as they'd come, they climbed up the stone steps and started walking down the stone quay again, their hands lightly linked. The pose fell somewhere in between romantic and friendly, which, Holly realized, was what she and Pierre might always be toward each other.

"So," Pierre said, breaking a long stretch of silence. "What was this you were telling me about a . . . tracking meeting?" Shrugging his shoulders, he shot Holly a curious glance.

"Track meet," Holly said, remembering her nonsensical rant. Suddenly, she started to giggle, feeling her spirits lift. After the intensity of the night, laughter felt like a pure release.

Pierre began laughing, too, shaking his head. "Yes, yes, a track meet," he chuckled. "And then something about an argument with my dear cousin? I am very interested to hear."

Holly quickly checked her watch. It was three in the morning, which meant she'd only get an hour or so of sleep — especially if she planned to explain everything to Pierre. But Holly figured she'd make do somehow; she could always sleep on the train.

"Oh, God," she groaned, rolling her eyes. "Track. Alexa. Where do I start?"

And then, for no real reason — other than the fact that they were still tipsy, and sort of embarrassed by their encounter — she and Pierre started laughing again. Holly realized that whether or not she'd been *in* love with Pierre, what she had loved about him was his easy laughter — the way he made her feel hilarious and sexy at the same time. Holly knew she'd miss that quality more than anything when she went back to New Jersey.

Well, that and having someone call her *'Olly*.

CHAPTER THIRTEEN
The Party Crashers

"Holly? Holly!"

With excruciating slowness, Holly let her eyes flutter open. Her head pounded, and her mouth felt cottony. Light was pouring in from somewhere, making her want to shut her eyes again. It couldn't be morning yet, could it?

"Holly, what are you doing here?"

Where am I? Holly wondered, blinking and lifting her head off the lumpy pillow. She took in the small room, the shuttered windows, her green safari-print dress pooled on the floor, and finally, the blonde girl leaning over her, looking bewildered.

Alexa, Holly realized. *Paris.* Then, as clarity and panic hit at the same time, Holly grabbed her travel

alarm clock off the floor by her bed and stared in horror at the numbers there.

12:00 P.M.

She screamed.

Alexa jumped back, clutching Xavier's sketch to
her chest as Holly sprang out of bed, holding the miniature alarm clock up to her face. "No no no no no,"
Holly cried, rattling the clock so hard Alexa was sure
she'd break it. "Tell me you're joking. Tell me this is
a joke." She was speaking directly to the clock now,
and Alexa worried for her friend's sanity.

"Hol," Alexa said gently, putting one hand on
Holly's shoulder and forgetting that, fifteen hours
earlier, she'd wanted to throttle her. "I don't think the
clock is joking."

Alexa held her breath as Holly looked up, her gray-
green eyes enormous and her freckled skin pale. "You
missed your meet?" Alexa whispered, already knowing the answer. She'd guessed as much when she'd
drifted into the room on a cloud of Xavier-induced
bliss only to find Holly passed out on her bed in
the classic drunken-sleep pose — mouth open, covers
kicked down, tank top riding up her belly.

"My meet — my train — my *life*!" Holly wailed,
breaking into a little jig of madness. As often happened whenever she thought of Wimbledon, Holly's
ankle began to throb. She pictured the Eurostar train

pulling out of the station, Holly-less, and zooming on toward England, where Meghan, Jess, and the rest of her teammates waited in vain for her. She was their captain, and she'd let each and every one of them down.

And Coach Graham was going to eat her alive.

At this thought, Holly had to cut her jig short and sink down on her bed, her breaths coming fast and shallow. She had *no idea* what to do. Rushing back to England now seemed pointless — the meet would be long finished when she arrived in the late afternoon. And she didn't want to turn on her cell phone, where a million *you're-in-such-deep-shit* messages from Meghan surely awaited. Or maybe it was Jess who had called, to inform Holly that all three girls would not be graduating in June.

"Stop hyperventilating," Alexa ordered, trying not to roll her eyes; Holly's nervous breakdown was understandable, but Alexa had only so much tolerance for hysteria. Adjusting her minuscule white skirt on her hips — Xavier had sort of broken the zipper last night — Alexa sat down beside her friend, sketch in hand. "Weren't you supposed to leave last night?" she asked massaging Holly's back. Alexa couldn't hide the curiosity in her voice; her sixth sense for boy-gossip told her that Holly's change in travel plans *somehow* involved her hot cousin.

Holly, who always paid close attention in health class, now had her head between her knees in case she fainted. "Pierre — ballet — beers — fooled around — came home really late," she managed to stammer. How had she been so stupid? Through the fog of her searing headache, Holly remembered coming back with Pierre, her throat raw from talking and her emotions still tumbling. She remembered changing into her boxers and tank and collapsing facedown in bed. Then, very vaguely, she remembered hearing the buzz of her alarm in the darkness and slapping her hand down to silence it. And the next thing she knew, Alexa was hollering her name.

Maybe oversleeping was punishment for kissing another boy.

"I *so* called it!" Alexa exclaimed, giving Holly's unkempt ponytail an excited yank. "I predicted from, like, day one that you and Pierre were gonna get it on!" Alexa felt a flood of satisfaction; she didn't know where Tyler Davis fit into this whole scenario, but Holly and Pierre made a too-cute-for-words couple. *Maybe Holly and I will* both *move here to be with our respective French boys,* Alexa mused. *Holly's practically related to me anyway, so it would make sense for her to end up with my cousin —*

"But we're not together now or anything," Holly said, unwittingly putting an end to Alexa's daydreaming. She straightened up, feeling marginally calmer now that she had something other than Coach Graham's snapping fangs on her mind, and turned to Alexa, grateful that her friend was there to soothe her. Holly, too, had momentarily forgotten last night's argument. "I mean, it *was* nice and all," she clarified with a sheepish smile. She knew Pierre was in classes all day, so at least she didn't have to worry about him overhearing. "But we stopped before it got too intense. I told Pierre all about Tyler, and —"

Holly paused at this mention of Tyler and, with a jolt, remembered her and Alexa's serious clash from the night before. Alexa seemed to remember as well, because her mouth tightened and her blue eyes went cold. An abrupt silence fell between the two girls, like a sheet of ice. *Oh, yeah. We're supposed to hate each other*, was the unspoken realization. Alexa chewed her bottom lip and Holly cleared her throat as they each sought safer places to rest their respective gazes.

Holly chose the sheet of paper in Alexa's hand, and saw that it was a charcoal sketch of — without question — Alexa herself. "Who drew that?" Holly asked quietly, glad to be able to fill the stark silence. She wasn't about to forgive Alexa, but Holly *loathed* awkward moments like these. Plus, after the over-sleeping disaster, she no longer had the energy to remain truly mad at her friend.

"Xavier," Alexa answered shortly — but she felt herself soften at the memory of the artist and their knee-weakening night together. Alexa *was* still pissed at Holly, but the girls' snipefest seemed borderline trivial compared to Alexa's all-consuming love.

"Oh," Holly mumbled. In all the chaos, she'd also managed to forget about Alexa's hot date with Monsieur Shady. Now, Holly took stock of her friend — the loose, tangled hair, the top on back-wards, the unglossed, slightly swollen lips — and realized that Alexa had only just come home this morning. After an obviously eventful night. But Holly also noticed a little-girl vulnerability in Alexa's expression — a hopefulness — that contrasted with her trashy walk-of-shame look. *She's* beyond *into this guy*, Holly thought, feeling a twinge of regret that she'd been so harsh on Xavier. Maybe he deserved another chance.

"Will you see him again?" Holly asked, trying to sound contrite. She could feel some of her tension with Alexa dissipating, though things weren't exactly warm and fuzzy yet.

"Tonight," Alexa sighed, and flopped back on the bed, staring up at the moldings on the ceiling. "I'm going to his glitzy gallery opening on the place des Vosges."

What Alexa failed to mention was that Xavier had no *clue* she was going.

That morning, she'd meant to ask him about the opening, but there'd been no time. Xavier had woken her with a kiss on her bare shoulder, whispering that he had to run, but that she should let herself out of the studio, since the door was self-locking. After a lingering kiss on the lips and a request that she call him later, Xavier handed her the sketch — and was gone. Stretching across the sofa with a contented sigh, the silk throw draped over her body, Alexa decided that instead of bothering Xavier (who must have been super-stressed) with a phone call, she'd simply show up to the party on her own, looking her most devastating. And surprise him.

Much sexier.

"A gallery opening, huh?" Holly asked, glancing down at Alexa. "As in, people standing around in a white room drinking wine and analyzing, like, sculptures of someone's feet?" Holly couldn't think of anything more pretentious or irritating. "Can I come?" she asked in the next breath, startling both herself and Alexa.

But Holly knew just why she had posed the question. She was desperate for a distraction — *any* distraction — from the gigantic, hovering, elephant-in-the-room problem of Wimbledon. She wanted to cast everything off, to pretend track and Coach Graham and her parents didn't exist. And having an event to attend in Paris that night — even if it was a snobby gallery opening — would allow Holly to do just that — keep stalling, keep pretending.

Holly Jacobson, welcome to the happy Land of Denial!

Lying flat on her back, Alexa studied Holly's anxious face, weighing the pros and cons of the situation. Naturally, Alexa had been envisioning sauntering into the gallery alone, people murmuring appreciatively as Xavier rushed over to sweep her into a kiss. But maybe it wouldn't hurt to have a friend by her side as a fallback in case Xavier was busy mingling. Yes, the event was open to the public — and she *was,* after all, Xavier Pascal's muse — but Alexa still hadn't been officially invited. It was one thing to arrive unannounced at a house party in Oakridge, as Alexa had done on a dare from Portia sophomore year (she'd gotten drunk off bad keg beer and wound up making out with a hot senior in the upstairs bathroom). It was something else entirely to crash a grown-up Parisian bash where there might be tons of celebrities.

She just hoped Holly wouldn't do something to embarrass her.

"Well, if you don't *need* to run back to England . . ." Alexa began with a shrug — her passive-aggressive way of saying yes. "But," she added, raising a warning eyebrow at Holly, "I'll probably be with Xavier and his crew most of the night, so you might need to fend for yourself."

Holly felt her hackles go up at Alexa's condescending tone — until she saw the humor in her friend's words. Knowing Alexa, she probably had this elaborate fantasy of being the star of the show — people murmuring appreciatively as she sauntered past, Xavier rushing over to kiss her, cameras going off in her wake . . . Holly bit back her smile.

If she was a citizen of Denial Land, then Alexa was the freaking prime minister.

Alexa spent the afternoon napping, while Holly went out for a defiantly big lunch comprised mostly of pastries, so both girls were feeling a little mellower when they arrived at the Galérie Paradis that evening.

Once the bouncer confirmed that they were not, in fact, paparazzi, he let them inside the packed, dimly lit gallery — which was not at all the stark, snobby scene Holly had been picturing. The floor was painted to look like a cloud-filled sky, the walls were exposed brick, and light-filled paper lanterns swayed from the beams in the ceiling. What sounded like the French equivalent of The Shins blasted from the speakers, and hipsters congregated in groups, sipping flame-colored martinis. Holly decided that if it weren't for the paintings displayed on the walls, the gathering would feel like a party at some cool college-age person's apartment.

But instead of getting intimidated by the trendy crowd, Holly felt surprisingly at ease in her new black cami with a burgundy sash, black cardigan, reliable denim mini, and crushed velvet flats. Maybe it was just that she'd been so turned off by coming here, but was pleasantly surprised at how chill the vibe was. Holly was certain that Alexa, for her part, would be totally in her artsy element — only, when she glanced at her friend, Holly saw that her glossy lips were white with fear.

Why am I so nervous? Alexa was asking herself at that very moment. Her palms were clammy and her stomach hurt — both rare conditions for her.

Yes, Alexa knew she looked hot in her new high-necked, backless paisley halter dress — cinched at the waist with a thick, burnished-orange belt — toeless apricot pumps, and big amber hoops. Her hair was swept back in a loose chignon and held off her face with a wide paisley headband. The effect, Alexa felt, was very Twiggy. Then, glancing around, she caught sight of a super-skinny Asian girl with bleached-blonde hair who was wearing nothing but an oversized, raggedy brown sweater and moon boots. Alexa sighed; it was impossible to stay a step ahead of cutting-edge

Parisian fashion. But as long as Xavier appreciated her outfit, that was all that mattered. And speaking of which, where *was* he?

Holly, of course, wasn't looking for Xavier at all, which was probably why she spotted him immediately. He was standing on the opposite end of the gallery, surrounded by a tight circle of admirers — among them a girl with a scarlet-red bob who wore a short white dress that looked as if it had been slashed to bits and a skinny guy with chunky glasses and a chipped front tooth. Xavier was talking animatedly to someone else, someone Holly couldn't make out, and gesturing with one hand while the other held a martini and a cigarette. Holly had to grudgingly concede that the artist looked really, really good in a black button-down shirt tucked into black trousers, a red silk tie, and his paint-stained, scuffed-up boots.

Still on her giving-Xavier-a-second-chance kick, Holly elbowed Alexa and whispered, "He's over there." If anything, Holly thought, that would at least put an end to Alexa's fidgeting — she'd been giving herself whiplash every two seconds, clearly dying to find her loverboy.

Alexa's heart leaped as she followed Holly's gaze, and there, at long last, was the object of her affection. He was talking with a few of his friends that Alexa recognized from last night. But the friends — along with Holly, Ms. Moon Boots over there, and everyone else in the gallery — went blurry, and all Alexa saw was Xavier. His artfully messy auburn hair, his smoky-gray eyes, the mouth she had kissed so many times . . . Alexa felt a small explosion of joy and pride in her belly; this yummy guy was the reason all these people were here tonight. And he was all *hers*.

"Xavier!" she cried, waving to him across the gallery. He didn't seem to hear over the loud music and the din, so, without even a backward glance at Holly, Alexa began making her way toward him, her feet barely touching the cloudy floor.

Holly watched Alexa float off and rolled her eyes. *Fend for yourself* was right; she should have known that Alexa would ditch her the minute she spied Xavier. Toying with her chunky silver ring, Holly hovered alone in the middle of the chain-smoking, French-chattering mob, her stomach sinking lower by the second. Holly *sucked* at fending for herself, period, and the fact that she didn't speak the language — or know a soul — didn't make matters any easier. Despite her lingering unsettled feelings toward Pierre, Holly desperately wished that he — or Raphi — had been able to come along. But both St. Laurent siblings were tied up elsewhere for the night.

A waiter carrying a tray of the dark red martinis walked by and Holly — just to have something to do with her hands — grabbed a drink. But when she took a sip, the tangy-sour taste — pomegranates, she guessed — made her grimace. *Ugh.* Holly was wondering if she could discreetly find a place in which to pour out the icky concoction when, suddenly, her ears pricked up at the most beautiful sound she'd heard all evening: someone speaking English.

Holly spun around to find the source of this heavenly sound, and saw two young women positioned in front of one of the brightly colored paintings on the brick wall. "I don't know," one of them, who had straight brown hair and dainty tortoise-shell glasses, said to the other, who had curly red hair and wore slouchy rhinestone-studded boots over pencil-thin jeans. "It's not what I expected."

For the first time since entering the gallery, Holly took a good look at the artwork on the walls — *Xavier's* artwork, she reminded herself. All the paintings, she quickly noticed, were of the same, astonishingly beautiful girl, a girl with long, flowing black hair and big dark eyes. In some paintings, the girl's face was bisected into green rectangles, and in others, into purple squares. *And Alexa says he's a genius?* Holly thought dubiously, raising her eyebrows at the purple painting nearest her. She didn't remotely see the appeal, but then again, she wasn't remotely an art expert.

"It's juvenile," the redhead pronounced, scribbling something on her notepad. "Simplistic."

"And the geometric shapes are *so* last season," the tortoise-shell girl added with a sigh.

As the two women turned around to face Holly, she saw that they each wore a laminated badge pinned to their respective blouses. Both badges bore the women's names and the words THE NEW YORK TIMES. *They're art critics*, Holly realized as she watched the women saunter over to the next painting, still scribbling on their pads. *They're reviewing Xavier's show!*

And, from what Holly could tell, the review would be far from glowing.

Eager to tell Alexa what she'd overheard, Holly glanced across the gallery. She saw Alexa approach Xavier and his entourage, wearing an expression that was very bright and eager — and very not Alexa. Immediately, Holly felt a distinct tug in her gut that told her, unquestionably, that she should join her friend. Holly knew Alexa would vastly prefer *not* to have her there, but she couldn't shake off her nagging intuition. To steel herself, she took another sip of her drink — which made her grimace again — and began elbowing her way through the gallery.

Meanwhile, Alexa, her pulse tapping, was almost at Xavier's side, and when she spoke his name for the third time, he finally glanced her way. For an instant, he looked startled; his eyes narrowed and his brow furrowed. Then his face brightened and he held one arm out toward her in a "come-join-me" motion.

"Alexa!" he said warmly. "I didn't expect to see you here tonight."

Alexa bit her Bourjois-glossed bottom lip, wondering why Xavier wasn't swooning over her surprise appearance. Her first impulse was to fly over and wrap him in a hug — God, she wanted to feel his body against hers again — but Xavier made no move to come forward and kiss *her*, so Alexa hung back, standing between Etienne and Ms. Scarlet.

"I — I read about it in *Pariscope*," Alexa explained, flashing Xavier a sparkly smile.

The girl standing right next to Xavier, who had short dark hair and big dark eyes — and whom Alexa didn't recognize from the night before — made a sound that was somewhere between a titter and a snort. "*Pariscope*? You're kidding, right?" she asked, and her voice reminded Alexa of ice cubes clinking in a glass — light and melodic, but cold enough to sting.

Instantly, Alexa felt her cheeks color. *Um, dork much?* It wasn't at *all* like her to be so unsubtle. Not allowing herself to get too flustered, Alexa coolly met the gaze of the snarky girl, who was sizing her up at the same time.

It was one of those classic pretty-girl show-downs — *Which one of us is cuter?* — that Alexa usually won without breaking a sweat. But now there was no denying that her competitor was absolutely breathtaking. She must have been about nineteen or twenty; tall and slender, she was also far curvier than Alexa would ever be. She had luminous alabaster skin that didn't need a lick of makeup, enormous, onyx-colored eyes, and shimmering black hair that was cropped short and worn slicked back, almost like a boy's. But there was nothing boyish about her tight black bustier, low-slung camouflage Capris, and four-inch metallic silver sandals. A silky, silver scarf knotted at her throat, a tiny diamond stud in her nose, and an antique-looking diamond ring on one finger were her only accessories. She was so French it made Alexa's teeth hurt. Suddenly Alexa felt very pastel-y, very blonde, and very — God, no — *boring* in her paisley dress.

Clearly aware of her victory, Mademoiselle Va-Va-Voom glanced away, shrugging one shoulder, and Alexa crossed her arms over her chest, pissed. Who *was* this girl to dangle Alexandria St. Laurent over the pit of insecurity?

"Alexa, this is Monique," Xavier explained help-fully, putting one hand on the girl's bare shoulder. "My muse." He shot Monique a grin, and then lifted his martini glass toward one of the paintings on the walls. "The show is dedicated to her."

Slightly dizzy, Alexa shook her head, positive she'd heard wrong. Maybe, for some weird reason, she'd mis-understood Xavier's rapid-fire French? After all, the role of muse was already filled — by *her*. Alexa put one hand on her hip, ready to remind Xavier of that fact, but then Monique let out a short laugh, her silver-stemmed cigarette holder quivering between her crimson lips.

"Xavi, you silly boy," she purred, her pure black eyes fixed on Alexa. "Now it's your turn to tell me who *she* is. No, wait — let me guess. One of your little amusements?"

Alexa's fiery temper flared, and she narrowed her eyes at Monique, *so* ready to take this bitch on. "Get a clue," she snapped, her trembling fingers digging hard into the paisley clutch she held. "I'm Xavier's *girlfriend*." Alexa flung the word out there boldly, waiting for Monique to blink and back off.

Instead, Monique only gave a lazy smile, removing the cigarette holder from her mouth. Casually, she reached for the drink in Xavier's hand, with an easy intimacy that made Alexa's stomach turn cold. "Isn't

259

that sweet," Monique replied in a soft voice while Xavier remained silent and motionless at her side. "I'm his fiancée."

Alexa felt as if someone were punching her in slow motion, draining the wind out of her. *Fiancée*. A French word in English. *Such a funny word*, Alexa thought vaguely, as her knees wobbled and threatened to give out. It definitely wasn't one that came up in conversations with her friends back home. Why had Monique even said it?

But, as Alexa's eyes — slightly blurred from shock — drifted toward the bling-bling rock on Monique's ring finger, the word suddenly made sense. The horrible weight of understanding settled on Alexa's chest, and she lifted her eyes to study Xavier. He stared back at her, his eyebrows raised in a *who-little-old-me?* expression. There wasn't even a hint of shame or guilt in the face Alexa had so loved.

Desperate to look away, Alexa stumbled back a few steps, and glanced, for the first time all night, at the paintings displayed on the walls. Then, openmouthed, she dropped her paisley clutch.

Every single painting was of Monique.

Monique with long hair — Xavier must have painted them some time ago, Alexa realized with a fresh pang of pain — but Monique nonetheless. Her face seemed to be *everywhere*, freakishly multiplying, like clones in a bad science fiction movie. *She* is *his muse*, Alexa understood in one heartrending instant. Of course. And it had been Monique as well in that painting Alexa had seen in Xavier's studio.

Last night.

When he'd said — when she'd said — when they'd —

"No," Alexa whispered, turning back to Xavier. She wanted to lash out at him, to scream, but instead she felt weak and trembly, scarily close to breaking down. "I — I — don't understand," Alexa went on, using every last ounce of willpower to fight back her tears. She could feel the haughty gazes of Monique and Xavier's friends — judging her, testing her. "What about last night — and — everything? You — you *lied* to me." Alexa heard herself hiss these last words as she took a step closer to Xavier. Anger swirled in with her hurt, mixing like two colors of paint.

Xavier shrugged, his hand lightly rubbing Monique's shoulder. "Alexa, *calme-toi*," he murmured, his expression still maddeningly innocent. "I never lied about anything. I assumed you knew we were just . . . playing." Xavier chuckled, and he and Monique exchanged a brief, what-are-we-going-to-*do*-with her? eye roll. Alexa was filled the nauseating certainty that this exchange — hapless, lovesick girl facing off against a blasé Xavier-and-fiancée — was an all-too-common occurrence. "Come on, Alexa," Xavier sighed as he turned his indifferent gray gaze back to her. "Let's not make a big deal out of this — you're an adult, aren't you?"

Alexa had never fully understood the word "heartbreak" before, but now she felt it in her chest — a sharp, splintering pain, like an invisible hand was squeezing her rib cage. Suddenly she was remembering fragments that, in hindsight, made perfect sense: Xavier's mysterious phone calls, how he hadn't taken her back to his apartment, the knowing way his friends had smirked at her in the bar . . . She — street-smart, savvy, Paris-born Alexa St. Laurent — had been duped. Big-time. And now, in front of Xavier, Alexa didn't feel at all like a grown-up. She felt like a tourist. A naïve, bumbling tourist, who didn't speak the language and couldn't count the currency and got tricked into spending all her money on a shitty reproduction of a famous work of art.

Maybe Alexa didn't know all there was to know about Paris. *Or* boys.

"Come on, Alexa," Xavier repeated, only this time he had switched — appropriately — to English. His mouth curled up in a half smile as he let his hand drop from a yawning Monique. "Stop looking at me that way. I'm not the devil."

"That's true — you're not," a familiar voice spoke

firmly from behind Alexa, also in English. "You're just a raging asshole."

Alexa — along with Xavier's friends — gasped, and turned around to see who *dared* insult the great artist.

And there stood Holly, her face so white with rage Alexa could practically count her golden-brown freckles. Alexa had no idea how long Holly had been listening to the exchange — or, since it had been in French, how much she'd understood — but clearly she'd gotten the gist of it. Alexa's first impulse was to whisk her friend away and tell her to stop mortifying them both. Then she realized — with a flood of gratitude — that Holly was sticking up for her. With a close friend at her side, Alexa wasn't so defenseless anymore.

Plus, it was beyond empowering to hear polite Holly spit the word *asshole*.

"*What* did you call me?" Xavier asked Holly, looking far more amused than upset, while Monique narrowed her eyes at the new girl.

"An asshole," Holly repeated, amazed at how clear and strong her voice sounded. "I don't know the equivalent in French, but whatever it is, you're that, too."

Am I really speaking these words? Holly wondered. But she was filled with the courage of her convictions, and forgot to feel frightened. Instead, she felt almost heady with triumph. Maybe Holly *did* know more about boys than she gave herself credit for. She'd realized that as soon as she'd seen Xavier touch the girl at his side — the girl from the paintings — and smirk at Alexa. Holly hadn't needed a translator after that; she'd understood everything immediately. And Holly knew she couldn't stand by in silence while her friend's heart was publicly stomped on. Holly Jacobson was definitely *not* avoiding this confrontation.

Xavier seemed momentarily taken aback by Holly's retort, but he quickly recovered and shot her a charming smile. "I remember you," he said, his voice lilting. Taking the martini back from Monique, he finished off his drink and dropped the empty glass on a passing waiter's tray. "We met last night. You never answered my question about American girls, did you?"

Alexa, bowled over by Holly's gutsiness, turned back to her friend, wondering what her response would be. And what had Xavier even *asked* about American girls? Alexa felt her skin start to crawl. She'd never really known Xavier, had she? Alexa watched as Holly rocked her martini glass back and forth in her hand, clearly formulating her answer. But, just as she was opening her mouth to respond, Scarlet-Bob Girl suddenly spoke up beside Alexa.

"Wait — you're American?" she asked Alexa in French, clearly surprised.

"You didn't know?" Etienne cut in, rolling his eyes. "It even said so in the paper today."

Excuse me? Alexa thought, glancing from Holly to Etienne in bewilderment. The *newspaper* had announced her Americanness to the world? How was that possible? But, as Etienne reached into the back pocket of his low-slung jeans — French boys, Alexa randomly reflected in that moment, seemed to carry all their earthly possessions in the pockets of their Levi's — and pulled out a folded piece of newsprint, things began to click. In a really bad way.

"I brought this to show you, Xav," Etienne explained as he unfolded the scrap of paper and held it up for Xavier to see. "I know you hate the 'ratzies, but publicity is publicity."

Alexa felt her eyes widen in horror as she stared at the full-page, black-and-white photograph ... *of herself.* Herself, and Xavier, standing outside Café Mercerie. Xavier's head was half-down, and he was glowering at the camera, while Alexa had one hand on Xavier's arm and the other on her hip. Her face was stretched into a huge, eager smile, and Alexa shuddered at the sight; she looked like a shameless wannabe — D-list, at best. But worst of all, was the evil caption waiting beneath the train-wreck photo: XAVIER PASCAL OUT BAR-HOPPING WITH HIS FLAVOR OF THE WEEK,

AN ANONYMOUS AMERICAN TEENAGER. SEEMS HIS BLONDE STREAK IS CONTINUING! BUT IN THE END, HE ALWAYS COMES CRAWLING BACK TO HIS BELOVED BRUNETTE, MONIQUE.

Everyone — including Monique — broke into raucous laughter as Xavier tore the paper from Etienne's grasp. Only Alexa and Holly — the party crashers, the outsiders — stood still and silent.

"Is that from last night?" Holly whispered, nudging Alexa with her elbow. Holly felt a dash of excitement over seeing her friend's photo in the newspaper — even if the usually photogenic Alexa looked not-so-hot. But one glance at the Alexa standing beside her made Holly's stomach sink. Her friend's face was bright red, and her eyes were swimming. Holly didn't think she'd ever seen Alexa so upset — not even when she'd skinned both her knees learning how to bike-ride when she was nine, *or* lost her beaded choker necklace in the school cafeteria when she was eleven. Holly realized she needed to get Alexa away from Xavier as soon as possible.

Alexa swallowed, unable to respond. *An anonymous American teenager.* Alexa didn't know how *Le Soleil* had figured out that she was American, but it didn't matter. At this moment, that was *all* she longed to be — a nameless, faceless anygirl. Why had she *ever* wanted to be famous? Why couldn't she be back in New Jersey, happily roaming the bland Oakridge Galleria, instead of here, humiliated out of her mind in beautiful Paris? Alexa felt a sudden, surprising wave of homesickness, and knew then that she had to escape the gallery. Immediately. If she stayed a second longer, she'd break down in tears — the kind of tears that were impossible to hide. She might even need to wail.

And to think she'd been worried about *Holly* embarrassing her.

Thankfully, Holly seemed to be working the mental telepathy thing tonight. She put a hand on Alexa's elbow and gently pulled her away from the group, her other hand still holding the martini glass. "Let's blow this joint," Holly whispered, clearly trying to make Alexa smile, but Alexa felt like smiling was something beyond her — something she might never do again.

She allowed Holly to lead her away from Xavier, into the swarming crowd, but all the while Alexa was dying to turn around, to say one last thing to the artist who'd never really loved her. But what could she tell him? Alexa remembered whispering *au revoir* to Diego — who really *had* loved her — and felt the fracture in her heart deepen.

When she and Holly made it out of the gallery, onto the silent place des Vosges, Alexa finally let the dam burst. As the tears cascaded down her face, she reached instinctively for her clutch, and the tissue she'd stashed in there (to blot off excess lip gloss, of course) but her hands were empty.

"My — my bag," Alexa sobbed, glancing over her shoulder into the gallery. "I — left it — I dropped it —" *Next to Xavier*. She couldn't speak his name.

"I'll get it," Holly said briskly, giving Alexa's arm a quick squeeze and handing her friend *her* mint-green bag. She'd been secretly hoping for a reason to return to the gallery, even if it meant leaving a wounded Alexa alone momentarily. "Wait right here — I promise I'll be back in, like, five seconds."

Or however long it took to bring down Xavier Pascal.

Storming back into the gallery, Holly made her way over to the pretentious little posse, who were still huddled around the newspaper clipping. Holly quickly retrieved Alexa's clutch from the floor, straightened up, and immediately locked eyes with Xavier. Holly may have had trouble sticking up for herself when *she'd* been hurt. But if somebody made her *friend* cry — look the hell out.

"Hey, Xavier," Holly said through gritted teeth, gripping her martini glass in her fist. Her heart was beating a staccato rhythm, but she forged ahead, her boldness growing. "I really hate to interrupt your fifteen minutes of fame, but if you want to know all

268

about American girls, I suggest you ask *them*." Fiercely, Holly gestured with her martini glass to the two women from *The New York Times* who were standing several feet away, shaking their heads in disdain over another painting.

"Who are *they*?" Xavier scoffed, glancing in the journalists' direction, but Holly thought she saw his face turn pale.

"Your future," Holly replied, her cheeks flushing as the words miraculously came to her. It was true, she realized — maybe Xavier was on his way out. "They're big-time art critics from New York, Xavier, and guess what?" she continued breathlessly. "They think your show *sucks*."

Xavier and Monique exchanged a glance, but this time, Holly saw, there was clearly a sense of wariness passing between the power couple.

"You don't know what you're talking about," Monique snapped in accented English, looking icily back at Holly.

"Hmm, 'simplistic'?" Holly quoted, tilting her head to one side. "'Juvenile'? 'So last season'?" She shrugged at a startled-looking Xavier. "Fine — don't believe me. Just wait for the review tomorrow morning." Holly *didn't* quite know what she was talking about, but she felt that discussing art was kind of like crashing a party — you just had to bluff your way through it.

Trembling only a little, she tucked Alexa's bag under her arm and turned to go. But Xavier's hand on the small of her back — *inappropriate much?* — stopped her.

"Just because your little friend found out the truth —" Xavier began viciously, but he never got the sentence out because — before she could think too clearly — Holly had flung the rest of her pomegranate martini straight into his face.

She *had* been wanting to get rid of the drink somehow.

Holly watched, half-stunned, as the rosy liquid dropped down Xavier's chin and onto his matching red tie. Xavier blinked madly, obviously too astonished to get angry. Holly heard Monique shriek and several other bystanders murmur in confusion as someone shut off the music. Clearly, now was the time to flee.

"She can do so much better than you," Holly murmured, not caring if Xavier heard her or not. She backed up, bumping into various people, and then turned and made straight for the exit. By the time she got outside, Holly was grinning, her heart swelling with pride at the memory of Xavier's befuddled expression. She *had* to tell Alexa.

Who wasn't there anymore.

Holly glanced frantically up and down the long arcade, feeling a stirring of panic; the place des Vosges was deserted at this hour. "Alexa!" Holly cried, her voice echoing against the stone arches. But there was no trace of her friend — not even the sound of weeping. Holly bit her lip; had tempestuous Alexa dashed off to do something rash, like set fire to Xavier's studio or jump into the Seine? Drawing a deep breath, Holly started off down the empty street. Paris was *huge*, and Alexa could have gone anywhere. Holly could only hope that she'd be able to find her.

CHAPTER FOURTEEN
Best Bets

"Don't you dare say *I told you so*," Alexa sobbed as soon as Holly found her. She was sitting on the edge of a fountain several streets down from the gallery, her shoes kicked off and her head down. Her shoulders shook from weeping, and she barely glanced up.

"I wasn't going to," Holly protested softly, immensely relieved at the sight of her friend. "I just wanted to make sure you were okay." She, too, slipped off her flats — it seemed appropriate somehow — set down Alexa's clutch, and joined her friend on the cool marble rim. Behind them, carved nymphs emptied their jugs onto a sleeping Cupid. The tinkling sound of the water was calming.

"Do I *look* okay?" Alexa asked rhetorically, staring at her feet. She wasn't bothering to wipe her tears as they fell; her face felt like she'd dunked it in the fountain. Alexa remembered the last time she'd sobbed on the streets of Paris: the infamous night of the Diego breakup and luggage-snatching. Tonight felt eerily similar, but much, much worse. Back then, Alexa had feared that her true love wasn't being faithful; now, she *knew*. Back then, she'd had her possessions torn from her; now, her dignity.

"Well, considering the circumstances, you could look worse," Holly began, but hesitated as Alexa continued to sob. Clearly, her attempt at humor wasn't going to work. And what she'd said wasn't even true; Alexa, for possibly the first time *ever*, looked crappy — her face was puffy, squiggly lines of mascara decorated her cheeks, and her careful chignon was coming undone.

Frowning with concern, Holly slid closer to Alexa on the bench and put a comforting arm across her friend's shoulder. But the gesture only seemed to make Alexa cry harder.

"He — he said he loved me," Alexa hiccuped, her words coming out in small gasps, her face crumpling with hurt. "He — called me — his muse — I thought I could tell — I *know* about guys —" She swallowed hard, her body shuddering with sobs as Holly watched her worriedly. "I was — so sure —" she choked out, before burying her face in her hands.

The girls sat together, Holly's arm around Alexa, the nighttime silence punctured by Alexa's quiet weeping. The fountain whispered behind them while the lights of the place des Vosges glimmered up ahead. The air blew chilly and brisk off the river, but both girls were too preoccupied to notice the cold.

"I'm so sorry," Holly finally spoke, her voice soft. Alexa still had her face in her hands, but at least she seemed to have stopped sobbing. Something she had said earlier resonated with Holly. *I know about guys.* And that was the whole problem, Holly suddenly understood. Alexa *thought* she knew about guys — *everything* about guys — but tonight, she'd been proven wrong.

Holly mentally reviewed Alexa's extensive history with boys — starting with Eliot Johnson in junior high and ending with Diego Mendieta — and realized that Alexa had never officially had her heart broken. Yes, things had clearly been painful with Diego, but Holly knew that Alexa had been the one to initiate the break-up — she was always the dump*er*, never the dump*ee*.

Until now.

"I just wish . . ." Alexa lifted her tear-streaked face, running one arm under her nose. "I wish I hadn't fallen in love with him," she whispered miserably, her voice raw from crying. Why did she always have to fall in love so easily, so deeply, Alexa wondered with a sigh. Her head felt heavy, so she rested it on Holly's shoulder, closing her eyes.

Holly briefly leaned her own head against Alexa's and let out a sympathetic sigh. She thought back to some of her own boy agonies — Diego last year, Tyler last week — and realized that she, unlike Alexa, *had* had experience with heartbreak. Enough experience, at least, to help steer an adrift Alexa back to sanity.

"No matter how bad it hurts right now," Holly began thoughtfully. "After a while — I don't know how long, I think it's different for everyone — you'll get past it. I promise." She reached down and took Alexa's hand in hers. "Actually, I think you're gonna be *relieved* that jerk is out of your life."

Alexa sniffled. "I guess he *is* kind of a jerk," she conceded, even though it pained her to admit it. In a twisted, masochistic way, she still felt like she loved Xavier. "But when you went back inside the gallery," Alexa added, feeling a pang of false hope, "did he seem to care that I'd left?" Alexa got that Xavier had a fiancée, but maybe, just *maybe*, his feelings for Alexa transcended that fact.

"No," Holly replied, and oddly enough, Alexa thought she heard a smile in her friend's voice. "He got a little distracted by the martini running down his face."

Alexa lifted her head off Holly's shoulder. "What

275

do you mean?" she asked Holly, who was biting her lip and raising her eyebrows, managing to look sheepish and proud at the same time. Alexa felt a burst of surprise that lightened her sorrow. Alexa had always suspected that Holly could get seriously badass when provoked, but she felt floored by her friend tonight. "You — you *didn't*," Alexa whispered, a ghost of a smile on her lips.

Holly nodded, now grinning fully. "What can I say? I'm an athlete. I've got good aim."

"Oh, *Holly*!" Alexa cried, and unexpected laughter rose in her throat. Apparently, Xavier hadn't known whom he was messing with. Picturing the flummoxed *artiste*, Alexa started to giggle, and soon Holly was cracking up as well. The two of them laughed together, clutching their bellies as they doubled over, almost falling off the fountain's rim. When Alexa saw a passing couple glance their way, she knew what she and Holly must have looked like — two trashed girls having a silly night out.

If only.

As their laughter died down, Alexa swiped at her wet cheeks, feeling about fifty percent better. "You know, you never cease to amaze me," she said nudging Holly in the side. Holly modestly rolled her eyes, her freckled cheeks turning predictably pink. "I mean it," Alexa insisted, thinking about how often she underestimated Holly. "You're a lot stronger than I am sometimes." Alexa felt herself tear up again. She'd always considered herself thick-skinned, but now she realized she was more vulnerable to getting hurt than she'd ever thought.

Holly laughed, quietly this time. "Oh, come on, Alexa," she said. "I think we've both accepted the fact that I'm a humongous wuss." But, even as she spoke, Holly was remembering how pumped she'd felt during the showdown in the gallery. She remembered swallowing the scary French food at the St. Laurents' dinner. She remembered walking across Waterloo Station to board that train. For a self-proclaimed wuss, Holly had done some gutsy stuff of late. But Holly knew that she wouldn't — *couldn't* — have done any of it without Alexa backing her up. It was Alexa who made her fearless.

"Well, you're smarter than I am, in any case," Alexa sighed, leaning back on her hands and stretching her long legs out in front of her. "Smarter about reading people." Turning to Holly, she gave her friend a long, serious look. "Hol, I feel so bad about last night — how I freaked when you tried to warn me about Xavier." Alexa shook her head at how insanely defensive she'd gotten — and how insanely on-target Holly had been.

Alexa rarely — if ever — liked to apologize, but at this moment, it felt *more* than necessary. "I should have listened,"Alexa finished simply, giving Holly a shrug.

I told you so, Holly thought with a small smile, but of course, she didn't utter those words. "You were too in love to listen," she replied understandingly. "But you *were* kind of a pain about it," she couldn't help but add, as Alexa nodded soberly. Holly realized that being so up-front with Alexa felt natural — healthy. Not every confrontation had to turn into a fight. Holly knew then that the girls' friendship was strong enough to bear the brunt of honesty. "Like, when you brought up the whole Tyler thing," Holly continued, feeling her face grow warm.

"I shouldn't have said that," Alexa told Holly regretfully. But remembering Holly's cryptic remark from last night she couldn't help but add, "Though *will* you finally tell me what's going on between you guys?"

Holly drew a deep breath, prepping herself for the big confession. Alexa had her on the spot, but this time — after everything they'd been through tonight — Holly finally felt ready to tell her friend the whole truth. So, she did just that, recounting everything from the car-tastrophe to the phone avoidance to her see-sawing between Tyler and Pierre. "And I'm sorry I kept all this from you," Holly concluded with a sigh. "It's not that I didn't trust you, Alexa, it's just that you were – *part* of the problem, so . . ." She trailed off, shrugging.

"Let me get this straight," Alexa began. She wriggled closer to Holly on the fountain's edge, momentarily forgetting her own troubles in favor of her friend's juicy story. "You think Tyler's not attracted to you?" she prompted, and Holly nodded, her cheeks dark pink in the moonlight. "And you think he was *more* into *me*?" Alexa asked. When Holly nodded again, Alexa grinned and shook her head.

"What?" Holly asked warily, hugging herself as the river breeze washed over her. Was Alexa making fun of her?

"Holly Rebecca Jacobson," Alexa pronounced dramatically, crossing her legs at the ankle. "Let's consider Tyler Davis, shall we?" Alexa paused for effect, while Holly watched her wide-eyed. "He's, like, the *definition* of old-fashioned polite," Alexa continued, remembering Tyler's opening-doors-and-pulling-out-chairs personality with a mix of fondness and irritation. "Especially when it comes to sex," she added wisely. "He never wants to be that kind of guy that pressures girls, so he holds back, you know?" Holly nodded emphatically, looking aggravated, and Alexa smiled. "But he's really into making sure the girl is completely comfortable first — which *is* pretty cool," Alexa mused aloud, wondering if she sometimes sold nice guys short.

"The thing is," Holly replied in frustration, eager to finally get her host of issues off her chest, "when we were in the car the other night, he *knew* he wasn't pressuring me, so why —"

"It would have been your first time together, right?" Alexa cut in, and waited until Holly gave a short, shy nod. "*That's* why, Hol," Alexa went on softly. "Tyler's all about the location, the setup. Everything has to be . . . just so. God, once he blew me off just because my dad happened to be downstairs." Alexa rolled her eyes at the memory; incidentally — or not — that had been the same day she'd broken up with Tyler. "So come on — his car? On the way to *Newark*?" Alexa shook her head, and Holly smiled in acknowledgment. "That's so not his style."

"But was he really the same way with you?" Holly asked Alexa, still dubious. She dropped her arms and rested her hands in her lap. "I mean, you guys *did*, you know, do it, after all. . . ." Holly's cheeks burned; it felt kind of bizarre — but also surprisingly normal — to be discussing this super-private stuff with Alexa.

"Well, only because I initiated it," Alexa admitted, after a moment's hesitation, recalling the cute/

awkward New Year's Eve at her house. "He thought we were rushing into sex too soon — even though we'd been together four whole months!" Alexa shook her head in amazement. "But maybe he was right — it was after we slept together that things started to go downhill for us."

Holly blew her bangs up off her forehead, deep in thought; four months *was* kind of short — at least, by her standards. Then, suddenly, Tyler's words from the night in the car echoed in her head: *I guess I sort of feel like we're . . . rushing*, he'd said. *I've made that mistake before.* Holly's heart leaped. So he *had* been talking about Alexa — to explain why their relationship had turned sour. But Holly's insecurities had kicked in right away, blinding her to all that. She couldn't believe she'd been so dense.

"Maybe . . ." Holly mused aloud, leaning back on her hands and looking up at the expanse of stars overhead. There was a lightening in her chest that felt very close to relief. "Maybe because *we've* been together longer, he feels like the stakes are . . . higher?" She thought of how she'd felt on the riverbank with Pierre — how wrong the moment had seemed. With Tyler, she realized, she'd want the moment to be even *more* right. And Tyler must have felt the same way. Of course.

"Oh, totally," Alexa affirmed, nodding at her friend. "He doesn't want your first time to be anything but perfect — because he knows you're worth it." Alexa grinned as she pictured Tyler running around Oakridge, buying roses, strawberries, and candles for his big night with Holly. "He loves you, Hol," she said matter-of-factly. "Anyone can see that."

Holly bit her bottom lip and studied Alexa's face. "You think so?" she asked, her voice shaky.

Alexa nodded, a lump forming in her throat. "Tyler and I weren't ever *really* in love," she whispered, trying her darndest not to make the mental leap to Xavier. "But, just from watching you guys in the cafeteria or wherever, I can tell what you have is so much deeper. More meaningful."

Holly's own throat closed with emotion as she thought of her sweet, considerate boyfriend, and felt a swell of unfettered affection for him. *I* do *take love seriously*, Holly realized, thinking back to her conversation with Pierre the night before. *But so does Tyler — and that's just why I love him.* How had there been any confusion? She'd loved Tyler all along, even when she'd been distracted by Pierre. But it had also taken Pierre to help Holly understand the depth of her feelings for Tyler.

"What about now?" Holly asked Alexa anxiously. "After what happened with Pierre, and not speaking for a week . . ." She shrugged, biting her lip. "Will things still be the same when I get back?"

"I'd bet on it," Alexa said confidently, and reached over to squeeze Holly's arm. Alexa realized how much she was enjoying this role of advice-giver; it let her take a break from herself for a while. "I'd bet my — I don't know — my new pumps," Alexa declared, pointing to the covet-worthy apricot shoes, and Holly giggled. "You guys just need to *talk*," she added, and rose to her feet, stretching her arms over her head. "And besides, it's not like Tyler knows anything about what happened with Pierre, right?"

And he probably doesn't need to know, Holly thought with a sigh. She got to her feet, too, assuming Alexa was ready to go back to the apartment — she was definitely feeling the cold now, especially by the fountain. But to Holly's surprise, her impulsive friend turned to face the fountain, hopped up on the rim, and stepped right in.

Holly watched, half-amused, half-worried, as Alexa, hiking up the short skirt of her paisley dress, began tiptoeing through the ankle-high murky water. "Are you okay?" Holly asked, taking a step closer. "Is this about Xavier?" Alexa seemed calmer, but maybe her unexpected fountain-visit was some sort of troubling response to the trauma.

Alexa — who had stepped in for no other reason

than, in that moment, wanting to — turned around, the cold water covering her feet, her soles flat against the slick marble bottom. She felt like the blonde girl who waded through the fountain in *La Dolce Vita*, a stylish 1960s Italian movie Alexa's dad was obsessed with. She felt airy and free and, for the time being, not focused on her heartache. She knew the pain would return later that night, or tomorrow, but she'd worry about it then.

"I'm fine," she promised Holly, smiling at her friend's concerned expression. It was so like Holly to always look out for her, even when they'd just been discussing *Holly's* problems. Alexa realized their whole trip had been about that: Holly selflessly putting aside her own issues — boy- or sports-related or otherwise — to help Alexa with hers. Alexa choked up; she couldn't think of a single other friend who would have done that for her. Definitely not Portia and Maeve, her supposed bests.

Alexa's eyes welled with fresh tears as she studied her generous friend, who was still motioning for her to get out of the fountain. "Hey, Hol?" Alexa said softly, remaining where she was.

"Yeah?" Holly asked, taking a step closer to the fountain, putting her hands out for Alexa to take.

"I know we aren't as close as we used to be, back in the day, but . . ." Alexa swallowed her tears and put her hands in Holly's. "You know you're my best friend, don't you?" In that moment, Alexa understood both the full weight of those words, *and* how true they were. Holly *was* the best — the best friend Alexa could have had at her side throughout her various crises. The best friend to make Alexa laugh after having her heart broken. And the *only* friend with whom Alexa would have wanted to spend her last spring break of high school. Right then, Alexa could think of no other way to express her immense gratitude than telling Holly that plain, simple truth.

"I am?" Holly asked, holding on to Alexa's hands. Hearing the once-familiar title filled Holly with a warm glow, but she also was a little wary. *Been there, done that*, Holly wanted to say, remembering how close the girls had been in grade school — and how much it had hurt when Alexa had decided to ditch her in junior high. "But, Alexa," Holly argued pragmatically. "We hardly even spend time together back home — and our other friends —"

"I know," Alexa sighed in disappointment. "But we can change that — like, we *should* sit together at lunch if we want to." That wouldn't be too hard, Alexa thought, considering she no longer planned to sit with Portia and Maeve every day, anyway. "And I promise to be better about calling you to make plans on the weekends," Alexa swore, once again feeling a small — and utterly random — stab of pleasure at the thought of returning to Oakridge. "Besides," she added, as she finally stepped up on the rim of the fountain, letting Holly help her down onto the pavement, "I think there's more to our friendship than how often we hang out, don't you?"

Holly nodded, knowing how right Alexa was. She and Alexa *did* have a rare bond — one that ran far deeper than how much time they spent together at the mall. And though Holly didn't doubt she'd maintain her closeness with Meghan and Jess (providing the girls were still speaking to her after the stress she'd put them through this week), it was comforting to know she could turn to Alexa whenever she needed to discuss serious boy matters.

Leaving wet footprints on the pavement, Alexa retrieved her bag and shoes, and Holly followed suit, both girls laughing quietly over Alexa's fountain escapade. As Holly was straightening the heel of her crushed velvet flat, she caught sight of the time on her silver wristwatch — it was after midnight. "I should go to bed soon," she told Alexa. "I can't oversleep *again*."

"So it's England tomorrow?" Alexa asked as the two girls circled around the fountain and began wending their way home through the silent, moonlit streets. "For *real* now?"

"I have no choice," Holly replied as they crossed the rue St-Gilles. "The whole team flies back together on Sunday morning." Holly knew she could no longer hide from Wimbledon. Whatever fate awaited her there, she simply had to face it. And, more important, Holly finally felt like she *could* return to England: She even wondered if she'd been destined to miss her train that morning, just for the purpose of being at Alexa's side in the gallery. After the encounter with Xavier — and seeing Alexa much more subdued now — Holly could safely know that she'd come to Paris for a valid reason. Her work here was done.

"I just hope Ms. Graham isn't too harsh when she explains to my parents that I've been expelled," Holly added blithely, linking her arm through Alexa's as they walked.

Alexa laughed, bumping Holly's hip with hers. "Listen, don't worry — I bet it's actually going to work out okay."

"You'd bet your shoes again?" Holly teased. "Or maybe one of your bags from Frou-Frou?" she offered, gesturing to Alexa's paisley clutch. "St. Laurent, watch out — I'm going to end up with your whole wardrobe."

"Well, I definitely owe you *something*, for, oh, I don't know, asking you to jeopardize your entire future for me," Alexa replied as the girls arrived at the rue de Sévigné. They walked toward the familiar shut-tered house, and Alexa took out her key.

"You don't owe me anything," Holly assured Alexa as her friend unlocked the door. She leaned over and kissed Alexa on one cheek, non-Parisian style. "If it wasn't for you, I'd never have come to Paris. And I'd never have had the best week of my life." Right then — drunk off the emotional night — Holly did feel like her time in this incredible city would more than make up for any punishment she'd have to endure.

But she'd probably feel a *little* different tomorrow.

∩ew Jerrey Kirr

I bet it's actually going to work out okay.

Alexa's words rang in Holly's head, mocking her, as Holly climbed the steps of the Wimbledon hostel. Waking up before dawn in Paris, Holly had felt fairly calm, but during her Chunnel ride back to England, the first tendrils of dread began to take root. Now, as she unlocked the door to the room she shared with Meghan and Jess, Holly's pulse skyrocketed. She was sure she'd walk in to find her friends tearing their hair out, rending their clothes, and wailing in agony.

But stepping into the quiet room, Holly found both girls fast asleep. Jess was sprawled across her top bunk, one arm hanging off the edge, while Meghan lay curled up on the bottom bunk, snoring softly. Holly felt a momentary flash of relief — maybe this was a good sign. As she shakily set her duffel on the single bed next to the bunk, Holly realized that it was only nine o'clock, and that today, Saturday, was supposed to be another free day for the team — since it would be their last in Wimbledon. So it made sense that Meghan and Jess were still in bed — though maybe the girls were sleeping off the effects of their hysterical sobbing from the night before.

Holly considered waking her friends, but then decided that she'd rather postpone hearing the bad news. First, she'd treat herself to a hot shower; she felt achy and grimy after the long train ride. Still, she figured she should let her friends know that she'd returned safely, in case they woke up and saw her bag. From her duffel, Holly pulled out a pen and the spiral-bound notepad her parents had given her before the trip — "You never know when you'll need to write information down!" her mom had clucked — and scrawled Meghan and Jess a note that she was back and in one piece and fully understood if they never wanted to speak to her again.

Holly had had some practice writing notes that morning; before leaving Paris, she'd penned three separate ones for the sleeping St. Laurent cousins: A *love-you-see-you-in-Oakridge* note for Alexa; a *thanks-for-the-hospitality-and-handbag* message for Raphi, and, working up her nerve, a heartfelt *I'll-never-forget-*

you note for Pierre, which included Holly's e-mail address. Regardless of what happened with Tyler, Holly did hope she and Pierre would stay in touch as friends.

Towel, flip-flops, and Herbal Essences shower gel in hand, Holly crept out of the room and headed for the hall bathroom. She was pushing open the door when a familiar voice behind her chilled Holly to the bone.

"Holly Jacobson."

Her heart lodged in her throat, Holly turned around as slowly as possible. Coach Graham stood in the door frame of her room, wearing long-sleeved gray cotton pajamas printed with small sheep. Even though Holly's parents were teachers, she always found it freaky to see any adult authority figure looking like, well, a normal person. And since Coach Graham had been particularly authoritative on this trip, seeing her in PJs was *doubly* weird — and, somehow, also made her a little less scary.

But only a little.

Holly tried to speak — *Ms. Graham, please let me explain!* — but her tongue was glued to the roof of her mouth. Frozen in terror, Holly watched as Ms. Graham advanced toward her, one arm extended menacingly. Holly gulped, her knees buckling; was her coach actually going to *hit* her? Wasn't that illegal or something?

Instead of smacking Holly, though, Coach Graham rested one hand on Holly's shoulder and stared right into her eyes.

"Holly," Coach Graham said quietly, her voice full of concern. "Tell me. How *are* you?"

Huh?

"What — I'm — um — I'm all right, I guess," Holly stammered, even though *all right* was the opposite of how she was feeling. What did Coach Graham *expect* her to say? *Well, I'm about to have my life ruined, but other than that, I'm cool?*

"Your ankle's better?" Coach Graham went on, gesturing down to Holly's left foot. "It must have healed more or less by now."

"Uh — yeah, it's actually fine," Holly said, automatically rotating her ankle and realizing that Paris must have been good for it — there was not a hint of pain now. But why was Coach Graham even bothering to ask about her ankle when she was so furious at her?

Coach Graham nodded, and a look of — was it *relief?* — passed over her face. "It's good to see you up and about," she replied, giving Holly's shoulder a quick squeeze while Holly gazed back at her, thoroughly bewildered. "Though you are a little pale," Coach Graham added, frowning. "Is your stomach still bothering you?"

My stomach? Holly thought, shaking her head. *What is she talking abou —*

And then Holly got it.

In wild disbelief, she remembered what Meghan had said to her over the phone: *So now Coach Graham thinks you've got food poisoning, chronic headaches . . .*

No.

It couldn't be.

"It — well, um, it still kind of hurts," Holly managed to squeak out, putting a hand to her belly. None of this was making *any* sense, but Holly thought it best to attempt to play along for now.

Coach Graham nodded sympathetically. "But I hope at least your migraines are gone by now? Those were probably a side effect of the stomach problems."

This is a trap, Holly realized, her mouth going dry. Coach Graham wanted Holly to fess up to her ludicious collection of illnesses, and *then* she'd have her cornered. Holly knew there was *no* conceivable way that four whole Holly-free days — including Friday's big final meet — could have passed without Coach Graham figuring out the truth. After all, Holly didn't see why her coach couldn't have done something as simple as barge into the girls' room to see for herself if Holly was really an invalid.

"I felt your pain, by the way," Coach Graham was

saying, now clutching her own stomach. "Just like you — bad shepherd's pie. I had two portions at some London pub on Wednesday and was flat on my back — or over the toilet — for the rest of the week." Coach Graham shuddered. "I'm only just starting to feel better today."

Holly blinked, trying to wrap her mind around this startling development. Coach Graham had been . . . *sick*? For the first time since they'd started talking, Holly noticed that her coach did look sort of haggard; her face was drawn, her curly ash-blonde bob was matted, and there were shadowy circles under her eyes. With a burst of wonder, Holly realized that if Coach Graham had been out of commission for most of the week, she *wouldn't* have been able to check up on Holly.

"God, I'm — um, really sorry," Holly replied, a great wave of hope cresting in her. She'd never imagined she could feel so happy about someone's food poisoning. "That must have been awful. I mean — um — I know exactly what you went through," she added hastily, her cheeks warming up. "I'm surprised I didn't run into you in the bathroom." *Easy there,* Holly told herself. *Maybe that's pushing it.*

Coach Graham rolled her eyes. "Can you believe it? The coach and the captain both sick at the same time? I had to ask Coach Saunders from the Canadian team to cover for me during the meets, and Meghan and Jess became acting captains."

Holly felt a wash of pride and gratitude toward her friends, who, she was sure, had stepped up to the task nicely. They'd obviously carried off their *other* task — of covering for her — just brilliantly. How could Holly have ever doubted them? Between Alexa's insight into Tyler last night, and Meghan and Jess standing strong for her this whole week, Holly vowed never to second-guess her friends again.

"My biggest regret was missing Friday's final meet," Coach Graham was musing, and Holly snapped back to attention.

"Wait — did we win?" she asked, realizing in the next second that if she *had* been at Wimbledon this whole time — even bedridden — she should have known the answer. *Oops.*

But to Holly's boundless relief, Coach Graham was looking at her with sober understanding. "I see," she said softly. "Meghan and Jess didn't have the heart to tell you, did they?"

Holly bit her lip. "The German team?" she guessed.

Coach Graham shook her head. "Apparently the Bulgarian girls came out of nowhere at the last minute and swept the whole show." She let out a heavy sigh. "We came in tenth."

Holly hung her head, consumed by guilt, and she

felt Coach Graham reach out and pat her shoulder again. "There, there," Coach Graham said. "I know it's a lot to take on top of everything else you've been going through"— she lowered her voice —"with your family and all."

Right. Meghan and Jess's fallback excuse. Holly glanced up at her coach, wishing that she were a better actress — or at least as naturally dramatic as Alexa. Channeling her friend across the Channel, Holly opened her eyes as wide as they would go and whispered, "It's been really rough." Holly didn't feel like she was completely lying; after all, she *had* had issues with someone from home. Remembering Tyler — to whom she now hadn't spoken for a full week — Holly didn't have to fake the sadness that crossed her face.

"I understand," Coach Graham assured her. "Problems from home can really interfere while you're away. It's probably not appropriate for me to tell you this"— Holly immediately perked up at these words — "but my husband and I had an argument right before I left and I've been . . ." She shrugged at Holly, looking embarrassed. "Pretty torn up about it ever since."

Surprise Number Three Hundred and Twenty. Holly felt a tingling of sudden understanding; maybe *that* was why the coach had been so irritable on this trip — *and* why she may have been too distracted to think too deeply about Meghan and Jess's multiple excuses. Holly remembered how, on the plane to London, she'd assumed that Coach Graham didn't know jack about relationships, and felt instantly humbled; apparently, she and Alexa didn't have the monopoly on romantic crises. She pictured Coach Graham sitting at a café with her and Alexa, complaining to the girls about her lame husband. Holly almost giggled out loud at the unlikely image, until she remembered she was supposed to be torn up, too. She straightened her face and returned Coach Graham's gaze.

"I guess we had sort of parallel weeks," Holly told her coach, surprised at how easy it felt to talk to her like this. The sheep pajamas definitely helped. But, a little unsteady from her unforeseen victory, Holly decided to quit while she was ahead. After urging her coach to get better soon, Holly was turning back toward the bathroom, when Ms. Graham spoke up again.

"Holly? One thing," she said.

Holly glanced over her shoulder, wary once more. "Yes?" she whispered.

"Because you did miss most of the competition this week," Coach Graham began, crossing her arms over her chest and returning to teacher mode, "I'm afraid I'm going to have to bench you for another couple of weeks." She sighed, shaking her head. "I hate to penalize team members for illnesses or problems beyond their control, but I don't want to set a precedent for the others so they think they can skip meets, too."

"Oh," Holly mumbled, her heart sinking. *Reality check!* She should have known she wouldn't get off one-hundred-percent free. And not being able to run once she was back in Oakridge was going to suck. But considering what her punishment *could* have been, that seemed a minor price to pay.

As Coach Graham waved and returned to her room, Holly finally surrendered to the excitement that had been building inside her. Alexa had been right! Only this was better than just *okay* — this was miraculous! All of her anxieties in Paris had been for naught. While Holly had savored every moment of her secret trip, she surely would have had an even *better* time had she not obsessed over Wimbledon so much. Maybe that was the thing about doing something that risky, Holly thought as she headed into the bathroom. You just had to go for it, helter-skelter, banishing worry or fear.

Still, Holly mused as she started for the shower, even though she *had* pulled off her vanishing act, she felt horrible about abandoning her team in their time of need. And she knew enough not to push her luck; fate might not be so friendly to her in the future. She definitely didn't plan on repeating a stunt like this anytime soon.

The next morning, at seven o'clock, New Jersey time, Coach Graham led the jet-lagged girls' track team through the Virgin Atlantic arrivals gate at Newark Airport. As the team started up the escalator to baggage claim, Holly lingered behind, holding her duffel in both hands and taking in the wonderfully familiar sights: the crowded Starbucks kiosk to her left, the Pizza Hut to her right, the empty Krispy Kreme bag crumpled on the floor. The very air — stale coffee and lemony cleaning solution — smelled comforting, like home.

"Holly? Are you coming?" Meghan asked, grinning over her shoulder as she and Jess rose up on the escalator. "You don't want to go somewhere *else,* do you?" she added, lowering her voice. The rest of the team had — also miraculously — remained unaware of Holly's breakout, thanks to the combined efforts of Meghan and Jess.

"No," Holly replied, laughing. "Not for a while, anyway." She hurried to rejoin her friends, still enormously grateful that they weren't mad at her. Meghan and Jess had both been so relieved that the scheme had come off without a hitch that neither of them bothered to harbor any ill will.

The team gathered around the circular baggage carousel, but since Holly and a few other girls only had carry-ons, Coach Graham urged them to go ahead and meet their families in the waiting area. Holly hugged Meghan and Jess fiercely, said good-bye to the rest of the team and Coach Graham — who was beaming as she chatted with her husband on her cell phone — and practically sprinted out of baggage claim and into the huge waiting area.

Squinting into the sea of faces, Holly searched for her mom's square red-framed glasses and her dad's dark bushy eyebrows. She'd called her parents from England last night, apologizing for being out of touch for a few days (without, of course, the slightest mention of Paris). Her parents had promised to be at Newark the next morning to pick her up, but now they were nowhere to be found. Holly felt a prickle of worry and was reaching into the pocket of her Kangol hoodie for her cell when she finally spotted a familiar face in the crowd.

Wavy, dark-blond hair, amber-brown eyes, chiseled features. *Wow,* Holly thought as she gazed at him. *I'd forgotten how beautiful he is.* He was scanning the crowd, his brow furrowed, a bouquet of yellow roses in one hand. Holly felt herself swell up with joy — and surprise. He must have arranged all this with her parents. In spite of everything, he had come to meet her.

"Tyler!" she called, her heart bursting. He looked her way, his face lighting up in a huge smile, and he lifted the bouquet in greeting. Holly could feel it then — across the crowded airport, almost like a piece of rope that connected them — the strength of what she and Tyler had.

Grinning uncontrollably, Holly broke into a mad dash and Tyler, not a shabby runner himself, also raced toward her. Before Holly knew it, they were together, Tyler taking her duffel from her, handing her the gorgeous bouquet, and wrapping one arm around her waist. Holly drew close to her boyfriend, inhaling his clean, soapy scent as it mingled with the heady perfume of the roses. But she and Tyler didn't kiss — yet.

Tyler set down her duffel at his side, and then straightened up, his face etched with concern. "Holly," he murmured, gazing down at her. "I'm so glad you're finally back. This week was — um — was really hard."

"Tell me about it." Holly sighed, admiring her boyfriend's golden-flecked eyes, and realizing how much she'd missed all the small details about him. "Tyler?" she added quietly, and he nodded at her attentively. "I'm sorry I never called," Holly went on, choking up a little. "If you knew how many times I thought of you —"

"Me, too," Tyler murmured, reaching up to tenderly cup Holly's face in both his hands. "I did call you once, but I didn't have the nerve to leave a message. I felt like there was all this stuff I needed to tell you in person. . . ."

"But not now," Holly whispered, touching one finger to Tyler's upper lip. "We'll talk about everything later. We have so much time." *And we do*, Holly thought. There really *was* no rush for her and Tyler.

"That's true," Tyler agreed, his face breaking into a grin. "But sometimes you can't wait anymore, you know?" And, with that, he leaned in and kissed her.

The kiss was warm and deep, both gentle and passionate, and so blissfully familiar that Holly thought she might pass out from happiness. It was a kiss that contained all the sweetness of her and Tyler's past kisses, but held the tantalizing promise of something . . . *more.* Holly returned the kiss enthusiastically, twining her arms around Tyler's neck and burying her hands in his soft, wavy hair. Holly thought of her last kiss and how different and exciting it had felt to kiss a French boy in France. But now, with Tyler's lips on hers, Holly realized that a kiss in the middle of New Jersey, from the regular American boy she loved, could be just as thrilling.

They were pulling apart when Holly's cell phone — as if feeling left out — chimed in with a loud

302

ring. "Parents," she and Tyler said in unison, laughing as Holly removed her cell from her pocket. On the screen, however, Holly saw not the word HOME, but — as she had that fateful night in Wimbledon — a plus sign followed by a string of digits. A Paris number.

"I should take this," she told Tyler apologetically, pressing TALK and bringing the phone to her ear. "*Chérie?*" she asked with a grin. Tyler raised his eyebrows, clearly surprised to hear Holly speak another language.

"Oh, my God, the cuteness!" Alexa laughed from the other side of the Atlantic, where it was one P.M., Paris time.

In Paris, Alexa was striding up the sweeping, sunlit Champs-Elysées, clutching her new pearl-studded mobile phone — a post-Xavier consolation gift she'd bought that morning, after she'd gone to breakfast with her cousins, who were being very supportive. From Alexa's free hand swung a colorful array of glossy shopping bags; after all, she'd needed a *lot* of consolation.

"Hol, did you make it home safely?" Alexa asked breathlessly.

"I'm home all right." Holly smiled at Tyler, who was watching her, intrigued. She reached down to take her boyfriend's hand. "When does *your* flight leave?"

"Sometime this evening," Alexa sighed, maneuvering around a street musician. "I'm hoping to *God* that Diego changed his ticket and won't be on the plane." She heard Holly giggle and realized her friend sounded . . . happy. Not at all like someone who'd been expelled. "So spill it," Alexa urged. "Can you still graduate in June? Did you make up with Tyler? I've been *dying* over here!"

Holly bit her lip, hesitating. Yesterday, she hadn't had a chance to check in with Alexa from England, and now — with Tyler right there, and her teammates milling about — was clearly not the moment to divulge. "Let's put it this way," Holly replied teasingly. "I think your shoes *and* your clutch are perfectly safe. . . ."

"I knew it," Alexa declared, gazing ahead at the grand Arc de Triomphe. "Am I not psychic?" She felt a wave of relief for her friend, but a twinge of melancholy for herself; *her* spring break hadn't ended quite as, well, triumphantly.

"Are you doing any better?" Holly asked, hearing the note of sorrow in her friend's voice. Holding hands, she and Tyler headed for the airport's exit.

"Not really," Alexa admitted, swallowing hard. Her heart was still brimming with raw pain and unchecked anger toward Xavier. Though yesterday, in the apartment, after tearing out and crumpling up his magazine photos, she'd been ready to rip his charcoal portrait of her to shreds — but had stopped herself. With uncharacteristic calm, she'd decided to keep the sketch — as a reminder that even she, Alexa St. Laurent, could get completely stupid over a boy.

Or she could always sell it on eBay.

"We'll talk more when you're back," Holly was promising on the other end, but Alexa was distracted by someone bumping into her right shoulder — hard. Still holding the phone to her ear, she spun around, glaring at the wayward pedestrian.

Who happened to be a smolderingly hot guy.

"Pardon," he told Alexa, his dark green eyes crinkling up in a smile as he pushed a hand through his mop of brown hair.

Ooh, Alexa thought, smiling back at him, and for the first time in two days, felt a spark of hope. But then she tossed her hair over one shoulder and kept right on walking, her espadrilles carrying her confidently forward. *No thank you, monsieur.* It was time for Alexa to *really* get her independence on. And if there was anything she had learned from Xavier, it was *never* to get tricked into falling in love so easily again.

At least, not for a while.

"Sorry — I'm still here," Alexa told Holly. "And definitely yes to the talking-when-I'm-back thing," she added. "How about we go to the mall after school one day? We'll pretend the Galleria food court is our little café on the place des Vosges."

"I can't wait," Holly laughed, stepping out with Tyler into the New Jersey sunshine.

Neither can I, Alexa realized, surprising herself. This unexpected feeling had been building in her for a few days now, but right there, on the elegant Champs-Elysées, Alexa knew it for sure: She missed Oakridge. A lot. Paris might have been all shimmer and romance but, to Alexa, New Jersey would always be about friendship. Which, at the moment, felt so much more important than anything else.

"So I'll see you tomorrow?" Alexa heard Holly asking.

"Tomorrow," Alexa echoed happily. Snapping shut her cell phone, she paused in the middle of the wide, bustling avenue and smiled with anticipation.

She was going home.

About the Author

Aimee Friedman is the *New York Times* bestselling author of *South Beach,* the romantic comedy *A Novel Idea,* and the forthcoming graphic novel *Breaking Up: A Fashion High Graphic Novel.* Aimee was born and raised in New York City, where she still lives and works as a book editor. But she loves to travel as much as possible—especially to Paris.

Don't miss the gripping new *Point* novel

« Rewind

by Laura Dower
Available everywhere in April 2006!

Chapter Twenty-Eight

Prom Night, June 15, 10:25 PM
Cady

Cady Sanchez adjusted her red bra strap and took a deep breath.

Next to her, a serious-looking boy with biceps the size of bread loaves shot a look at a blond girl fixing the T-strap on her sandal.

"We just took some killer stuff," the boy whispered. "Want some?"

The girl twisted her head and glared. "I don't take candy from strangers," she said, shaking her taffeta hips confidently.

Cady watched as the girl headed toward a group of guys and girls singing off-key, a capella, in a corner. Biceps quickly shoved his hands into his pockets to avert the glare of a class chaperone. Orange-carpeted floors vibrated with the heavy boom of DJ Beat's music and the loud pound of more than a hundred feet jumping up and down and up and down.

You know you want it. You know, you know, you know you want it.

The entire school year had been leading up to this?

Most girls had been shopping for their prom dresses since the start of senior year at Chesterfield High School. Now they wandered in and out of the massive ballroom at the Chesterfield Suites like lacy, frosted mannequins, half-dazed with heat, emotion, and the wonder of it all. Cady felt different, looked different, from the rest. Her dress was scarlet; although she didn't wear lipstick or shoes to match, she had painted each toenail the same shocking red.

It had taken Cady all of her seventeen years to get used to most parts of herself, like the downward curve of her nose and the pattern of pale freckles on her right shoulder that looked like a miniature constellation. Her skin was so light, too light, Cady thought, considering that her father was from South America. She wished she looked more like her brother, Diego, whose skin was more olive toned. Cady's light skin came from her mother, Sara, whose own Irish skin was so pale it was almost translucent, like a china doll. Cady didn't want to be anything like china. She didn't want to break.

From inside the ballroom, strobes flashed red, and then yellow. Even from a distance, the disco light pulses gave Cady a headache.

DJ Beat popped his lips and pumped up the volume on one song, a ballad neatly mixed with new wave and rap.

"This one's for Hope," he shouted into the mic.

As soon as Cady heard the name *Hope*, she scanned the faces in the crowd, searching. She hadn't seen Hope White since the start of prom.

The mob of guys from the basketball team (and the mob of girls who liked them) walked by, rapping to each other.

"Hot dress, Sanchez," one player named Darius West called out.

Cady flashed a wide smile. She'd known Darius since sixth grade, but they'd never been "real" friends. Life was funny that way. You could know people for so long but never know them at all.

"Nice tux, West," Cady whispered. He wore a T-shirt with a picture of a tuxedo on it.

As Darius walked on, Cady glanced at herself in a wall mirror but quickly looked away. What was going on with her hair? The dress was hot and itchy and she already had the makings of a blister on her little toe. And where was Lucas? He promised Cady one dance.

But she'd lost him.

Weaving her way through the endless throng of seniors was worse than navigating a driving test obstacle course. These were the cones and roadblocks of Cady's senior year: the jocks, the jokers, and of course, the beautiful people. Cady narrowly missed knocking a glass of orange punch (definitely spiked) out of one jock's hand. She almost stepped on the open-toed sandal of a girl she hated from music class. Carefully, Cady edged past a cluster of clucking girls who complained about how unfair it was that they couldn't smoke anywhere at the hotel, not even on the outside patio. The hotel had installed cameras to make sure no one broke the rules.

"Cady!" someone cried from the crowd. "Where have you been?"

"Marisol." Cady sighed, relieved to have found one of her friends again. "I was looking for you. Where's Ed?"

Marisol shrugged. "Getting my bag. I think we're gonna go."

Cady tipped her head to the side and squinted. It was the face she always made when she wasn't so sure about something. "Well," Cady said, "I was thinking of hanging out a little while longer. Just in case. You know."

Marisol grabbed Cady's shoulders. "You look good, girl. You should be working it on some boy who's worth it instead of waiting around for *him*."

Cady laughed. "I don't know how to work it, Marisol. I'm better on back-up guitar. Actually, I brought mine with me tonight."

"You did?" Marisol said. "Big surprise. Well, I think it's time you play something loud and kiss that boy's butt good-bye. You know Emile is having a rave later. You're coming, right? Oh — wait — I see Ed . . ."

Marisol waved to her boyfriend from across the room. Of course they'd only been dating since the winter, but Cady could tell it was true love. Or at least she hoped it was. Cady wanted to believe in true love more than anything. No matter what happened, she was determined to believe.

"Maybe I'll go to the rave," Cady said thoughtfully. "Maybe."

"You better!" Marisol commanded. She gave Cady a "see you later" kiss and hustled away toward Ed.

Cady watched her best friend disappear and scanned the room again. Lucas was still missing. But she spotted a hotel-sized couch along one wall. Sitting down seemed like a good idea.

"Excuse me," Cady said weakly as she squeezed onto the cushions next to a boy named Fly. She recognized him from calculus. His girlfriend, who didn't go to Chesterfield, was at his side.

"Mmmnh," Fly grunted. He had crystal blue eyes. Cady couldn't help but stare. His girlfriend looked stoned.

"What are you looking at?" Fly's girlfriend asked.

"Nothing," Cady said, fanning herself with an open hand. "It's just hot."

"Hot," the girl said as she put her hand on the inside of her boyfriend's leg. Without even turning around, Fly slid his hand halfway up his date's skirt, revealing more of her fishnet stockings. They both moaned.

Cady tried not to look. She'd come without a date, and so the sight of two kids feeling each other up made her bristle with utter, total, complete disgust.

And a teeny bit of jealousy.

After all, she'd gone to all this trouble with the red dress.

You know you want it. You know, you know, you know you want it.

The music thumped again. Cady fussed with her long brown hair. She'd stupidly sprayed hair gel into it earlier that evening and now it was sticky like a spider web. She could barely comb her fingers through the top.

"Ouch."

Make-out Boy elbowed Cady in the side as he raised his hips and pressed into his girlfriend.

Where was a chaperone when you needed one?

Cady stood up again and walked toward an exit. She needed air.

Through a set of sliding glass doors, Cady wandered onto an enormous mezzanine-level patio and perched over the wide iron railing. She'd begun the night with a group of friends. Now she was alone.

Cady gazed across a field at the main road behind the hotel, tracing the red and white paths of taillights and headlights on cars and trucks moving toward unknown destinations. The traffic made her dizzy. And although the hotel patio was cooler and much quieter than the flashing ballroom, Cady's head still ached.

All around, kids gulped night air and stole French kisses. Cady wished Lucas Wheeler was here, too, with his square shoulders and sweet tongue. Kissing her. She wanted to finger the lock of curly hair that swept across his forehead. She wanted to gaze into his deep-set brown eyes. He always smelled like burned incense and his voice was rough, like he smoked, even though he said he hated cigarettes. He was warm all the time, even in winter.

Everything about Lucas Wheeler was made for kissing.

Prom noise filtered upstairs to guest rooms on the third floor, so hotel security came around with their buzzing walkie-talkies, trying the best they could to keep the rowdiest graduates quiet.

No one was listening.

Students stumbled to the elevator bank, half-drunk with the alcohol they weren't supposed to be drinking. Some headed upstairs to rented suites where they planned to hook up, watch movies, drink some more, and stay up all night long. Others made their way toward the hotel parking lot and lined up for their limousines.

Everyone needed someplace to go, and anywhere was good, as long as it wasn't home. Not yet.

The distressed wooden clock on the mezzanine wall read eleven o'clock. There was still time for Cady to salvage prom. If she hurried. She grabbed the hem of her dress and moved swiftly toward the coat check area. When she got there, Cady leaned into the table, drumming out a song beat with impatient fingertips, and waited for the coat checker to return.

Most of the musicians in her class hoped for a late night prom jam, since it might be one of the last times they played together. A group planned to meet at Big Cup, a makeshift coffee house for teens that was set up in the basement of a local art gallery. Cady wished she'd brought her faded jeans and a tee to change into. How was she going to jam in this dress?

"Um, can you hurry it up?" Cady asked the checker, who seemed lost in a maze of bags and coats. "My bag's cowhide with a big silver buckle and it should be sitting next to a guitar case. I mean, how many Fenders are back there?"

Through the loudspeakers, music sped up. There would be a few more fast songs before the end of everything.

Off in the distance, Cady observed a girl standing alone, fingering a blue tassel fringe on a scarf around her neck. Cady guessed that girl had been waiting for a dance since prom began. Sometimes strangers seemed so familiar, Cady thought. Nearby, two other girls jokingly lifted up their shiny tops for just a nanosecond while a cluster of guys applauded. But no one paid much attention to them or their belly-button rings.

Where was the damn bag?

Not so far away, a couple appeared, arguing, just outside the main doors to the main ballroom. Cady couldn't see the guy at all. He stood hidden behind a pillar. But she knew the girl right away. Cady recognized the low dip in the back of Hope White's long prom dress.

Cady moved her eyes over the curve of Hope's shoulder, down her naked spine, down the V-line of her silk dress, and ending at Hope's slender ankles. Everything about Hope's form was perfectly sewn, buttoned, and zipped. But the poker-straight blond hair was down now, not up, like it had been earlier that night. And Hope's normally eggshell white skin was flushed.

Cady could tell something was wrong.

Then the boy stepped into view.

"Lucas?" Cady said weakly.

He waved his arms wildly in the air, as if he and Hope were doing a dance.

But they weren't.

Cady's pulse raced and she edged closer.

8

"Leave me —" Hope said.

Cady could only hear some of the words.

"Cut the —" Lucas said.

"Don't —"

"Lies —" Lucas cried.

Then he raised his left arm up high over his head.

SLAP.

Cady clasped a wide hand over her gaping mouth.

Hope fell to the floor.

Someone nearby screamed and the room spun on its axis. Biceps boy, Darius West and his basketball crew, Fly and his stoner girlfriend all turned.

Everyone stopped. Time stopped.

"Hey!" a guy cried from halfway across the room. "Wheeler. What the hell did you do?"

It was Jed Baker, one of the biggest kids at Chesterfield.

"You're hamburger, asshole."

Jed lunged and body-slammed Lucas into a wall. A few more guys came over quickly, muscles pumped, knuckles primed.

"Watch out!"

"Did you see that?"

"He hit a girl!" someone screamed.

From out of nowhere, another kid tried to sucker-punch Lucas right in the face. Lucas bobbed to the side and stumbled back, coughing.

"Let — me — go —" Lucas mumbled, tugging at his own collar.

But no one let go. The crowd moved in tighter, like a vise.

"What just happened?"

"He hit a girl."

"You piece of—"

"Stand BACK!" a chaperone shouted. "Stand back! NOW!" He clapped his hands.

Reluctantly, the guys pushed away from Lucas, and Cady raced over. She kneeled down beside Hope, who sat on the floor in a crumpled pile, prom dress bunched up around her like purple icing on a dirty cake.

"Oh my God, are you okay?" Cady asked, touching Hope's arm.

"No . . ." Hope said. She touched her own cheek. There was a handprint. "My face . . . burns . . ."

Cady leaned in closer. Her insides were grinding. The whole crowd was grinding.

"Can you stand?" Cady asked Hope.

Another teacher rushed over. "Does someone want to tell me *exactly* what happened here?" she yelled.

Pale yellow organza and floor-length pink satin swooshed as girls hurried to give their own scattered versions of the story. But everything was happening too fast to make any sense.

"Lucas Wheeler just lost it."

"Someone call hotel security."

"Oh my God, oh my God."

Cady squeezed Hope's hand. "Can you stand?" she asked again.

"No." Hope shook her head.

Then Cady looked up, and saw Lucas clearly for the

first time. He wiped the corner of his mouth and stared down at his shaking palms.

There was blood on his mouth and hand.

"Oh, shit," Lucas said aloud. "This is bad."

A few more muscle-heads shoved their way toward him, but a chaperone got in the way. "Stand back, I said! Stand back!" he wailed.

The angry crowd moved in and out like it was breathing.

"Just—wait—*please*—let me explain . . ." Lucas said.

Cady saw Lucas thrust his arms into the air, surrendering to the chaos. She'd never seen him look so scared. His eyes appeared to cross and then uncross like he'd had too much to drink, and Cady guessed that he had. His buddies had probably laced a cup of punch with hard stuff.

"Incident on the mezzanine level. Send up the manager, please."

Out of nowhere, two hotel security guards appeared, pushing through the mob, walkie-talkies in hand. They each grabbed an arm and started to lead Lucas back toward the elevators.

"Hey! Where are you taking him?" a girl yelled.

The taller security guard waved the girl away.

"Out of my way," the guard growled. "This is an accident, and we'll handle it from here. . . ."

"It was no accident!" Hope sobbed, trying to be heard above the crowd. "HE HIT ME!"

"He hit her!" the crowd repeated loudly, eyes rutted with angry judgment.

Cady gazed deep into Hope's eyes, across from her. The truth had to be there. Where was it? Then Cady looked over at Lucas. He stared back, jaw locked. He spoke softly — too softly — to be heard above the din. But Cady could read his lips.

"I screwed up so bad," Lucas said. "It wasn't her. You were the one."

Cady's chest clenched. She knew what he meant.

In one instant, she understood everything.

Cady pulled herself up from the floor and stretched out the fingers of her left hand. She grabbed at air like she was grabbing for Lucas, even as he was being dragged away by the two security guards. And in spite of everything that had just happened, she still wanted that dance.

She still wanted.

Chapter Twenty-Seven

Prom Night, June 15, 8:12 PM
Hope

Girls crowded around the sink inside the marble bathroom at the Chesterfield Suites. The air reeked of jasmine perfume, baby powder, and antiseptic. A restroom matron sat in a small black leather chair off to one side, passing out hand towels and checking to make sure no one sneaked cigarettes or worse inside the stalls. She had a tip dish on the counter next to her, but it was empty.

Everyone had to pee. The line wound halfway out the door. Girls whispered excitedly about their prom dates or their outfits or, in most cases, about someone else's outfit — and how tacky/ugly/slutty/fill-in-the-blank it was.

"Hey, does anyone have any deodorant?" one girl called out to everyone else in the room.

Hope pressed in front of one sink mirror. She looked up while washing her hands. The pale pink gloss she'd applied an hour earlier had all but disappeared. She spotted Cady Sanchez in the mirror.

"There you are," Hope said, sidling up to Cady. "I wondered if I'd find you."

"You look . . . amazing," Cady said. Her face glowed.

Hope smiled. "Like the dress? It's an original Vance. Dad insisted."

Cady nodded. "Wow."

"Your dress is nice, too," Hope said, stroking the fabric. Her fingers slid lightly across Cady's wrist. "You really need lipstick, though. Something red hot."

"I put some on when I left the house," Cady said. "But then I forgot to take the tube with me. Dumb, right?"

"I'd give you some of mine, but this is too pale and it just wouldn't go. Sorry," Hope said. She blew a kiss into the mirror.

"So where's your date?" Cady asked. "You come with Rich?"

Hope grinned. "Uh-huh. He's outside with his friends."

"I bet *he* likes your dress," Cady said.

"What's not to like?" Hope countered with a shrug.

"What ever happened to that text-messaging guy?" Cady asked.

"Him?" Hope flinched a little. "Who cares?"

"He stopped texting."

"Well." Hope paused. "Not exactly. Actually, he might be here tonight."

"Here?" Cady blurted, taken aback. "At prom? Are you kidding?"

Hope shook her head. "He goes to Chesterfield."

"What? Cady asked, looking concerned.

"I know. I should have told you, Cady. I wanted to tell you. But then I couldn't. Please don't make a big deal . . ."

"Your stalker goes to our school," Cady said with disbelief. "How can you not make a big deal out of that? Who the hell is the guy?"

"Please," Hope said sternly. "Just drop it." She looked around to see if anyone was listening. This whole time she'd led Cady to believe that the "stalker" was a guy from her part-time job over at the medical building, but now the cat was out of the bag — with claws.

"Look, I know you're wondering why I didn't tell you before who this guy is," Hope continued. "And the reason I didn't tell you before and why I'm not telling you now is . . . well . . ." Hope clutched at the garnet stones on a delicate silver choker she was wearing.

"Hope," Cady pleaded, reaching for both of Hope's hands. "You can trust me. Are you scared? I really think we should tell someone . . ."

Hope looked down at Cady's fingers, now intertwined with her own. Cady's nails were short, with no polish, contrasting starkly with Hope's French manicure. But the two hands fit together nonetheless, like opposing pieces of an interlocking puzzle.

"What's that?" Cady asked, staring at Hope's arm.

Hope looked down. "Nothing," she mumbled. "I bumped into a —"

"Come on. Did *he* do that?" Cady asked. Gently, she pressed her fingertips into Hope's shoulder, and Hope winced dramatically. She'd tried to cover the mark with makeup, but it wasn't hard to tell what lay underneath. This bruise was fresh.

"Hope, talk to me. Now."

"Cady, you have to forget it."

"I can't —"

"Don't—"

"Fine," Cady said, throwing her hands up in the air. "I won't ask you anything else."

Hope took a deep breath and unbuckled the silver sequined clutch that she'd been carrying and slid out a palm-sized bottle.

"Want some?" Hope asked Cady.

"Hairspray? Uh . . . I don't think so."

"Suit yourself."

Hope lifted the bottle and sprayed around her head until every stray hair sat back in place, reprimanded, ready to face the dance. She prided herself on the fact that her hair was always perfect. Hairspray was her force field.

Cady sniffed the air. "Strong stuff," she said. "But it looks pretty good. Maybe I should try a little?" Cady held up a strand of her long dark brown hair and examined it.

Hope lifted the small aerosol bottle and pumped.

"Stop! That stuff really reeks." Cady coughed, fanning the air around her head. She checked her reflection and frowned. "Oh no. Look at me."

"It's not too terrible," Hope said, pasting on a smile. But she knew it wasn't too good either. Cady's hair poked up at the top, and the sides looked like they'd been glued down.

"Maybe he won't notice," Cady said softly, sounding dejected.

"Who won't?" Hope asked.

"You know," Cady said, rolling her eyes.

"Lucas Wheeler."

Hope saw Cady swallow hard. Cady never liked talking about boys, especially not Lucas, and Hope knew that.

"Look, Hope, we're not prom dates or anything, if that's what you're thinking," Cady said. "Lucas and I said we'd see each other here. That's all."

"That's all?" Hope said.

"Let's quit this, Hope," Cady interrupted. "I know you don't think Lucas is the right guy for me. You've only said that to me like a hundred times. You think he's some kind of freaky loner. I see how you look at him. . . ."

"You do?" Hope said with disbelief.

"Yes, I do." Cady tugged up her bra strap again with determination. "Look, Hope, I know Lucas Wheeler acts a little mysterious, but why do you and everyone else think that makes him some kind of closet . . . *fiend* or something? I mean, what would you do if you had to start a new school for senior year? I know I'd die."

"All I'm saying—all I've ever said—is that Lucas isn't the guy you think he is, Cady."

"Come on, Hope. Is anyone?"

"I know you *think* that the two of you are real friends . . ." Hope said.

"I don't think. We *are* friends. He gets my music. I can talk to him."

"Like you can talk to me?"

"That's different."

"Incoming!" A girl dressed in a skin-tight black dress shoved Cady out of the way to get to the sink. Cady nearly toppled over.

"What's your problem?" Hope asked.

"What's *your* problem?" The girl scowled.

Hope nudged the girl so hard that she fell back against the sink.

"Watch it!" the girl shrieked.

"You watch it," Hope said firmly.

"You wrecked my dress."

"Who cares?" Hope said.

"*What* did you say?"

Hope's insides roiled. She wasn't about to let some cow in leather ruin her prom. But before Hope could say anything more, Cady stepped in.

"Come on, let's go," Cady said softly.

The girl backed off and Hope reluctantly followed Cady through the bathroom door.

Prom music pounded hard outside in the hall. Hope glanced around at other seniors decked out in their black and blue and creamy white dupioni silk. Her purple gown stood out in the crowd, although Cady's red dress stood out even more. But was anyone really looking? She searched the crowd for familiar faces.

"This is a good song," Cady said as she moved her hips from side to side. Everything moved except her new helmet hair.

"Oh, look. I see Rich over there by the refreshment table," Hope announced. "I don't see your date, though." She grinned.

"Very funny," Cady said. "I *told* you Lucas is not my date."